"Will intrigue you from A to Z and then so on... Paige Shelton has come up with a unique combination of characters and setting."

—*New York Times* bestselling author Susan Wittig Albert

"Clare is a charming protagonist who loves her work. The minor characters and subplots accelerated the novel's pace to add intrigue and suspense. . . . I love cozy mysteries that are fast-paced, riveting, and intriguing, filled with exciting characters. *To Helvetica and Back* fits that bill nicely, and I can't wait to read future releases in this great, exciting, and lovable new series."

—MyShelf.com

"I really like Clare, Jodie, Chester, and Baskerville (the shop cat) as well as the side characters. Seth and Mutt look to be keepers. . . . I think I've found a new favorite!"

—Kings River Life Magazine

"All of the characters in this book are memorable, from cranky kitty Baskerville to Clare's BFF/cop Jodie to her love interest, geologist Seth. . . . It didn't disappoint in the least."

—Melissa's Mochas, Mysteries & Meows

"A refreshing, imaginative start to a new cozy mystery series. . . . I highly recommend this exciting new mystery . . . to those who like well-crafted cozy mysteries, unique settings, and the first blush of a sweet romance."

—Open Book Society

Berkley Prime Crime titles by Paige Shelton

Dangerous Type Mysteries

TO HELVETICA AND BACK

Farmers' Market Mysteries

FARM FRESH MURDER
FRUIT OF ALL EVIL
CROPS AND ROBBERS
A KILLER MAIZE
MERRY MARKET MURDER
BUSHEL FULL OF MURDER

Country Cooking School Mysteries

IF FRIED CHICKEN COULD FLY
IF MASHED POTATOES COULD DANCE
IF BREAD COULD RISE TO THE OCCASION
IF CATFISH HAD NINE LIVES
IF ONIONS COULD SPRING LEEKS

Specials

RED HOT DEADLY PEPPERS

Bookman Dead Style

A Dangerous Type Mystery

PAIGE SHELTON

BERKLEY PRIME CRIME
New York

BERKLEY PRIME CRIME
Published by Berkley
An imprint of Penguin Random House LLC
375 Hudson Street, New York, New York 10014

ISBN: 9780425277263

First Edition: February 2017

Printed in the United States of America
1   3   5   7   9   10   8   6   4   2

Cover art by Brandon Dorman
Cover design by Lesley Worrell
Book design by Kelly Lipovich

For Carole, Kathy, Fran, Walt, Steve, Astrid, and Jim

Acknowledgments

Thanks to my agent, Jessica Faust, and my editor, Michelle Vega, for their continued enthusiasm, support, and hard work.

Cover artist Brandon Dorman and designer Lesley Worrell as well as copy editor Michele Alpern sprinkled their magic all over this book. I'm eternally grateful to them, and to everyone at Penguin Random House.

My husband and son never tire of cheering me on. Thanks to Charlie and Tyler for always being on my team. I adore you.

"It's my good luck you're here. I saw your shop last year but didn't have time to stop in. You have the best selection of this kind of stuff I've ever seen. When I needed the note cards, I thought of you right away," he said with a genuine smile.

Silence. The uncomfortable kind.

Even Baskerville the cat was quiet as he surveyed the scene from his seated position on the corner of the counter.

Finally, I elbowed my niece, Marion.

"Oh, of course," she said in a voice so breathy I thought she was going to either faint or throw up. Unquestionably, surviving this moment would be difficult for anyone, but maybe more so for a teenage girl in the throes of fangirl-ness.

He smiled again. Close-up and in person or on the big

screen, when his face and his teeth and his smile were all enormous—at any size, his was a beautiful smile.

The Star City Film Festival had been a part of our Januarys for going on two decades now. We'd all seen our fair share of movie stars. Most of them were friendly. Most of them in person looked close to what you might expect. But a few of them were, frankly, disappointing, though not because of their looks. Many Star City residents had experienced a random moment or two of actor surliness or arrogance, giving us the overwhelming desire to tell someone who thought they were being "creative" that they should learn how to mind their manners and not think themselves so wonderful.

Matt Bane, however, did not disappoint. He'd been friendly from the moment he came through the door. He'd walked in with a humble smile already on his stubble-covered face. All the guys had at least a little stubble during this festival; clean-shaven wouldn't be cool. Matt's dirty-blond hair wasn't necessarily brushed, but it was clean and he'd removed the ball cap he'd been wearing. He wore a thin khaki ski coat over some black jeans, a white T-shirt, and black work boots. They were heavy boots, and the thought that he wore them to help keep his legs in such great shape had crossed my mind. He was unquestionably easy on the eyes.

He also smelled good, like laundry detergent and oranges. I know because I *accidentally* stepped close enough to him to covertly sniff once. I straightened my glasses as I breathed him in, so he wouldn't know what I was up to. He might have noticed, though, because he smiled a little sideways at me when I did it.

A few years before he'd been cast as a superhero. Two

movies of the franchise had already done extremely well worldwide. I was sure there were many more set to be produced. But we Star City residents and businesspeople didn't ask those kinds of questions. There were some unspoken rules about the way we behaved toward the "movie people." Sometimes some of us got to know them well, or at least as well as a brief acquaintanceship might allow. But mostly we just tried to leave them all alone. For ten days in January we wanted them to feel comfortable walking into our stores without worrying about wearing disguises or ducking from hidden cameras. We didn't want them concerned that they'd be photographed shoveling pie into their mouths or consuming carbohydrates; they should feel at ease when ordering something loaded with too many calories. Though not everyone in Star City cooperated and there were specific media events that broke all the unspoken rules, for the most part we were welcoming and easygoing, and they were . . . well, nice.

Matt Bane, though. Even my beautiful, intelligent, snowboarding, potential Olympic-qualifying niece couldn't be expected to be normal around Matt Bane. I was going to have to intervene with more than an elbow.

"We'd be happy to get these finished in an hour or so," I said. "Right, Marion?"

"Wow," she said.

Baskerville meowed and rolled his eyes, I think.

"I'm sorry," I said to the movie star.

"Not a problem," Matt said. "I appreciate the rush. I like to write handwritten thank-yous and I forgot to pack the cards I bought in LA a month or so ago. So many people here I need to thank. I've been treated very well."

"So, you'd just like your initials? MB at the bottom-right corner?" I asked, thinking his mom would be so proud of him and his handwritten thank-yous.

"Yep, that's all I'll need."

"Easy," I said, knowing Marion could print the cards while he waited if I told her to. I was worried she'd fall apart if he remained in the store too much longer, though. If he stayed while she worked, I was sure a disaster of some sort would ensue. "Would you like them delivered?"

"No, I'll just swing back by again," he said. "I'm walking around shopping this morning. It's cold out there, but sunny."

"The snow's perfect at the moment if you ski or board."

We had fresh powder, the right temperature, and only a few clouds in an otherwise clear blue sky. As was normal for us, a storm could roll in at any moment, but conditions were currently ideal for hitting the slopes.

"Not allowed. It's in my contracts that I don't take those sorts of risks, but I plan on watching other people conquer the slopes today."

"Conquer" was such a good word for a superhero.

"That's fun too," I said.

My grandfather Chester came through the door between the retail part of the store and the back workshop. He cradled an old typewriter in the crook of his left arm and he wore a plastic band around his head with an attached magnifying glass, lit and positioned over one eye.

"Clare, where in the world are all the small wrenches? Oh, pardon me—I didn't know we had a customer." He dialed the magnifying disk to the right and flipped off the light.

"It's all right. I was just . . . Hey, is that an old Royal?"

Matt said as he stepped around the side of the counter and eyed the inky machine that Chester held. Once the return was repaired, we would also clean off the grime and make the red, otherwise undamaged case look as good as it had when it had first been used back in the 1950s.

"It is, young man. A red Royal Quiet Deluxe." Chester laughed. "Not quiet by today's standards, of course, but back when it was first invented, it was. You know your typewriters," Chester said, though I was fairly certain that he had no idea he was talking to one of the most popular movie stars in the world. He often mentioned that he'd lost track of all "those people" when Gene Kelly passed.

"Actually, just that kind. I have one. My grandfather gave it to me. Are you fixing this one?"

"We are. It's part of what we do. We rescue words," Chester said.

"The Rescued Word. I get it. Stationery, typewriters. I like that. I didn't even notice the typewriter part because I was so impressed by your paper and pens."

"We also restore books," Marion blurted out.

We all looked at her as her face reddened and her fingers went up to her now-pinched lips.

"Very cool," Matt said with a smile.

If Marion didn't faint or throw up in the next ten seconds, this would turn out to be a great memory for her.

"Yes, we keep busy," Chester said cheerily, as if to draw the attention away from his seemingly embarrassed great-granddaughter.

"That's good to know. Mine still works pretty well, but if it ever starts acting up, I'll know where to send it."

The front door slammed open, so loudly that we all jumped before we turned to see who had come in. A brief low growl came from Baskerville, but I signaled to him to be quiet. His return expression told me he'd think about it.

"Matt, I've been looking all over for you," the man said. "You need to take a call."

Our new visitor was short and mostly bald, though the dark stubble on his face was duplicated on top of his head, as if he'd shaved everything above his neck a couple days ago and all the hair had grown back at the same speed. His John Lennon glasses reminded me of Chester's, though the man's were much thicker and his eyes were severely magnified behind them. Farsighted, not nearsighted like Chester and me. He wore a thin, ragged green jacket, a red and blue scarf that had seen better days, and black jeans. But it was more his attitude than his clothing choices that filled the room. He'd pushed open the door and let it slam without one hint of apology or an excuse-me. He might have stomped a foot if we hadn't all noticed him.

"It's my morning off," Matt said. He glanced back at us with an apologetic smile before turning again to face the man.

"It's . . . well, it's *the* call you've been waiting for," the man said.

"Oh, I see. I'll be there in just a second," Matt said, much less enthusiastically than I would have predicted regarding something that was *the* call.

The man hesitated. "All right. I'll wait out here for you. Come as soon as you can."

"Will do." Matt turned to us again. Before the man at

the door had made it back outside, Matt said, "I'm so sorry about that."

"No problem." I wanted to break the unwritten rule and be nosy. I wanted to know what was going on. Some movie deal? Maybe the call would include a big-time name like Steven Spielberg. Though I wasn't prone to fangirl moments, it was impossible not to be curious. It was Matt Bane, after all. *The* call must be something important. I bit my lip, working to keep my curiosity under control.

"I'll be back this afternoon to pick up the cards." His eyes moved to a cup full of shamrock pens that I'd placed on the end of the counter just that morning. They weren't expensive pens, but novelties—bendable and squishy with glittery bright green shamrocks sticking up from their tops. They were comfortable to hold, but the writing part—the business part, according to Chester—wasn't high quality. A pen salesmen had given them to us. He'd had "The Rescued Word" and "Bygone Alley, Star City, Utah" printed on the squishy green part. Despite the addition of our shop's name and address, Chester despised them, thought they were a waste of ink. He understood, though, that some people might think they were fun, even though we were still two months away from Saint Patrick's Day. He'd agreed to let me put them on the counter, but only give them away, not take "even a pittance" for them. Matt grabbed one of the pens. "I know someone who would love this—believes in good luck, four-leaf clovers and all. I'll take one of these too."

He pulled his wallet out of his back pocket.

"Oh, you can pay for the cards when you pick them up," I interjected. "The pen is on us. My grandfather"—I nodded toward Chester—"would love for someone to enjoy one, but they're not very high quality."

"Piece of crap, really," Chester said.

"Please just take it," I said. "Can I put it in a bag for you?"

"Thanks. No, I'll just . . ." Matt slipped the pen into his back pocket.

Before he could turn to leave, the door slammed open again.

"Matt Bane. You probably thought you could hide from me."

"Gracious," Chester said as we all looked at the woman who'd come through.

She was not dressed in typical film festival attire. Her hair was pulled back into a tight bun and the long dress she wore was reminiscent of the style that pioneer women had donned: blue, buttoned-up high neckline, long sleeves gathered at the wrists, an apron around her waist. I'd seen plenty of women dressed the way she was dressed, but that was only because I lived in Utah. Tucked into pockets of the state were families who still practiced polygamy, and some of the women in such families wore this sort of simple, old-fashioned, hand-sewn clothing.

We had our own polygamous compound in a small valley outside Star City, but the three sister-wives in that family all dressed modernly, and two of them had jobs out in the real world. Though most of us thought the whole polygamy thing was weird, I'd gone to high school with one of our local sister-wives, so I'd tried to remain mum when the subject matter was brought up. How the party girl Linea Riley had transformed into Linea Christiansen, sister-wife number three, would always be a mystery to both me and my best friend, Jodie, though.

Our current visitor wasn't demure in her body language, like many of the polygamists were. And she knew Matt Bane. It wasn't tough to peg her as an actress, but a not very well-known one. I didn't recognize her, and though I wasn't fanatical, I did go to movies.

"Cassie, hey. I wasn't hiding," Matt said.

"Right," she said as she stepped forward, marching with noisy shoes halfway through the store and throwing her hands on her hips. She stopped and struck a pose directly next to the dark wood shelves that displayed pastel-colored writing papers.

Matt sighed and looked at us again. "I'm sorry. I should know better than to think I might have even a few minutes of private time anymore. It's the price we pay, I'm afraid. Thank you. I'll be back this afternoon."

"Sure," I said. "The cards will be ready."

Marion nodded. Chester moved the typewriter to his other arm, and Baskerville flicked the end of his tail.

Matt met the woman next to the pastel papers and swooped his hand toward the front of the shop. Once they were both there, he opened the door and let her go through first, her shoes still clomping loudly. He sent us one more apologetic smile and a friendly wave before he followed her out the door. A brief moment later, we lost sight of him, the woman, and the man who'd been waiting.

Marion let out a loud breath and then took a seat on a high stool that had been placed at the end of the counter. Baskerville padded over the counter to comfort her.

"You okay?" I said.

"Fine. But that was Matt Bane. O-M-G, that was Matt Bane. I'm making personalized note cards for Matt Bane."

I smiled as she put her hands to her face and shook her head slowly. She'd be okay in a few minutes. The young were resilient.

"Nice-looking young man, though he could use a haircut," Chester said. "Is he here for the festival?"

Marion and I looked at each other and smiled.

"Yes, he's a movie star. Come on, Chester, let's go see if we can find some wrenches," I said. "Marion, let me know if you need any help up here. I'll be in the back. Work on the note cards while you can. We could have more business at any minute."

The film festival always brought something different to Star City. Different events and stories marked the years. A car had burst into flames one year and a famous director had saved three kids from burning up inside it. It had been so unseasonably warm once that a famous actress had stripped and walked into the final awards ceremony in only her underwear. We'd also had sad moments, with fatal heart attacks and deadly accidents on the slopes.

The Rescued Word had never had its own festival story before. Now we had Matt Bane, his unusual friends, and his note cards. The Rescued Word, and more specifically Marion, would now have something special to mark this year and to share with other Star City retailers and residents. I was sure it would be like any good fishing tale and would get bigger and better with time. However, I couldn't have predicted how little time would have to pass for it to get disturbingly better, and out-of-control bigger.

2

Jodie, my best friend since high school, repositioned her foot on the chair. She sat on the edge of my desk and had hooked the chair and pulled it toward her with her ankle. She was dressed for work, which meant she wore her police uniform, heavy boots, and a loaded gun in the holster at her hip. It was cold enough that she also wore a department-issued black winter coat, made especially for police officers, with a special attachment that held the microphone of her police radio on her left shoulder. By nature, she wasn't a delicate person, but when dressed for work, she was better described as rough-and-tumble tough—in the most professional way, of course.

Her bleached blond hair never took on a natural shade, but it somehow looked right on her even when she pulled it back into her favorite work style, a tight ponytail. Despite the lack of froufrou, she was a pretty woman with green eyes that could spot a lie from about twenty feet away.

"Matt Bane, huh? I'll be. He's quite the star," she said, feigning fascination. Jodie had no time for movie stars, particularly during the film festival. She'd seen the misbehaving side of celebrities over the years. The movie people held much less charm for her than they did for us regular civilians, Chester included.

"He seemed like a pretty nice guy. Extremely handsome in person, though that's not too surprising. I felt a little sorry for him," I said as I placed a type plate onto the replica Gutenberg press that Chester had built when he first opened The Rescued Word back in the 1950s. I had some printing assignments ahead, but the press had been acting up and I was doing a test run to see if I could determine and then fix what was causing one side of the ink to print too heavily.

My most urgent assignment was to reprint three pages for a Sylvia Plath book. *Ariel* was treasured by its owner, but this copy was of very little monetary value. Lately I'd been doing lots of those types of repairs. For many of my customers, books were their trade, or the items they collected; those customers bought and sold. But lately I'd seen a surge in customers with only sentimental value attached to their books. Someone's grandmother had read something to her, or he'd purchased a book on a trip with his loved ones and the story inside never failed to bring back memories of that time together; a missing or damaged page or two made the memory incomplete. I'd been completing lots of memories lately.

Though I never offered up my opinion about the contents of any customers' books, the second the customer called about bringing *Ariel* in, I wondered at least briefly if the owner had dark moods like the writer. I couldn't help it; it was a side effect of the job—trying to better understand people by the books they read, or more precisely by the books that were so important to them that they felt the need to repair them or clean them up. I'd enjoyed a Plath poem or two, but in small doses and usually only when I was feeling melancholy.

My unspoken curiosity was answered shortly after the customer, a pretty, middle-aged woman in jeans and a pink puffy ski coat, handed me the book over the counter with the mandate that I was to take extra good care of it, that it was something she cherished because it had been given to her by her own mother shortly after the customer's sister had committed suicide.

I'd blinked, straightened my glasses, and tried to think of what to say. She smiled as if acknowledging the speed bump she'd thrown in there, and to let me know that she didn't require any sympathy on my part.

It was all very morbid, but she seemed in a good place about it. I told her that I took extra care with all the words I rescued, be they a part of a book, the memories of an old typewriter, or the faded scribbles of a well-used pen. The book would be safe with me.

She'd sent Sylvia one last worried look before she smiled cheerily and left to go hit the slopes.

"Why in the world did you feel sorry for Matt Bane?" Jodie asked as she inspected her cuticles.

"No privacy. Ever, it seems." I loaded a piece of paper into the paper holder.

"He has enough money to buy his own island. I don't think you need to feel too sorry for him."

"I know, but still. I can't imagine how it would be not to be able to stop in a shop somewhere without being bothered by someone who knows you, or knows who you are."

Jodie laughed. "Sure you do. You live in Star City. Everyone knows everyone. You can't go anywhere without seeing someone you know."

"I can be as anonymous as I want in Salt Lake, though. He can't."

She frowned at her cuticles and then waved away my concern. "He'll be fine. I like my men real, much less polished, a few calluses on their hands, you know."

I smiled at her. She was, in fact, dating a very real man named Mutt. He was a long-haired motorcycle rider with a heart of gold and an unparalleled work ethic, and probably a few calluses on his hands. He lived in Salt Lake City, which was about half an hour away from Star City. Between his contracted computer-programming hours and his volunteer work with a number of children's charities, and Jodie's police schedule, their relationship was made up of infrequent dates and late-night meet-ups at the gas station / café located at the halfway point in the canyon between their two towns. It seemed to be working okay. I'd never seen her happier.

"When do you see Mutt next?" I leaned over and inspected the wood platen, the piece that pressed the paper against the type. I pushed up my glasses, smudging one of the lenses with my finger. I took them off and grabbed a cloth out of my desk drawer. It wasn't the first smudge of the day, and it most likely wouldn't be the last.

Jodie shrugged. "Probably tonight. You know us—we can't plan much of anything in advance."

"Right."

"When do you see Seth?" she asked.

Seth, my fairly new romantic interest, and I were also both very busy with our jobs—mine at the shop and his doing his geologist things, which currently included the reclamation of a number of mines around Star City. However, we lived across the street from each other, so I saw him almost every day, or evening when we were taking turns fixing dinner for each other.

I shrugged too, not wanting Jodie to think I was one-upping her on the boyfriend time, and then put my glasses back into place. "Probably tonight."

"It's an amazing thing, you and I both dating happily, at the same time."

"I know. Weird, huh?"

Jodie had always been my best friend, but she became the lifelong titleholder when a few years earlier I'd broken up with her brother Creighton, also a police officer, because he'd cheated on me. It wasn't strange that she'd chosen my side in the battle, but her vehemence over his cheating was still extra strong even today. I tried not to bring it up too often, but I did appreciate her loyalty, and sometimes it was just fun to get her riled up.

"When are you and Chester going to get some help around this place?" Jodie asked.

"We have Marion."

"Your Olympic-bound, gorgeous niece who might find her appearances on late-night television talk shows more important than her hours in the shop?"

"You've already got her on late-night television talk shows?" I looked back at the platen and thought it might be slightly off-kilter. I'd need a level to confirm. I looked over toward one of the back shelves, the one that held only tools, no typewriters or typewriter parts. I walked around the press and toward the shelf, then spied the level.

Jodie shrugged. "It doesn't take a Jedi to see the future for that one, Clare. Unless she gets hurt—God and Goddess forbid—there are big things in her future that won't leave much time for Star City."

"Jimmy will freak." My brother, Jimmy, took his role as overprotective father very seriously.

"Yes, he will, but he'll get over it. And he'll see that it's what she wants, and what she wants will become important to him at some point."

"I suppose," I said doubtfully as I carried the level back to the press. Jodie sent me a wry smile.

"I suggest you find someone sooner rather than later," she said.

"You want to quit the police force?"

"No, ma'am. Besides, I doubt you could handle my subtle and delicate ways all day, every day."

I laughed. "I don't know when we'll hire someone else. Chester made me his apprentice. Maybe I need an apprentice. You might be onto something. I'll talk to him."

Jodie's radio buzzed, pulling my attention away from the press.

"Jodie, you there?" The voice of her partner, Omar Miller, sounding far-off and full of static, came through.

"What's up?" she said as she bent her neck toward the microphone and pushed the button.

"Need you. We've got a problem over at The Fountain."

"On my way. What's going on?" she said as she stood to leave. The Fountain, a small hotel on Main Street across from Bygone Alley, where The Rescued Word was located, would normally be a quick walk or drive, but you never knew when or where the festival crowds would swell and hinder all traffic.

She was almost out of the workshop and her footfalls were so hard and loud that I couldn't be exactly sure of what I heard come from her radio next, but I thought it was something like: "Movie star stuff. Matt Bane, you know him?"

She'd moved through the swinging door between the workshop and the front of the store by the time I deciphered the words. A moment later I hurried after her.

She was almost out the shop's front doors by the time I made it to the counter that hid Marion's computer and small worktable from customers.

"What's up?" Marion said as she turned and looked at me.

"Don't know. You okay here without me for a minute?"

"Sure."

I didn't take the time to go back for my coat, but I'd be somewhat warmed by the sun once I got off Bygone and out from the shadows of its old buildings. I hurried toward Main Street, passing the newly added Old-Tyme Chocolate Shop and the Loom, a fiber and yarn shop, before I stepped out into the middle of groups making their way either up or down the street. The bulging hordes of people would be a common sight for the next ten days, and then the crowds would mellow back to their normal large size through the rest of the ski season. I wasn't complaining. Visitors and tourists were the reasons our little town thrived. But at the moment I didn't have a good visual of the hotel entrance across the street, and while everyone was in my way, I got in their way too when I started to thread my way through the crowds.

After a slew of "pardon-me's," I was at the curb and could finally see the hotel. It was an old brick two-story building, having been a saloon and brothel back in the day. An extension had been added to its back side at one point, and the saloon space and the three upstairs rooms had been transformed into a total of eight hotel rooms and a small but grand front lobby. It was difficult to book space at The Fountain, even during non-festival times. It was one of our more highly sought-after places to hang your hat, and always the place where the biggest movie stars stayed. I'd never seen inside the rooms, but I'd heard they were cute and old-fashioned with scuffed-up wood floors and antique furnishings.

I didn't see Jodie anywhere, so I assumed she'd already made her way inside the hotel. A police car was parked in front, situated like all the other cars on the street, aligned against the curb, not at an angle that might indicate the officer driving it had been in a hurry. Also, its lights weren't flashing, making me think that maybe the emergency inside the hotel wasn't dire. It was unusual that anyone, police officers included, managed to get such a good spot— street parking this time of year was even more difficult than booking a room at The Fountain.

Both the cold air and the shining sun bit at my nose and cheeks. It was so bright under the mostly blue sky that I squinted and my eyes started to water. Carefully, as I wove through thick vehicle traffic moving more slowly than the pedestrians, I made my way across the street and to the bottom of the steps leading up to the hotel doors.

I saw nothing to make me think I shouldn't go inside.

I took the few steps up to the wide double doors and opened one of them, then stepped into the lobby, my glasses fogging slightly at the sudden warmth. A wood-burning fireplace on my right blazed with medium-sized yellow flames that crackled behind a grate. Two ornate red velvet chairs and a short table were placed in front of the fireplace, but the chairs were both empty and the newspaper on the table was folded too neatly to have been looked at yet.

The other side of the lobby, with the wood counter and the old-fashioned hooks for keys on the wall behind it, was also empty. I peered down the hallway in the middle, but didn't see any activity other than the sudden dimming of a bulb inside one of the iron sconces on the walls. I looked up to the landing at the top of the polished mahogany staircase and didn't see anyone there either.

For a place that was so popular, it sure seemed empty.

But that changed only a moment later.

From the second floor above, I heard noises. Rumbles of both voices and footfalls coming in my direction.

I debated running back out of the hotel, but instead I moved to a spot in between the front window and the counter. I'd be out of the way there, though not invisible, no matter how much I tried to blend in with the scenery.

As though they traveled only together, a group of people appeared on the landing: Omar; a man I didn't recognize, dressed in a plush, white robe; and the short man with the glasses and big eyes who'd come into the shop looking for Matt Bane. Jodie was there too, wrangling a handcuffed prisoner, who was the movie star himself. Matt was no less handsome with a deeply worried and scared frown on his face and even messier hair. I noticed what I thought must be drying blood on his hands and a bloodstain in the middle of his white T-shirt. I couldn't let myself focus on the blood—in fact, the reality of it didn't want to register with me.

Just a prop, or a special effect maybe, my mind said.

He no longer wore the khaki ski coat, and the thought that he was going to get cold out there occurred to me as I watched Jodie guide him down the stairs.

His frantic eyes caught mine momentarily and I thought I saw brief but uncertain recognition in them. Weirdly, I nodded at him. Our silent communication didn't make any sense and he looked away quickly.

Omar, Matt's friend, and the robed man were all talking at once. I didn't get the specifics, but things like "I couldn't believe it!" and "Be tough!" and "He's so well-known!" came through. Those snippets didn't give me much of anything to go on, but there was no doubt that Matt was being arrested for something, and whatever it was, it included the shedding of blood, which was never a good sign.

No, just a prop. It's not real. It can't be.

As the group moved off the stairs and through the small lobby toward the front door, Jodie looked at me and silently mouthed, "What are you doing here?"

I lifted my eyebrows above my now fog-free glasses and shrugged a tiny bit. She sent me a Jodie-glare. I'd been the recipient of a few of those over the years. She'd want to discuss this later.

Omar pulled himself away from Matt's friend and the man and held the front door open for Jodie and Matt, and then spoke to the other two inside. Omar wasn't a big man and he was as fair as the winter snow on the slopes, but he knew how to command respect.

"We've got more officers on the way and you'll both need to answer some questions. For now, please remain in the lobby. Clare, I have no idea why you're here. Did you just come in?"

"Yes."

"Well, you need to leave. Everyone else, stay," Omar said. "And no one else is to leave. I'll be out front. Are there any back doors?"

"I don't think so," the robed man answered, his face seemingly becoming greener with each passing second.

"What does that mean, you don't know?" Omar said.

"No back door that I saw."

"Where's someone from the hotel? Is anyone working?"

No one had an answer for Omar.

"All right. Just stay put, you two. Out, Clare."

I nodded and moved toward the door, but couldn't resist asking, "What happened?"

Omar didn't answer, but the robed man spoke up, as if he needed to say the words, get them out of his system maybe.

"A woman was killed. That movie star killed her! So tragic."

"What?" I said.

The man who'd come into The Rescued Word after Matt shook his head and groaned.

"Come on, folks," Omar said with a glare in my direction that almost rivaled Jodie's. "Let's just settle down."

I took my cue and scooted through the front doors, finding an empty space where the police car had been. Jodie had been quick about getting Matt out of there. Before I could climb down the few stairs, a Subaru pulled into the space and I could see the two young women inside high-five each other. They'd managed to snag a great parking spot.

I was distracted as I stepped onto the sidewalk and crossed the street, but I made it in one piece. The crowds were currently oblivious to what had happened inside The Fountain, but the news would spread quickly. The story of this year's festival wouldn't be about Matt Bane purchasing personalized note cards from The Rescued Word so he could politely thank people. Marion wouldn't even get a bit part in this year's festival story.

It looked like the script would be all about Matt Bane killing someone.

The plot had most definitely thickened.

3

"No, I had no idea," I said as I looked at Marion, Seth, Chester, and Baskerville.

Baskerville seemed unimpressed by the news as Chester rubbed the back of his finger over each side of his mustache and shrugged. "Don't look at me. I don't pay attention to those sorts of things."

"Yeah," Marion said. "It's why he's here. Well, I did also hear that he's working on another project, but, nevertheless, his superhero movies aren't independent films. The movie he's here for is supposed to be his big 'serious' breakout film. *Kill Night.* He plays a cop who is also a killer, not like that serial killer who killed only other serial killers. No, Matt Bane's role is that of a vicious killer who likes to play mind games with the other cops, leave evidence to challenge them. That kind of thing. I hear it's gruesome and creepy and wonderful."

"Sounds it," I said. "Well, gruesome and creepy at least."

Seth smiled. "I heard it's so well written that you actually start to root for Matt's evil character even if you can't understand why. It's one of the few films I wanted to try to see. I bet it will be sold out just as soon as news hits the streets."

"Oh no," I said. "You don't think this is all a marketing ploy?"

Chester laughed. "You think Jodie would participate in such a thing?"

"No," I said.

"No, never," Marion agreed. "I just can't believe what has happened. He was so nice when he came in, and he's known for doing nice things. He's always visiting children's hospitals. He was supposed to be one of the good guys."

"Well, we don't know what happened yet. Let's wait and see," I said.

"I got his note cards done." Marion looked toward the short stack of note cards and envelopes she'd placed on the end of the counter. She'd wrapped the soft brown cards and envelopes with a bright red ribbon. She'd used a bold Bookman Old Style font to set "MB" in the bottom right corner of the cards. Though it had been a simple project, Matt's thank-yous would have been masculine and classy.

"We should have made him pay when he ordered," Chester said. We all looked at him. "I'm kidding. Sorry. I can see you all are fond of this fellow. I will reserve judgment until we better know the details of the crime. Gracious, you're all so sensitive."

He put his arm around Marion and pulled her close. "I'm sorry, dear girl."

"It's okay, Chester. You can't help yourself," Marion said.

"So true," he agreed.

Chester announced that he had some errands to run, and Marion asked if she could take a few minutes to dash up the hill to one of the festival's local ticket booths to see if any tickets were still available for *Kill Night* and some other films she wanted to see. I didn't have anywhere else I needed to be, but the conversation I'd had with Jodie about some additional help at the shop crossed my mind. We'd done fine so far, but Jodie was correct—Marion's life was potentially about to take her to places that would turn into more serious commitments than her part-time job. I didn't bring it up then, but I decided it would probably be a good idea to discuss it with Chester later. I said I'd watch the shop, and we all gave Marion some money so she could buy us tickets too. Even Chester—though hesitantly— became caught up in the Matt Bane frenzy we expected to unfold any minute and gave Marion some cash for tickets for him and his girlfriend, Ramona.

"What the heck, I might as well catch one film every ten years or so. I'll come with you and then run my errands afterwards," he said as he held the front door for Marion and then followed behind her.

When it was just Seth and me in the shop, he gave me his rock look, which was something I'd come to call his deeply curious inspection eyes. He loved rocks and geology. I think I realized he felt almost the same about me when one day he started looking at me in the same way he inspected the giant geode in his apartment. He said, "You okay?"

"Yeah, fine. I didn't see anything gory other than a little blood"—I swallowed hard—"but I'd like to know what's going on."

"Jodie will tell you," he said as he leaned a hip on the counter and crossed his arms in front of himself. "Maybe it's not what we think it is. Like you told Marion, let's get the facts first."

I wished I could open those arms and wedge myself inside them, but it didn't seem like a work-appropriate move. Yeah, I was smitten with the tall fellow who liked to read but had more rocks in his nerdy apartment than books. As befitted a scientist, at least a part of his mind was always taken up by his work. Even when I was the main focus of his attention, which was often, I knew his job never vacated his thoughts entirely. I didn't hold it against him. In fact, his immersive devotion to his career was one of the things I found so fetching about him. The others things included his clever sense of humor and the way he always pushed his glasses up his nose a second or two after I did the same thing to mine. Then there was the way we could talk for hours about anything, or say nothing and just sit silently together.

"Definitely, and I'll get Jodie to talk," I said. "Eventually."

Seth smiled. "Depends on her mood, I suppose."

"Everything depends on Jodie's mood." I pushed up my glasses.

So did Seth.

We were a couple of mostly opposites. I was on the shorter side, fair with long blond curls that drove me crazy more than they behaved. He was tall, thin but toned, not wiry, and molded with a defined softness that on him was somehow masculine. His dark curly hair was perpetually just slightly too long and looked in need of a good brushing. His skin was fair, but more alabaster than my peachy tones, and you could see the blue of his eyes from a couple of blocks away. He was a numbers guy; I was a words girl. We filled in each other's spaces.

"She's been in a good mood lately. Girl power makes it difficult for me to say this, but I give some credit to Mutt. I think they make each other happy," I said.

"They're a good couple. Last time we had dinner with them, he told me more about the work his motorcycle group does. I don't know how he has time to get everything done and see Jodie every now and then. Their mid-canyon meeting place is more like a hole-in-the-wall than a spot for a romantic rendezvous."

"Must not matter." I shrugged. I also liked that Seth said things like "romantic rendezvous." For a numbers guy, he still had some word surprises up his sleeve.

"So," Seth said as he bounced away from the counter. "I brought something for you."

"Oooh, really?" I said.

"Don't get too excited. It's more work related than personal."

I'd only halfway noticed that he'd placed a shoe box on the top of one of the middle paper shelves when he came in. He grabbed it, brought it back to the counter, and put his hands on the lid.

"I got this box from one of the geologists who helped with one of the reclamation projects. His mother lived in Salt Lake City. She passed away last week, and he's been cleaning out her house. I stopped by there yesterday to help him with some heavy lifting. He knows what you do for a living and said he thought you might be interested in these. He wanted you to have them."

"Intriguing."

With a bit more drama than the moment required, he lifted the lid.

"Ribbon tins!" I said as I peered inside the box. "So many of them!"

"By your happy tone, I take it this is a good surprise."

"It's a terrific surprise! Ribbon tins are fabulous." I reached inside and pulled out two. Both were round, about three inches in diameter. One was illustrated with a black background behind a decked-out equestrian on a horse that was jumping a pristine wooden fence; the other was decorated with a red cardinal sitting on a yellow tree branch, the black background on that one bringing out the red and yellow in bold relief.

"There are so many," I said. "I need to pay him for these."

"I told him that's what you'd want to do, but he insisted I give them to you. He thought maybe you might collect them, or go ahead and sell them if you want to. They are yours to do with whatever you please. He doesn't want any money. I got the sense that he was just glad to have one more box out of his mother's house, and it was a good way to thank me for my help."

"Typewriter ribbon tins are probably the most sought-after items associated with old typewriters. So many were created—it's difficult to know exactly how many—but they're small, and usually decorated with something interesting or weird. I think manufacturers started putting the ribbons in tins in the late eighteen hundreds. They're collectible, but none are all *that* valuable. People who love them *really* love them. We always sell them within a few days of getting them in the store. We don't even have to advertise. It's like there's some strange radar out there. I guarantee that within the next few days someone will come in asking if we have any ribbon tins to sell."

Carefully, I sifted through the box. Some of the art was bizarre; some of the tins didn't have any art but just words. But every single one was interesting. A woman seated in front of a typewriter with a bag over her head; a silhouette of an elk; a guy in a kilt playing bagpipes; a pigeon; the planet Saturn. And that was only the beginning.

"Glad I could contribute." Seth smiled.

I frowned. "I don't think I'd feel comfortable selling these. We'll see. Let me talk to Chester."

"Sure, but you don't need to worry. Seriously, do whatever you'd like to do with them. Daryl said that the only way he wants a cut is if you make over a million dollars."

"I'll keep that in mind. Thank you. Well, I'll thank him personally, but these are terrific."

Just as I dug my hand into the box again, Seth's cell

phone and the shop's phone rang at the same time. The shop's phone was an older model that still plugged into a landline. It didn't have caller ID, but it did have a tangled and knotted cord.

Seth looked at his caller ID, mouthed me a "See you later," and left out the front door just as I answered the shop's phone.

"Rescued Word," I said distractedly as I peered inside the box.

"Clare, s'me."

"Jodie? I can't think of the last time you called on the shop's phone. What's up?"

"I tried your cell. No answer. Hey, did you follow me over to The Fountain?"

"Yes," I confessed as I patted my pockets and looked over the front counter for my cell phone.

"Thought that's why you were there."

"What's going on?"

"I'll tell you because it will be all over the news any minute. We've arrested Matt Bane for murder. He's in one of our holding cells right now."

"That's horrible." My heart sank. "Who'd he kill?" I no longer cared about where my phone was hiding. I didn't know Matt well, but his movie star superhero persona and his friendliness in the shop that morning had given me a small connection to him. Or maybe it was just a sense of a connection. Either way, the news was deeply sad, and utterly shocking even after watching him being herded out of The Fountain in handcuffs.

"His sister. She was in town too. Some nobody actress

who was trying to ride his coattails to stardom, according to Omar. I don't pay attention to any of this movie star stuff. Anyway, there's another reason I'm calling. You already told me Mr. Movie Star was in your shop this morning. Got that, but he said his sister came in after him, and that he, his sister, and some guy named . . ." I heard some paper rustle. ". . . Howard Langer, Howie; he's Matt's guy. Matt called him his assistant, but I get the impression that he's more than that, maybe a kind of manager or agent; something more powerful than an assistant. Anyway, they all walked back down Bygone Alley together, and his sister—uh, Cassie—turned and headed down Main Street instead of crossing the street to go back to The Fountain. Mr. Bane is claiming that Cassie went somewhere and came back to The Fountain a little bit later. First, can you confirm that Ms. Cassie Bane and Mr. Howie Langer were in the shop?"

"Two people came in after Matt and they both seemed to be looking for him. A short guy with stubble over his face and head, glasses like Chester's but for someone farsighted; and a woman dressed like a stereotypical polygamist— pioneer stuff. I didn't get either of their names."

"Sounds like them. Okay, did you by chance see where they went after they left the shop?"

"Just toward Main Street. I didn't follow them outside to watch. No one did. Marion was too flummoxed by Matt coming in the store to do much of anything and Chester just didn't care."

"You've got that security camera outside the shop, right?"

"Well, yes, but it's not aimed down toward Main. It just gives us a view of who's directly outside by our front door."

Jodie cursed.

"Sorry."

"Not your fault. Gotta go, see if I can track down where his sister went after The Rescued Word, or if she really did go anywhere else."

"Jodie?"

"Yeah."

"Why would it matter if she went anywhere? Wasn't she killed at The Fountain?"

"She was, but Mr. Bane claims that someone came back to the hotel with her, that he heard voices coming from her room before he heard a big thud. At that moment Howie was in Matt's room. Matt ran next door and found the victim." She cleared her throat. "And then Matt grabbed the murder weapon, got blood on his hands and an interesting spatter pattern on his shirt. We don't think that's exactly what happened."

"How was she killed?"

"Knife to the gut. Quick and dirty. Crime scene folks will be cleaning up for another hour or so."

"Ugh. Wouldn't stabbing someone cause more blood?"

"Not necessarily. But good question. You're almost ready for cop school."

I smiled. Jodie had been razzing me about my overinvolvement in a murder that had occurred in town not too long ago. Typewriters had played a big part in that crime. It had seemed natural to be involved. For a brief moment or two Marion had been in danger as well. You can't help but jump into the middle of a murder when family could get hurt.

"I'm going to investigate every possible lead, including Matt's idea that someone else was in the room with Cassie. But at this time we don't having anything indicating that happened. If we had a recording of Cassie going right at the end of Bygone, we might have something more to go on."

"The hotel receptionist didn't see anyone go in with her?"

"No, no one was at the desk at that time. Hey, I gotta go, Clare."

"Okay. Bye," I said.

But she'd already hung up.

The news knocked me for a loop. Murder was always horrible, but the news that Matt had been arrested for the evil deed didn't sit right with me. He'd seemed like such a *nice young man*. My grandmother's words rang in my mind.

At the very least he hadn't seemed like a killer. However, I knew that some killers were the best actors. I shook away the disturbing thoughts.

I lifted the few pieces of paper on the counter in search of my cell phone, and then patted my pockets again. I hadn't been back to the workshop after returning from the hotel. Had I?

Baskerville had climbed to one of his sunning spots high atop the front shelves. He meowed down at me.

"Have you seen my phone?" I asked up to him.

He turned in a circle and relaxed into a naptime curl.

I hurried back to the workshop and glanced quickly over my desk. No sign of the phone. I returned to the front of the unmanned shop. I could do a better search in the back later when either Marion or Chester was back.

The few seconds I'd taken were enough for a slew of customers to come in from the cold. A group of four, two couples, and a woman who remained on the perimeter of the shop as the two couples perused and then decided on some paper and envelopes. I eyed the single woman as she walked around. She feigned an interest in the carved doors over the shelves that ran down the middle of the side walls of the shop. The carvings were mountainous landscape scenes and had garnered plenty of attention over the years, particularly when Chester entertained interested customers with stories he made up about each one. He enjoyed making up the stories almost as much as the customers enjoyed listening to and believing them.

But it was obvious that the woman in the black coat with the black scarf wound around her head wasn't truly interested in the doors. She faced them, but I could see the slight angle of her neck as if she wasn't really looking at them, but listening to the other customers' conversations instead.

She waited a polite two beats after the other customers left before she turned, looked toward the front door, and then toward me as she unfurled the scarf.

Her smile was big, white, and genuine.

"Hi," she said as she walked toward the counter.

She was even more stunning in person than she was on television and in movies. She wasn't young, but she didn't look her age, which I thought was probably close to fifty.

Her features didn't seem to have been altered with surgery though; there were pleasant laugh lines around her eyes, and I couldn't help but wonder about the brand of moisturizer she used.

"Hi," I said breathlessly. We had another movie star in the shop. And, coincidentally, she knew Matt Bane. For an instant, it was all a bit too much to process, but she gave me a second to recover. She was probably used to her ability to knock people momentarily speechless. "Welcome. How can I help you?"

"Thanks. It's great to be here. Star City is quite the place." She was friendly and looked me in the eye.

"Thanks," I said.

Nell Sterling wouldn't have been considered a serious actress. She'd been on a television sitcom for its full eight-season run. She'd transitioned into romantic comedies on the big screen, but I hadn't seen much from her lately. I had a fuzzy memory of reading about her frustration with the roles she'd been given over the years. She'd always wanted meaty, but had only been able to acquire fluffy.

However, her biggest claim to fame was that she'd dated Matt Bane. Though I despised the word, Nell had been Hollywood's most popular "cougar" for about seven months—a short time in most everyone's lives, but almost an eternity in Hollywood tabloid news. "Reporters" had managed to stretch the story about her and Matt, together and apart, for those long months. Eventually, their on-and-off relationship faded from the entertainment news and I hadn't heard much about her for some time.

She was tall, blond, and built (there might have been

some plastic surgery done below the neck, but I didn't want to stare) with a big, toothy smile that I was sure had just twinkled at me.

"I have a book," she said when she realized I was ready to move on. "It's a valuable book, but I don't want to sell it. I want to see if you can fix it."

She reached into the large, black leather bag over her shoulder and pulled out a manila envelope that bulged with a booklike bump. With another smile in my direction, she reached into the envelope and then pulled out the book.

"When I decided to come to the festival this year, I knew I had to see if you could help me. I'd heard about your shop and I could barely wait to come in. This was my father's book and I'd love to have it back in pristine condition."

It was a first edition—I confirmed by quickly lifting the cover to check the copyright page—of Charles Dickens's *Barnaby Rudge*. It was without a dust jacket, but the green cloth binding was in pretty good shape.

"I wish my grandfather was in the shop," I said. "He loves Dickens, tells everyone he was a childhood friend of the famous author."

Nell blinked. "That wouldn't even be possible, would it? Dickens lived in the eighteen hundreds, didn't he?"

I smiled. "See, he'd like you right away because you knew that. You'd be surprised how many people don't."

Of course, even my grandfather wouldn't be immune to Nell Sterling's beauty, even if she hadn't known that Dickens was a nineteenth-century author.

"Ah, I see," she said. "I'll have to come back when he's in. Do you think you can fix the book?"

"What's wrong with it?"

"Chocolate. Pages forty-eight, forty-nine, and fifty."

The edges of the pages were worn with time, but I'd seen much worse. I used my knuckles so I wouldn't add any oil to the paper as I made my way to forty-eight. There weren't just a few chocolate fingerprints but lots of them, so many that one paragraph was almost illegible. The same thing had occurred on the other two mentioned pages.

"What happened?"

"My niece, a few years ago when she was little, really liked chocolate, and I hadn't childproofed my library. She still likes chocolate, but is old enough now to be mortified when I tell the story of how she thought it would be fun to add her own touches to the book."

"It's a great book," I said. "Are you going to try to sell it?"

I'd never read the book, but I'd heard Chester discuss it with customers. Originally published in serial form, it was Dickens's first attempt at writing a historical novel. It was about a decades-old murder and those who covered up the crime. The clearest memory I had of one of Chester's discussions was a vibrant back-and-forth about the meaning of the birthmark on the character Barnaby's wrist. Chester had been fairly friendly with the customer, but after he left, Chester said, *"That man needs to learn how to read a book, not just skim it."*

"No. It's mine forever, or my niece's someday," Nell said. "Children don't look to be in my future." There was no sadness in her voice, or in her eyes. I looked closely because I knew that was one of the reasons the tabloids claimed had caused the breakup with Matt. She hadn't wanted to try to have kids at her age and he wanted a family.

"Do you know about the raven?" I asked.

"The talking raven in the story?"

"Yes."

"What about him?"

Now I really wished Chester were in the shop to tell her all about Grip. My grandfather collected stories about authors, and this was one of his favorites. It wasn't a long story, but he could tell it with much more appropriate drama than I could.

"The raven in the story was inspired by Dickens's own raven, Grip."

"Really?"

"Yes, Grip was a beloved pet. And there's more."

"I'm all ears."

"Two other interesting facts. One, it is said that Edgar Allan Poe reviewed *Barnaby Rudge* and thought Dickens should have given the raven a bigger part. Some say . . ."

"That Dickens's raven inspired Poe's?" Nell jumped in.

"Yes."

"That's wonderful." She smiled dreamily like I'd seen others do when Chester told the story. It was always interesting to think about the juxtaposition of the two authors and how the same bird might have inspired their work. Maybe I hadn't been so boring in the telling after all.

"And the bird is on display in Philadelphia, just in case you have any desire to see an old stuffed bird," I said.

She laughed. "No kidding? You know, I just might have .

to do that someday. Thanks for the story. I love that I know that now."

"My pleasure. Anyway, when it comes to your book, I might be able to clean it up a little bit, but I'd like for you to really think about if you want me to do too much. Clearly, you adore your niece, and the chocolate fingerprints make a good story. You don't want to sell the book—even if you did, I might advise against cleaning it up completely. Sometimes 'as is' is better than anything that's been worked on. Are you in town through the festival?"

"I am."

"Think about it a day or so. Do you really want to get rid of those fingerprints? If you do, bring it back in. If not, just come by sometime and give my grandfather a thrill. He's not much into movie stuff, but he'd know who you are, and if he had false teeth, I'm sure they'd fall right out when you came into the shop."

She smiled. "Thank you."

"You're welcome."

The front door opened again. Both Nell and I looked toward it.

"Uh-oh," I heard her say under her breath. I thought the same thing.

We'd gone from zero to three in our movie star count. And, oddly, they were all connected.

Adele White took up much more space than it seemed her tiny frame should allow. She was petite, and looked fierce, with all black clothing that included an oversized black leather jacket, Goth makeup, and short black hair. She was striking. She was pretty one moment, not so pretty the next. I thought her chameleon ability might be a good skill for an actress to have.

She was also, at least according to what I knew, Matt Bane's current girlfriend.

Before I smiled and welcomed her in, I wondered briefly if we were all being filmed for some silly festival candid-camera stunt.

I glanced back and forth between the actresses, as different as they could be. They looked at each other, away, and then back at each other again. Neither of them seemed happy to see the other one.

"Uh-oh" was right.

4

Nell sent me a friendly but quick smile and a thank-you before she said she'd be in touch about the chocolate stains. With her chin perhaps tilted a bit too high, she walked confidently down the middle of the store, past Adele, and then out the front door. They didn't really look at each other as they both muttered things I couldn't quite catch.

Once Nell was out of the shop, Adele seemed to become suddenly more comfortable in her skin. She smiled warily, shyly maybe, as she walked toward me. It was impossible to know if she had been uncomfortable about Nell or just uncomfortable. Maybe it was just her way.

Earlier last year Adele had been the star of a torturous movie about a teenage girl dying from cancer. For weeks, I'd observed people leaving our small Star City Main Street Theater in tears and wondered why anyone would want to see such horror. I'd heard Adele's portrayal of the girl would put her in contention for the big movie awards. It hadn't, though. She'd been over-looked, or ignored, or whatever it was that happened. Some said it was because of her relationship with Matt Bane, who was at the time known more for wearing a cape and saving the world than for portraying anything as gritty or serious as a serial killer. If Matt hadn't been arrested for murder and if his new movie did well at the festival, he might have been able to change not only his career but the careers of the people closest to him. Hollywood was a weird world.

"Welcome, can I help you with anything?" I said.

She was almost to the counter, and then she stopped. She cocked her head and bit her bottom lip. She looked around, at the shelves, at the counter, then slowly along the counter, and finally at me. "Was Matt Bane in here earlier?"

"Yes, he was," I said while my brain did a quick sift of the facts as I knew them to be. Matt and Adele were a couple, or maybe they were just a rumored couple. Either way, her asking the question wasn't quite like the typical starstruck fan asking it, so I'd answered honestly and hopefully without even a tinge of suspicion to my voice. When she didn't say anything more I continued, though I had no way to be certain she knew he'd been arrested. "I'm, uh, sorry about Matt."

"I know. Me too. It's so sad and scary. I can't believe it's real."

I nodded. "Did you come by to pick up his note cards?"

"Yes. Note cards. I'm a bit distracted, worried. I apologize."

"No problem. I understand. The note cards are ready." I grabbed them from the end of the counter and handed them to her. She took them and nodded, but didn't say anything as she slipped them into her jacket pocket.

"Hitting the slopes this year?" I said.

"I don't like winter. I really don't like snow. Skiing and snowboarding aren't things I'm interested in at all. I miss Los Angeles."

Though my experience in conversing with movie stars was limited, I felt uneasy about not being able to figure out what more to say to Adele. I was sure that Marion would have done just fine, but all I could think of were more comments about the normal stuff—slopes and snow—so I just smiled.

"Oh, what do I owe you?" she said another second later.

The transaction was completed quickly, and she sent me one last obligatory and almost sheepish smile before she looked around the shop again and then left. "Slunk away" came to my mind as I watched her go.

Suddenly, all became quiet in the shop. The silence radiated a feeling I knew, something I recognized after living in Star City and working at The Rescued Word for so long. The quiet changed inside the shop when a storm was on the way; it became heavier and closer, though explaining that to outsiders was difficult. Chester recognized it, and Marion was beginning to get it. We'd decided it was something about the history and the architecture of the old brick mining-office building—it pulled itself in a little tighter when bad weather was on the way.

Baskerville, a less-than-friendly calico cat, recognized it too. Though he spent most of his days resting on top of the high shelves, picking the best side depending upon which high window the sun was shining in, he decided it was time to join me, one of the mere humans, below. He felt the stormy silence too.

"We've been popular today," I said as I gathered him into

my arms. He let me hold him, but he didn't snuggle. Baskerville wasn't a snuggler. The offspring of the greatest cat ever and our first shop cat, Arial, Baskerville would be loved and cared for forever, even if he wasn't nearly as friendly as his mother.

I carried him up to the front, where we looked out the window together. I was much more interested in the large crowd inside the diner across the street than he was. But when some big, fat snowflakes began to fall, his eyes watched them carefully, suspiciously. Like Adele, Baskerville did not like winter weather. But I loved it. So did Chester and Marion; even Seth liked it and was seemingly intrigued by Marion's offer to teach him to snowboard. Cold noses and cheeks, blazing fireplaces, knit hats and scarves, and hot chocolate. I loved winter, and Star City did winter right.

The tranquil Bygone Alley snow globe scene was interrupted by the blaring of sirens and the blaze of bright lights. I jumped in my skin as Baskerville's eyes got wide and he dug a claw into my arm. I winced but held tight as a police car pulled up to the curb in front of the shop.

For a moment I was worried about what might happen next. But then Jodie got out of the car and waved. She was dressed in civilian clothing and had a big smile on her face.

I'd forgotten about our date—dinner and one of the less popular festival films she'd managed to get tickets to.

I hoped she hadn't caught my momentary confusion and then the clarity that had set in when I realized she wasn't here on official business. I waved back.

"Guess I'd better brush my hair," I said to Baskerville.

He meowed disagreeably.

5

I hurried back out to the front of the store after having dashed up to Chester's apartment for a quick freshening up. My phone had been on Marion's low work desk behind the shop's counter the whole time. I'd happened to see it out of the corner of my eye only when I was rushing to rejoin Jodie by the front door. The ringer had been turned off and I had no recollection of leaving it there. I must have been more shaken by the day's events than I'd thought.

When I reached her, Jodie's smile had been replaced with a marked frown.

"What?"

"I have to run back to the station first. Creighton needs some paperwork I didn't finish. His promotion will be the death of me." She glanced at the giant-faced watch on her wrist. "After that, we'll have to make dinner a fast one to get to the movie on time."

"No problem. I'll come with you down the hill so you don't have to make the detour here again," I said.

"Deal."

I bid the cat good night and left a note for Chester before I switched off the lights and locked the front door. Baskerville would join Chester up in his apartment later, where he would knead Chester's leg as he tried to read in his old chair. The cat would curl up next to Chester's face when he went to bed. It was a routine that neither of them would admit to enjoying, but one they both relished.

"A little early to be closing?" Jodie said.

"You're probably right about our needing some help. However, I think Chester will be back soon and we don't typically have too many customers this late. I have no idea if Marion will come back in or not. And it's beginning to snow. It's okay to close a little early."

In fact, the snow did little to deter our business, but it *was* close to dinnertime.

"Told you," Jodie said over the top of her police car as she opened her door.

"You did," I conceded. I hid the smile that pulled at the corner of my mouth. Jodie loved to be right. Sometimes I just liked to give her the opportunity. She did the same for me sometimes too.

Most of the time I thought Jodie abused her police power with her siren and lights, but during the festival I always appreciated the convenience; it was about the only way to get anywhere in a timely manner.

The flashing lights and one loud nasal honk were enough to get the crowds out of our way as we rolled back down the hill and toward the police station.

"So," I began as Jodie dodged two young festivalgoers who were taking their lives into their hands by crossing in front of us.

"What?" she said without looking over at me. She sent a stern grimace to the pedestrians, but they ignored her.

"Matt Bane is under arrest?" I said.

"Yes."

"He's in one of the cells at the police station?"

"For now."

"Has he had any visitors?"

"No visitors allowed right now. We'll let an attorney in, but no one else."

I paused.

"What?" Jodie said.

"Any chance you could look the other way for a minute while we're walking by the door that leads to the cells?" I said.

"No. And it wouldn't do you any good anyway. You have to be buzzed in."

"Would you buzz me in? Please?"

"No! Why do you want to talk to him?"

"I'm not sure, Jodie. Until this very second it hadn't even occurred to me, but we'll be in his general proximity. I met him shortly before the murder, and he seemed so . . . non-murderous, I guess. I'd just like to talk to him. I bet he could use a friend."

"All killers are lacking for friends. Unless you count those freaky prison pen-pal people."

Paige Shelton

"Come on. What harm could I do?"

"Clare, it's totally against policy."

"Will Creighton be there?"

"He's gone, but he said he'd be back later."

"He's the big boss now, right? If he's not there at the moment . . ."

"Clare."

"We're almost there. What harm could I do? Just think about it until we get inside."

We remained silent as Jodie pulled into the station lot and parked the car. I knew she was ruminating on my request even if she seemed disinterested. Once the flashing lights atop the car were switched off, the surrounding parking lot and streetlights became bland and boringly normal. Big snowflakes were still falling, but not heavily yet.

I pulled my coat collar up around my mouth and followed closely behind her as we went through the front doors toward the hallway that led to her office. She came to a hard stop before we reached the left hall that would take us to the holding cells.

"Why do you want to talk to Matt Bane, Clare? I know you're not starstruck, and I know you despise the paparazzi. It's not like you're going to snap a picture and try to sell it."

"Of course not. No, Jodie, but having met him, I feel like there's a connection. Nothing romantic, just something there. Believe it or not, I'm concerned about him." I looked around. No one was listening. "Coincidentally, Nell Sterling also came into the shop today. I liked her as well. I don't know. Maybe I'm making up the connections or I could be a little starstruck and not know it, but I don't think

· 48 ·

so. I just want to check on him. I don't have a file in my purse, like I would if it were you in there. I'd break you out for sure, but not Matt Bane."

She angled one eyebrow.

I held a small, hopeful smile.

"All right," she said a beat later. "We do allow visitors for prisoners—just not this one because he's so famous, but that's only Creighton's rule, not policy. I suppose you could talk to him for a minute."

"Thanks, Jodie."

"Whatever. If I get fired, you have to date Creighton again just so he'll give me my job back."

I was never going to date Creighton again, but I made a gurgled noncommittal noise to keep her from changing her mind.

We came upon a large, thick steel door. Jodie hid her fingers as she punched in a code. A buzz preceded the loud thunk of locking mechanisms before the door swung inward.

"Wow, I thought we were just little old Star City," I said.

"High-tech security. We might be small, but we get visitors from all over the world, Clare. We've got to be prepared."

"I guess."

We traveled down the starkly lit gray hallway, the sense of being in a vacuum coming over me. I swallowed the claustrophobia that was inching through my chest. It wasn't a tight space, but the closing door behind us and the fact that there was no sign of an exit or even a window ahead got to me a little.

"Jodie, what's up?" Linus said. Linus had been on the

police force for about a hundred and fifty years. He'd never climbed the ranks and had, in fact, mostly been given desk jobs. He was a well-known figure throughout town because of his friendly smile and his short stature. He wore short better than most tall men wore tall, Jodie once said.

"Linus, can you buzz Clare back to talk to the prisoner in number three?" Jodie said.

"Nope. Creighton said no visitors."

"Yeah, I know, but that's because of the whole press, paparazzi stuff. Clare's a friend of Mr. Bane's. She just wants to make sure he's doing all right. You know Clare Henry, don't you?"

"Sure, you and your grandfather have the word place up there on Bygone. Your grandfather fixed my typewriter twenty years ago and I haven't had to fight it once since."

"That's good to hear," I said.

Jodie and I both fell silent as Linus considered the request. I was sure Jodie was trying not to frown as much as I was trying not to over-smile.

"Well, okeydokey, then," Linus finally said.

"I'll be in my office," Jodie said to me. She turned to Linus. "Send her my way when she's done. Thanks, Linus."

I didn't watch her leave the hallway, but I heard her heavy, quick footsteps fade as she walked away.

"All righty, young lady. You may talk to the prisoner. You have to stay back from his cell by five feet. There's a line on the floor to keep behind. You may either stand or use one of those folding chairs against the back wall. I'm not going to work hard to listen, but there's no privacy in there, in case you were wondering. If he confesses to killing that young lady, or any other crime for that matter, those words could be used against him. Got all that?"

"I do. Thanks, Linus."

"Welcome."

Linus reached to the far side of the desk and pushed a hidden button. This time the buzz preceded an iron-barred door swinging open.

Again, it did not seem like I was in little ol' Star City, but I went through anyway. Fluorescent lights on the short ceiling came on as though they were on a sensor switch set to illuminate one at a time as I passed by. Suddenly, the black bars of the four cells seemed to become much more real—inky and cold.

"Hello?" a voice called from the far cell.

"Matt?" I said as I made sure I stayed behind the line as I approached.

"Yeah. Who's here?"

"Hey," I said as Matt's cell came into view. He was standing and holding on to the bars, just like they do in the movies. His disheveled hair matched his untucked shirt, but he was still movie star handsome. He still wore black jeans, but he'd been given a different white T-shirt; this one looked new with straight creases from where it had been folded. There was no blood on either the new shirt or his hands. I was surprisingly relieved.

I'd never once seen these holding cells. I'd never asked for the tour or Jodie would have obliged. They were stark with a mattress-free cot and a utilitarian toilet, but nothing else. I'd never given one thought to the holding cells inside the station, but they were just awful. At least they didn't smell bad.

Matt's eyebrows came together when he saw me. A beat later he said, "You're the woman from the note card place. The word rescuer."

"Clare Henry."

"Okay, Clare Henry. I'm confused. Why are you here?"

"Well, I wanted to see how you were doing." I cringed.

"Not well. But . . . thanks." His face was drawn and even though a night hadn't passed yet, dark circles had already formed under his eyes.

I grabbed the folding chair leaning against the far wall and set it precisely behind the line.

As I took a seat, I said, "My best friend is a police officer. We were here because she has some work to do, and I asked if I could check on you. I'm very sorry about your sister."

"That's very kind." He ran his fingers through his hair, making it even messier. "I can't believe she's gone. I can't believe they think I killed her."

"Do you have an attorney?"

"I believe so, but I haven't met him or her yet. My assistant is taking care of the arrangements, I hope. I haven't seen him either," he said as he took a seat on the edge of the cot.

Though it didn't smell bad, there was a damp scent that burned my sinuses slightly.

I nodded as I rubbed my finger under my nose. Now that I was there, I realized how really weird it was that I had wanted to talk to Matt Bane as he sat in a prison cell. How strange it must have been from his side of the bars.

"Matt, your old and new girlfriends stopped by The

Rescued Word today," I said, searching for something that might make my being there somehow more valid.

"Oh?" He blinked up from the depths.

"Yeah, both Nell and Adele stopped by. Adele picked up your note cards."

"Really? Huh. Well, that was nice of her, I guess. Do you want to know if we're really a couple? That's what most people want to know."

"No, I don't care much about that. I really liked Nell, though. She seems smart and friendly."

"She's also much older than me, which was no big deal as far as I was concerned. She didn't like the 'cougar' title."

"No. I imagine not."

We'd taken a tiny step forward. I could see Matt's shoulders relax a little bit. Despite the fact that he must have been distraught about his sister and concerned about his own freedom, I trudged forward.

"Matt," I said. He looked at me, his eyes less glazed over now. "Who do you think killed your sister?"

He shrugged. "I have absolutely no idea. None at all."

"Hollywood jealousy maybe?"

He blinked again as if he hadn't even considered the idea. Maybe he hadn't considered any idea. If he wasn't the killer, he was probably still in shock. If he was the killer, he was putting on his best performance. But I still hadn't seen *Kill Night*, so it might be too soon to judge.

"I truly don't know." He paused, seemingly considering my words. "I can't imagine why anyone would be jealous of Cassie." He blanched. "Oh my God, she's dead."

His head fell into his hands and I had the urge to get out of the chair and offer comfort or something. I stayed put.

"I'm sorry, Matt," I said.

The awkwardness stretched, but I couldn't find the right moment to jump back in, and getting up and leaving seemed rude. Fortunately, Matt moved us forward.

"I'm sorry, Clare. I'm sure I'll be fine. Actually, if I give it some thought, I might have a couple of ideas of who could have killed my sister. Maybe."

"Did you give the police any ideas of where to look?"

"No, and I wouldn't yet anyway. I'm waiting for my attorney before I talk to them."

"Of course. That makes sense."

"I didn't kill my sister, Clare."

"Good. The police will find the killer, then."

"I hope so. I have . . . Well, I just hope so. I wonder . . ."

"What do you wonder?"

Matt stood from the cot and moved to the bars again, lowering his voice. "I wonder about my fame. It can either work for or against me."

"Most likely for. At least that's been the history with these kinds of things."

He tapped on the bar twice with his fingertip. "Would you consider doing me a favor?"

"I guess. What is it?" Truthfully, I didn't want to do Matt Bane a favor. I didn't even completely understand why I'd wanted to talk to him, except for that weird sense of a connection that I couldn't quite shake.

"Is there any chance you could check on my assistant, Howie? See why he hasn't come to talk to me and ask him what he thinks might have happened to Cassie. He's in room four at The Fountain."

"I think the police will do that," I said. "And there's a chance that Howie has tried to talk to you, Matt. You're off-limits to all visitors except an attorney."

"Why? Oh, of course, that makes sense. Every trash tabloid reporter would be all over me. I guess I should be thankful for the protection. How did you get in?"

"My police officer friend. I twisted her arm."

Matt nodded. "All right." He paused. "Will you ask Howie why he hasn't sent an attorney yet?"

"Again, I bet the police are working on it, or they'll ask Howie."

"Howie won't be up-front with the police, probably won't talk to them unless they cuff him. It's what he does. He lies, particularly to media people, paparazzi, and the police. It's his nature. He doesn't trust anyone. He would do what he could to avoid them. He wouldn't lie to you, though, not if you told him I'd asked you to talk to him."

"Why would he believe that you sent me?"

"I'll give you a code word. We have to use them, like when we check into hotels under aliases. We have secret words, stuff like that. Part of the price of fame."

"Kind of like parents give their kids so they know who to trust if someone approaches them?"

"Exactly. Howie and I have used a particular one frequently. It helps."

"What's the code word?"

"You'll do it, then—talk to Howie?"

"I will." I wasn't sure I'd be able to manipulate another

meeting with Matt, but I was willing to try. Besides, now I really wanted to know what the code word was.

"Thanks. It's 'Sundance.' I loved *Butch Cassidy and the Sundance Kid* when I was growing up."

"Sundance. I can handle that."

"Thank you, Clare. Let him know I'm doing all right. Ask him to send an attorney. Ask him to come see me himself." I heard a smidgen of hope with his words. It was always good to be proactive, I guess, even if that just meant asking someone else to do something.

"Will do."

"I owe you," Matt said sincerely.

"Not at all." I stood and moved the chair back to the wall. As I headed toward Linus and the exit, I stopped in front of Matt's cell again and pushed up my glasses. He didn't remind me so much of a movie star anymore.

"What a mess," Matt muttered as he made his way back to the cot. "I can't even mourn my sister properly because I'm so scared I'll be falsely convicted for her murder. I go from devastated to scared to death and back again. Over and over. I'm sure I sound frantic. I'm sorry." He paused briefly. "And I'm sorry to ask you for a favor. You don't owe me a thing, but I really appreciate it."

"It's fine, Matt. I'm sorry for what you're going through, and I always believe in innocent until proven guilty." My heart hurt for him and that connection that I'd sensed grew a little bigger. I wondered if I'd feel the same way about all my friendly customers who got arrested for murder or just the ones who played superheroes in movies. And serial killers—I needed to remember that part too.

"I didn't kill her, Clare. There's no reason you should believe me, but I didn't kill her."

He was a good actor. Or he was telling the truth.

"The police will figure it out, Matt. They're a top-notch group."

"I hope so."

I doubted even the best of actors could have put as much emotion into the word "hope" as he'd just done.

But maybe he was just really, really good.

"I hate to even ask this," he said as he came back to the bars again, "but could I have your phone number? I don't know if they'll ever let me make calls, but I feel so lost. If I can't get to Howie, I . . . I guess I just need a connection, someone I know I can talk to if I need to."

"Sure." I recited the number and he memorized it.

"Thank you," he said, his voice full of relief.

I didn't know what it was like to feel so alone, and my heart hurt for him.

"See you later, Matt," I said.

"Thanks, Clare. Thanks more than you know."

6

"That wasn't one of the best. Sorry. I knew there was a reason I got the tickets so easily," Jodie said as we left the small theater.

"I kind of enjoyed it," I said. The plot about an elementary school teacher's drunken weekend had been pretty weak and predictable, but I'd relished the fact that I was able to spend an hour and a half in my own thoughts and not feel like I missed too much.

"Dinner was good."

"Dinner was great," I agreed.

We walked slowly toward the police car. Surprisingly it wasn't so cold that we felt the need to hurry. The clouds had cocooned us, and the snow had stopped. It would start again soon, I predicted.

The temperature was pleasant, particularly for a January

night in Star City. If we both didn't have to work in the morning, we'd probably stay out with the festival crowd. When we were younger, we'd spent an evening or two in search of movie stars. We might not be as interested in that sort of thing anymore, but the party atmosphere was fun if you were in the party mood—which we weren't, hadn't been for some time. A sudden wave of concern over Marion came over me. When I was seventeen and the festival was in full swing, I wasn't on my best behavior. But I had to remember that her father was my overprotective brother, Jimmy. He was probably standing sentry outside her bedroom door. I smiled to myself. When did I get so old?

"I'm surprised I liked it," Jodie said.

I blinked. "Oh. The dinner. You're surprised you liked sushi? Me too. I thought you'd hate it."

"Clare, what's on your mind?" Jodie said. "You're only half here."

"Sorry. Just a weird day."

"Your conversation with Matt Bane? The one where he told you nothing important but continued to proclaim his innocence."

That had been my story and I was sticking to it. "Yes. He definitely said he was innocent."

"Shocking. Most criminals confess right away."

"I know, I know."

Jodie sighed and looked up and down the street. "Don't know if he's innocent or not. Don't have a sense of it yet. But I will. He's the obvious one at this point. That's why he's under arrest."

"Right. Any less obvious suspects out there?"

"Not telling."

I sent her a Clare-glare, but they were never as effective as hers.

Jodie opened the passenger door for me. "After you."

"Thanks."

She didn't turn on the siren or the lights as we cruised up Main Street. At night the mere presence of the police car caused rowdier pockets to quiet down and jaywalkers to think twice before crossing, and though she was off-duty, she was looking around for potential trouble. As usual, the street was crowded, but the flow of people both up and down the sidewalks was brisk. The car traffic was much slower than the pedestrians and we stopped and started frequently.

As we came upon The Fountain, my attention turned toward its charming brick facade. It suddenly reminded me of a gingerbread cottage plunked next to more modern but still charming buildings. My admiration transformed to curiosity as I watched a tall woman walk into the hotel. I sat up straighter. Had that been Nell Sterling? The woman had worn a scarf around her head, but it was familiar, and had distinctly reminded me of Nell.

"What?" Jodie said.

"I . . . uh. You know, this is crazy. I'm going to get out here and walk the rest of the way up. You can turn around and head back down. It's such a great night. No need to fight all this."

"Well . . . ," Jodie began.

I was out of the car before she could complete the protest. "Thanks for the great evening, Jodie. We'll talk tomorrow."

"You're welcome. I know you're up to something. Just don't get in trouble, okay?"

"I won't." I laughed.

"Good night, Clare."

"Good night, Jodie." I closed the door, grateful she'd had a long day too and wasn't in the mood to interrogate me regarding my sudden exit.

I thought I would have to meander a moment so she wouldn't see where I went, but she flipped on the lights and siren and was turned around and out of sight only a few seconds later.

"Atta girl," I said.

Without further hesitation, I wove my way through the crowds and went into The Fountain.

A cozy fire was blazing again, but the newspapers from the side tables were gone, replaced by a couple of paperbacks I didn't recognize. There was no receptionist behind the narrow counter. There was no sign of Nell, of anyone. I saw a bell I could ring but decided not to before I dashed up the stairway.

The short hall that led to the four upper-level rooms wasn't well lit, leaving most of the space shadowy, but I could clearly see whether anyone was there, and the hallway was as empty as the lobby.

I stood on the balcony part of the second floor with my hands on my hips and pondered what to do next. I could knock on doors in search of Nell or knock on room four's door and share the secret word with Howie if he was there, but it was late and I was mostly curious about Nell. I wished I'd asked Matt if she was staying at The Fountain.

Jodie would know, but she'd turn the police car around and would have me in handcuffs if she figured out I was snooping.

The noise of a lock mechanism caused me to step back and find my way behind a tall waxy-leafed plant. I wasn't very well hidden, but my instinct was to not get caught and it was the best cover around. I peered through a spot in between two of the leaves.

A second later, I confirmed that I had, in fact, seen Nell Sterling. The woman clad in a black scarf and coat and boots now came out of the second room on the right, which was room number three. One piece of her long blond hair had escaped all the black and made a bold statement down the front of her coat.

She had the same big bag she'd brought into the shop with her, but it didn't seem weighed down by much of anything. She held an iPad clutched to her chest. Had I seen the iPad when she'd entered the hotel? I thought back and tried to visualize. I didn't think I'd seen it. In fact, I was pretty sure I hadn't. I remembered her pulling open the door and there'd been nothing in her hands at that time.

Had she taken an iPad from the bag or the room she'd been in? Whose room was it? Whose iPad?

I froze behind the poor cover of the plant. She was bound to see me.

But she couldn't have cared less about the plant or who was behind it. Her singular focus was on getting out of the hotel. Her eyes never ventured in my direction. Her head was tilted down as if she was attempting to hide her face. Her strides were long and fast. She passed by without looking up, let alone toward me. I got a whiff of her lavender perfume before she turned and hurried down the stairs.

I was out from behind the plant the second she pushed through the front door. With what sounded to me like Jodie's footfalls, I clomped down the stairs and out the door. There was still no one at the reception counter. Did anyone ever work there?

The good news was that the streets were still crowded, so Nell hadn't gotten far and I could spot her easily. The better news was that she was going my way, up the hill toward my house.

I followed behind, zigging and zagging, not too concerned that I'd be caught. Even if I was seen, I could have come up with a believable story. When she was only two houses from mine, though, she stopped and turned to look back down the hill. A rush of guilt tightened my throat as I froze in place. If she looked at me, I'd smile and wave. But her searching eyes skimmed over me without even a hint of recognition. She turned into a small walkway between two buildings. I knew it was a spot that held an old rickety stairway that led to some of the bigger chalet homes located higher up on the hill than my small house. Not many people knew about the stairs, preferring to use the much more reliable paved path that you could get to only by going all the way up Main and then circling around. The stairs were a nice, if slightly unsteady, shortcut. She knew her way around Star City.

Once she was out of sight, I hurried to follow behind, but I didn't go up the stairs. Instead, from outside the walkway, I watched her go up two short but steep flights and then take a narrow boardwalk toward the house directly above mine. If she went inside it, I could watch her from my side living room window.

I hurried to get to my house. The crowds were much lighter at the top of Main Street, where only homes, not bars or other businesses, were located. I was able to get inside quickly. I banged my knee on a side table as I darted to the window, but I still kept the lights off and slipped my glasses down to the tip of my nose to let the fog dissipate.

Though blurrily because I wasn't looking out my lenses, I saw a light come on behind a large picture window on this side of the big house above. A second later, by the time the pain from the collision with the side table kicked in full force and my glasses were mostly usable, I saw Nell as she took off her winter wear and dropped everything on the back of a big chair. She swung around quickly as if someone had come up behind her, and then went out of sight.

"Come on," I said as I tried to angle myself to have a better look at the house.

Another few seconds later, she came back into view, along with another person.

"Howie?" I said.

The other person stood behind a lamp next to the chair, so I couldn't be sure, but I thought it was Howie. Nell spoke adamantly with her hands and arms. The other person was standing still; therefore it was difficult to read his posture or see him clearly.

After Nell plopped her hands on her hips and became

still herself for a couple seconds, she turned and moved to the window. She looked out, to her left, to her right, and I thought maybe down at me. But it would have been impossible to see me in the dark.

With a dramatic flourish she closed the curtains, ending the better of the two shows I'd seen that evening. I was left wondering what was going on, if it meant anything to Cassie's murder, and if I should call Jodie and confess what I'd been up to and what I'd seen as a result. I thought Jodie might be irritated at my behavior, but there was no way to explain why I'd been compelled to follow Nell into The Fountain. For a moment I wondered if I had indeed become starstruck. If that was the case, Jodie would figuratively shake me and tell me to snap out of it.

After that shallow study of my own psyche, I decided two things—that I wouldn't call Jodie, and that I could never have been able to close those curtains with such style.

7

"Large or small?" Seth said as he held the two cups toward me.

"Large for sure. I've been up most of the night."

"Why?" He thought a moment. "And why didn't you call me to come keep you company?"

It was impossible not to duplicate his wry smile. Our relationship had progressed nicely, though we weren't ready to spend *every* night together. I had purchased an extra toothbrush for him, but I hadn't told him about it yet. One step at a time, even when you're almost thirty.

"I've been spying," I said as I took the large cup of coffee. It would be only the first of many today, I was sure. "Follow me."

Seth followed me to the side window. I'd turned a chair so I could be more comfortable as I watched the house above. I'd tried to go to bed, but the window kept drawing me down from my bedroom loft. Finally I'd moved the chair and hoped I'd just fall asleep there, and wake up to find I was magically over this weird obsession.

"Here. You sit in the chair. I'll lean against the window ledge and talk to you. It will look fairly normal if anyone can see in. Just let me know if you see anyone come out of that side door," I said.

"Okay. It's not a great angle, but I'll do my best." Seth leaned against the left arm of the well-used and comfortable chair, twisted his neck just right, and peered up and out, like I had done most of the night.

"I'm oddly and totally obsessed," I said.

"I'd say. But with what?"

I knew saying the words out loud would make the entire situation even crazier than I already thought it was, but I told Seth about meeting with Matt, my previous evening's activities, and my ultimate curiosity about who had gone in that house with Nell and why she had that iPad. Was Howie really her mystery guest?

He listened carefully and didn't scoff once, though a couple of times I saw him work to hold back a comment. I appreciated the restraint.

"Why do you need to know? What does it matter?" he finally asked.

"I think it's mostly the fact that Howie hasn't done anything to help Matt. There's been no attorney. I thought attorneys were supposed to get there quickly. Matt asked me to talk to Howie. Nell must have gone into a room that wasn't hers. I'm pretty sure she didn't have the iPad when she went in. I didn't know she was at the house right above mine. I'm not even sure any of it is important to the murder, but what are the people in Matt's life up to? I fell asleep a couple times in the chair, so I might have missed it anyway." I paused and looked up out the window. "What do you think?"

A sip of coffee later, Seth said, "I think you should have called me. We could have made better use of the time, and then you and I could have traded shifts spying on the Hollywood people."

I turned back and looked at him. His blue eyes were so intelligent that they sometimes verged on being unreal, as if they were windows to the wheels and dials of a computer that was behind them instead of just a human brain. I'd figured out early on that he was geologist smart. It was a little later that I learned he was just plain old smart with a head full of nerdy kinds of knowledge and a surprisingly large dose of common sense to complete the package.

"You don't think I'm crazy?"

"Not really, but I *also* think it's suspicious that Nell and Adele came into The Rescued Word on the same day, at almost the same time. I know it's a small town, but that's weird. Your subconscious is just working through things. Listen to it, particularly if you sense danger ahead. And then run the other way."

Waves of gooey things washed through me when I looked at him. These waves were new to me. My only other serious relationship had been with Creighton, and though I'd enjoyed most of my time with him, there had been no waves there, unless you counted the rocky variety when he cheated on me.

I wasn't quite sure what to do with all this new emotion. Sometimes I just gave in and threw myself at Seth, but many times we weren't in an appropriate place to do that. We might have been able to take some time this morning, but I decided I would have been far too distracted. Later.

"You're kind of awesome, you know?" I said.

"I am? Why, thank you. You're awesomer." His eyes smiled at me over the brim of the cup.

"Anyway," I said. "I should have called, but I didn't want to bother you. I knew you needed to drive south today. I didn't want to mess up your sleep schedule."

Seth laughed. "Clare, though I thought I'd made it pretty clear, I'll reinforce it now. You should mess up my sleep schedule as much as you want. Guys typically don't mind that sort of thing. I'm a guy. And there's always coffee."

"Got it." I blushed.

"All right. Well, unless we're prepared to take the morning off . . . hey, there's someone coming out of the house."

If he'd been looking in my direction, he would have seen my blond curls fluff as my head swung around.

"Howie," I said.

He didn't look guilty, as if he was trying to sneak away or not be seen. No walk of shame. He didn't seem to be either happy or sad. He was simply leaving the house.

"Now that you know it's him, what do you suppose it all means? Does it matter?" Seth asked as he stood from the chair and peered up toward the walkway Howie had taken. He was no longer in sight.

"All it means is that I'm glad to know it's him. I would have hated to spend a sleepless night for nothing."

"You going to tell Jodie?"

"Yeah. Well, I don't know. I didn't tell her that Matt asked me to find and talk to Howie. And she'll think I've lost my mind. I'm not sure what I'll do. Except . . ." Seth was so tall that I had to lift myself up to my toes to kiss him. He smelled like coffee and soap and I thought I saw a small dot of shaving cream behind his ear. "Next time call you."

"Good plan."

The police station parking lot was jam-packed, but not with the vehicles of law enforcement officers, victims wanting to report a crime, or criminals, but with news vans and reporters.

"Oh boy," I said as I pulled into the lot. I drove slowly around people wrapped up in winter gear and holding cameras and microphones, all of them visibly disappointed when they got a good look at me. If they knew that yesterday I'd been sent on a mission by the incarcerated movie star, I'm sure I would have been swarmed. The clouds above weren't keeping us as warm this morning. The cold air made all their exposed noses and cheeks rosy, and I knew snow was again imminent.

Miraculously, a parking spot was being vacated at the end of the row. Once it was available, I took it so quickly that my car rocked as I shifted it into park.

"Smooth," I muttered to myself.

I'd taken a book home a couple nights ago. A project passed on to me by Chester, it sat on the passenger seat, wrapped in a brown paper bag. I'd acquired the habit of taking book projects home, purely for security's sake. I could keep my eye on books inside my house much easier than if I left them in the workshop. Not that we had many visitors back there, but I was just paranoid enough not to fully trust our less-than-perfect security system, which was made up of a few unreliable cameras. *My First Summer in the Sierra*, by John Muir, was one of Chester's favorite books. Mr. Muir's diary of his trek through the foothills of the Sierra Nevada in 1869—driving a flock of sheep—was first published in 1911, long before the author, a Scottish immigrant, became known as a preservationist and wildlands advocate. The diary was not only interesting but rich with description and detailed sketches. The book, inside a paper bag and on my passenger seat, was an early printing, but there was no date listed on the copyright page. We'd been hired to see if we could find out more about the exact print date as well as the origin of a bookplate inside. Chester had been secretive about the identity of the client, but I hadn't pushed him too much to tell me a name. Sometimes Chester just liked to be secretive.

There was a chance that the author himself had signed the bookplate, but the writing on it was faded and almost impossible to read. I debated taking the book inside the police station with me, but decided it would probably be fine in the car.

I made my way, mostly unimpeded, into the station, and was greeted inside the front door by Linus. I wondered if he ever went home.

"Can you believe that craziness out there? I've been moved here to keep everyone out," he said authoritatively. "You're welcome inside, though."

"Thanks. Yes, it's definitely crazy. Matt Bane's pretty famous."

"Yes, ma'am, but this sort of thing can get people in trouble. Too much of a distraction. We need to get him moved to Salt Lake as soon as possible."

"Makes sense. Thanks, Linus," I said as I went through the second set of doors.

I didn't know if Jodie was at work yet. I'd called, but she hadn't answered. However, she frequently had to return calls that she'd been too busy to answer. Before Seth left for his trek to southern Utah for the day, we'd talked through everything again. We agreed that I should let Jodie in on my observations, even if they turned out to mean nothing.

The halls were buzzing with activity, but no one paid me much attention as I took the right hall toward Jodie's office, a large space she shared with five other officers.

I stood in the office doorway a moment as I searched for her. This room was even busier than the hallway and the parking lot, with at least twenty officers inside, most of them in uniform but a few of them not, some on a phone, some looking at something on a desk, or conferring with one another. Jodie wasn't at her desk and I didn't see her anywhere else, but I happened to lock eyes with Creighton as he talked on his desk phone. To be polite, I waved. He hurriedly hung up and marched toward me.

"You have a second?" he said as he took my elbow.

"Uh, sure," I said as I gently pulled my elbow from his grip.

He blinked. "This way."

I followed him deeper down the hallway and into an interview room. I'd been in it once before, being interviewed about a crime. The familiarity of the space and the memory of my last time there got under my skin and I was briefly bothered that Jodie hadn't done anything to prevent me from having to go through those few moments of terror. The past was the past. I pushed away the irritation and told myself to get over it.

"You talked to Matt Bane last night?" Creighton said.

"I did," I said. It would have done no good to lie.

"What did he say?"

"Not much, really. He was surprised to see me. He'd come into the store early yesterday morning. He was very friendly."

Creighton nodded. He wasn't angry that I'd spoken to Matt, or at least he wasn't showing any anger.

"Why did you want to talk to him?"

"Well, like I said, I'd met him earlier and he was nice. His old girlfriend and his new girlfriend came into the store yesterday too. I felt a strange bond. I was curious."

Creighton nodded. He was always so intense, but so was Jodie when she was working. It was probably a necessary trait to becoming a cop. He didn't understand my curiosity, but I wasn't sure I did either. Fortunately, he didn't push it.

"So, you chatted about the weather?"

"No, Creighton. He told me thanks for stopping by and that he was innocent. Didn't Linus tell you?" I crossed my arms in front of myself.

"Linus doesn't hear well—that's why I'm asking."

I nodded. "Well, the weather didn't come up once."

A tiny flash of irritation crossed his eyes. "I'd made Matt Bane off-limits for visitors."

I had to play this one right, not be defensive, which would have been my natural inclination. If I pointed out the difference in the department's policy and Creighton's need to be in charge of the entire world, this might end badly.

"Sorry. We thought it would be okay," I said. The apology didn't sound all that sincere, but at least I'd said the word, bitter as it had been in my mouth. And I uncrossed my arms just to make it better.

"You and Jodie?"

"Yes." I hated getting her in trouble, but it would have been worse to deny it. To move the blame off her, I followed up with a sheer gut reaction. "Creighton, I was actually hoping to talk to him again."

"Of course you were."

"Really. When I left yesterday, he was distraught. I was so concerned about him that I didn't sleep well last night. I'd like to make sure he's okay."

"He's an alleged killer, Clare. You just met him, right?"

I nodded.

"You're caught up in all the Hollywood stuff. It's great to have the festival in Star City, but some of us get carried away. That's what's happening."

I clenched my jaw for a moment. I took a deep breath through my nose. Reluctantly and with great effort I finally said, "Maybe."

Creighton had a judgmental way of lifting one eyebrow

I hadn't really planned on talking to Matt again. My request had been a diversion, something that had popped into my head with the hope of keeping Jodie out of the line of fire—make Creighton more bothered by me than by his sister. I was there, though, once again in the claustrophobic back room with no windows and four holding cells. I'd have to say something.

"Hi," I said as I approached the cell.

"Hey," Matt said. He was already standing at the bars, and he no longer resembled a movie star. It was more than the wrinkled clothes and the messy hair; it was the demeanor. No swagger there. "What's going on?"

There wasn't much energy to his voice. He didn't sound anxious or worried, just defeated.

I didn't grab the chair this time as I stood on my side of the line. "I just . . . well, I guess I just wanted to talk to you again."

"Okay. Did you talk to Howie?"

"No, not yet."

"Okay. Will you still try?"

"Matt, what room number were you staying in?"

"Three."

"Do you have an iPad?"

He hesitated, but then said, "Yeah, why?"

"Anything on it that might be worrisome?"

"I don't know what you mean." he said, his voice up a notch from defeated to semi-curious.

Quietly, and as I watched him closely for unspoken reactions, I told him about Nell's activities and Howie's joining her. As he listened, he stood straighter and his face became serious and then baffled and then serious again. I didn't really know why I was telling him instead of Jodie, except maybe to see how he reacted.

When he didn't say anything for a long moment after I finished, I said, "Matt? What does it all mean?"

"I'm not totally sure," he said.

"But you have an idea?"

"I might."

"Want to share with me?"

"It would only be speculation," he said, his voice back to defeated.

"Okay."

He moved to the cot and sat, leaned his elbows on his knees, and ran his hands through his hair.

"As for why Howie spent the night with Nell, I don't know. I'd like to think that it's nothing. They know each other. He's helped with her career too. He was staying at The Fountain. I can understand why he wouldn't want to stay there now. Nell's renting a big house. Howie being there doesn't have to mean anything other than that's where he stayed."

"Would that bother you?"

"I don't know. I can't imagine anything other than being accused of murder bothering me at the moment."

"Good point. But what about the iPad? Do you think she took it from your room?"

"Yes. There are things on my iPad. Nell wanted it," he said.

"Things about her?"

"Some. There's something about my sister too. Something

that might make me look like I might not have wanted her around. Maybe Howie told her about that part."

"I see." I paused. I felt that the tide suddenly had turned, the other shoe had fallen, and whatever other clichés that ultimately meant that everything had just changed. Like Seth had said, when my subconscious told me to go in the other direction, I needed to listen. I'd made a terrible move in telling Matt what I'd seen and observed. I'd gotten carried away or something. Maybe I really had become starstruck.

"Matt, it's time for me to bow out of this," I said. "Time for you and an attorney to talk to the police." I turned to leave, a sensation of wanting to flee coming over me. Whatever this was, it had just gone way beyond something I should be involved in. At least my instincts about something being wonky with Nell and the iPad were on target, but I should never have said one word to Matt about it. There could potentially be something there that might lead to a killer. Maybe not, but either way I now knew it was not my place to make any of this my business.

"Wait. Please. Now I'm really not sure who I can trust. I could still use your help."

"Matt. It's murder."

"I know! My sister's." He stood again. "I did not kill her, Clare. I didn't. I don't know exactly what's going on, but what if Howie is somehow involved? He's the one who's supposed to be getting me an attorney. What if Nell . . . I'm more confused than ever, and I can't do one thing to find any answers when I'm behind bars."

"You can request a different attorney."

He gripped the bars and held his head down. I should

have left, but I didn't. I watched as he tapped a finger on one of the bars and seemed to struggle with his thoughts. I waited. I couldn't help myself.

He looked up a moment later. "Please, Clare, I have another idea, a way you might find out more. It might help set me free, and might help find the real killer."

Man, he was a good actor, if he was acting. How was anyone ever sure?

"How about you just talk to a police officer? I can get Jodie. . . ."

"She might be the best police officer ever, Clare, but I will not talk to the police without an attorney."

"Of course not. And you shouldn't," I conceded. I suddenly realized I couldn't talk to them either. I couldn't tell Jodie anything I'd discovered. My observations might only muck up the system and get in the way of finding a killer. I'd painted myself into a corner, two corners actually if that was a way to make something worse. I should have just minded my own business.

"Please, Clare."

"What's on the iPad?" I said as I pushed up my glasses and crossed my arms in front of myself.

"Pictures. Recently taken pictures of me and Nell. We're . . . well, we're in compromising positions."

"Oh."

"We really did break up, but we're still very attracted to each other."

"Got it. How does Adele feel about that?"

"She doesn't know. She wouldn't be pleased. I was going to break it off with her after the festival. She'll be upset.

I'm sorry about that, but she will be. I love Nell. I wish I didn't, but I do. Nell knows and I think she's trying to figure it all out, but I was going to do whatever I could to make it right with her."

"You think she didn't want those pictures made public?"

Matt shrugged. "I guess."

"What's the stuff about your sister?"

Matt bit his bottom lip. "We were kind of just goofing around, and Howie recorded a video of me saying something unflattering about my sister."

"What specifically?"

"That I wished she'd never followed me to Hollywood, that she's a pain in my backside and my career."

"That's not great, but that's not too bad. It could be worse. Why didn't you just erase it?"

"That might seem like the obvious choice at this moment, but at the time I saw no reason to do such a thing."

"Hmm."

"What if Howie and Nell did something to the iPad to manipulate the stuff on it? What if they're in on something together and want me to look guilty? Something's not right with them."

Or what if Matt was setting me up to believe they were up to something? Manipulation was running rampant today.

"They would do that?" I said.

"I don't know. Was Nell so worried about our pictures becoming public or was it something else? I don't know what possessed her to get the iPad. Why hasn't Howie been taking care of things for me? It's what he does—takes care of things."

"You need to talk to the police. I don't know why an attorney hasn't come to see you, but you need one right away and you need to have a conversation with the police. Got it?"

"I do, Clare. I understand, but . . . and I will. I will right away. In fact, if you tell the police to go ahead and get me a public defender, I'll do exactly as you say I should. But I'd still like you to do me a favor."

"What's that?"

"It's . . . It's a little crazy."

"Sounds about right."

He moved back to the cot and sat down. He reached into his shoe, or maybe just his sock. I stepped back, thinking that he must have been checked for weapons but I should be farther out of his reach just in case. But I still didn't leave. I couldn't bring myself to go yet.

He stood and came back to the bars, moving an arm through and holding out something in my direction. "Go to this. Take a date. Everyone who's a part of my life will be there. This will get you in."

"They didn't take this when you were arrested?" I said as I looked toward the guard desk before stepping forward and reaching for the paper.

"They took my watch, phone, and wallet, but they didn't notice this. It's such a secret event that I had it hidden in my sock. They took my shoes, but not my socks."

I unfolded the paper, which was in the shape of a giant golden key: "Party. Bring this and you and your plus-one will be welcomed. Not for public notification. Dress is formal. No social media pictures allowed. We'll be watching." Then it listed a time, date, and location.

"Well, you're right—this is crazy."

"I know, but, seriously, everyone in my life will be there. You can maybe see what they're up to."

"It's tomorrow night."

"It is. It's *the* party. Go. Please. See what you can find out. Even though the invitation was sent to me, if you have it with you, they'll just ask for your name."

"Whose party is it?"

"Can't tell. It's the rule."

"Matt, I think you've lost sight of what's important here. How would my going to a party help?"

"Like I said, everyone will be there. Nell, Howie, Adele, and everyone else in my life. They might be upset about the murder, maybe upset about my arrest, but they won't miss this. No one who's invited even considers missing it."

"You want me to talk to them all there?"

"No, not really." He bit his bottom lip. "I think you should observe them. See what's going on between Howie and Nell, and Nell and Adele."

"Do you think one of them killed Cassie?"

Matt's eyebrows came together. "I don't think it would be fair to accuse anyone of such a terrible crime, Clare, but someone else killed my sister. Why would it be someone random? Doesn't it make sense that it should be someone in our circle of friends and acquaintants? And . . ."

"What?"

"Last time you were here, you said Adele came in and got the note cards."

"Right."

"I've given some thought to that one too, and I'm pretty

sure I never told her about them. She would never have known to come get them."

"Howie or Cassie told her?"

"Neither of them knew either, I thought. They weren't in your store when I ordered them and I don't think I mentioned to either of them what I was doing."

"So what does it mean that Adele knew about them?"

"She didn't know, I'm sure. For some reason she came into The Rescued Word. Was she following Nell? Was she tracking my footsteps? I don't know, but it's weird."

I thought back to when she'd come into the shop. Had I been the one to ask her if she was there for the note cards? She hadn't brought them up first. It might have just been a case of my planting the seed. I couldn't be sure.

"Yeah, you're right. Things are weird and crazy," I said.

A conglomeration of noises came from the guard's desk. A number of people were coming through, all of them looking mighty official. Creighton led the way. He was followed by other police officers, none of whom I recognized.

"Step back, Clare," Creighton said.

There was no way to squeeze past the crowd, so I did as he'd instructed and stepped back toward the wall with the chair leaning against it.

"What's going on?" Matt asked Creighton.

"You're being relocated to Salt Lake City."

"Why?"

No one answered the question, but I suspected it was because his arrest in Star City was causing too big a traffic jam in our little town.

It was all very precise and official. They had Matt out

of the cell, cuffed, and moving toward the guard station quickly.

As he was being herded, he strained to look back over his shoulder at me. His eyes were pleading.

Against my better judgment, I put the piece of paper into my pocket and nodded. I'd go to the party and I'd try to figure out what Matt's "friends" were up to. I wasn't sure I'd ever see him again in person, but his eyes told me how scared he was, how alone. One of the biggest movie stars in the world needed a friend.

I could play that part.

8

"Not much of anything, Creighton," I said. I looked at Jodie.

"She'd tell you if he said anything important," Jodie said.

"He's scared," I said. "He's just scared. That's all. Says he's innocent."

"We had to get him out of Star City. Things are difficult enough to manage around here during the festival. It was getting out of hand," Creighton said. I wondered why he was explaining.

"Makes sense." I watched the corner of his left eye twitch once. Something more was bothering him.

My phone rang and buzzed and I grabbed it out of my pocket.

"It's Chester. May I be excused?" I asked.

"Sure," Jodie said.

Creighton looked at me a long moment before nodding like he didn't really mean it. I hurried out of their office and into the hallway. It was much less crowded now.

"Clare, are you working today?" Chester said when I answered.

"I am. Sorry I'm late. I'll be in in just a few minutes."

"All right, dear. You're going to be busy. The customers are coming in like we're giving away paper with currency printed on it."

"I'll hurry."

After I ended the call, I peered around the doorway and caught Jodie's attention. Silently, I eyed her to come out to the hallway. She got the message.

"What's up?" she asked.

"You in trouble?"

"Not at all. Creighton won't say a word about me letting you talk to Matt first. He wouldn't dare. He's still stretching his 'chief' muscles. I'm prepared to fight back. And he's my brother before he's my boss. We're good. So, did Matt tell you anything important?"

"No, nothing. He says he's innocent. I'm glad you're not in trouble."

"Of course Matt says he's innocent. He might be, but it doesn't look good at the moment. We—and now the Salt Lake police too—will be thorough. Don't let an actor manipulate you, Clare. Criminals are good at that sort of thing, actors too. He's probably doubly good."

"Got it. Thanks for the dinner and movie last night. You're always a good date."

"Right. You too. You didn't get in any trouble after you darted out of my car, did you?"

"No. It was a nice walk home." I tasted something bitter at the back of my throat. I'd originally come to the station to talk to Jodie, to tell her about Nell, the iPad, and Howie. "Jodie, why hasn't Matt spoken to an attorney yet? Isn't that supposed to happen quickly?"

She looked at me a long moment with something in between a Jodie-glare and a question. "I gotta get back to it, Clare. Call you later?" she finally said.

"Sure." I nodded, trying to hide my reaction. She hadn't just dodged my question; she'd kicked it to the curb.

I watched her hurry back into the office. Was everything on the up-and-up around here? Despite my friendships and history, I was glad the Salt Lake police had come aboard.

I took a deep breath before I turned and left, thoughts of misplaced trust coming at me from every direction.

I wasn't too surprised to step out into a snowstorm. It was a gray-skied, fat-flaked, warmish storm. The slopes would be busy today. I pulled the collar of my coat a little tighter to keep the flakes from falling in, and enjoyed the moment. The snow took away my immediate concerns and put me in a better mood. The Salt Lake police would take care of Matt, and I would go to a secret party tomorrow. It wasn't a bad sacrifice.

Whatever vehicles had transported Matt to Salt Lake City were gone, and the news vehicles had mostly cleared out too. There was only one left and it was parked right next to my car. It was just an old white van with a magnetic sign on the side of it that read BLOG OF THE STARS. I'd never heard of the blog, if that's what it was really called. I had to cut a wide path around the back of it to get to my driver's side door. As could happen, the snow was building quickly on the asphalt, so I had to lift my boots, using a high-step maneuver. The combination of moves should have been easy, something I'd done plenty of times before, but this time something caused me to slip, and I was on the ground on my backside before I could make the turn behind the back bumper.

"You okay?"

I looked up, more embarrassed than hurt, at the overly padded young man, dressed in multiple layers of pristine winter wear.

"You're from California?" I said as I took his hand and let him help hoist me up.

"How'd you know?"

"Thanks for the hand. Your coat looks brand-new and you're dressed . . . thickly."

The young man smiled with only one side of his mouth. His dark eyes matched the short tufts of dark hair sneaking out from under his cap. "Yeah, I'm from California. Never been to Utah before. Not sure I can describe the pure fear I felt when I started up this steep canyon and saw those 'Runaway Truck Ramp Ahead' signs."

"There are mountains in California, right?"

"Not like these, and I've never driven in them before."

I inspected the side of the van and then his youthful face. "You're here with the blog?"

He glanced at the sign and then back at me. "I am the blog. It's just me. Toby Lavery." He extended his hand.

"How long have you had your license, Toby?" I shook his hand.

He laughed. "I'm actually almost twenty. I just look young."

"Nineteen is pretty young to be doing all of this."

He shrugged. "College didn't appeal to me. I'm pretty good at sneaking around. I live near Hollywood. It seemed like a good fit."

"You're a member of the paparazzi?"

He laughed again. "Yeah, but I try not to be too intrusive. I don't take naked pictures or anything."

He was wide-eyed innocent with dimples on each cheek. He seemed like a nice kid. "How's it going?"

His face scrunched slightly and he scratched above his ear. "I might have to start taking naked pictures."

I smiled. "Keep at it. You never know when you'll come upon a big story."

"You're not in the movie industry, are you?"

"No, I work at my grandfather's shop up the hill. The Rescued Word."

"That's a great name."

"Thanks. It's a great shop. It's on Bygone Alley. Stop by for some hot chocolate or coffee if you need a break." I turned slowly just in case my fall had been caused by unseen black ice, and resumed walking.

"What's your name?" he said.

"Clare."

"So, Clare, what were you doing in the police station?"

"My best friend is a police officer."

"I see. Any chance you could get me an interview with her, or him, about Matt Bane?"

"No chance at all, but nice try."

"Okay."

"Thanks for helping me up, Toby," I said.

He suddenly reminded me of a puppy with his sad, innocent eyes. The steadily falling snow had built up on the top of his red knit cap, and the ridiculous amount of layers he wore made me want to take him inside somewhere and fix him that hot chocolate with a huge dollop of whipped cream.

"How about I tell you something off the record?" I said.

"On the record would be better, but I'll take off too." His eyes lit.

"Off the record. Meaning you can't use anything I tell you for an article. But you might be able to use it to help confirm other things."

"I got it. I know what 'off the record' means." He put his hands awkwardly on his hips.

"Okay. Well, Matt Bane ordered personalized note cards from us. He was very friendly. He's a nice guy."

"I have no idea how that might help me with a story. But thanks."

"He was in the store, being friendly, right before the murder occurred. There was no indication that he might be someone who could do such a thing, kill someone. Use that to find out if he really is a nice guy. Maybe you can uncover his true personality."

Toby bit his bottom lip and looked at the ground a second, a bit of the gathered snow sprinkling off the cap. He looked back up at me. "A nice guy, huh? Arrogant at all?"

"Not even a little bit."

"Good to know. Maybe I can do something with that."

"Maybe."

"Thanks, Clare."

"You're welcome. Good luck!"

"I'll need it. Well, that or those naked pictures."

I smiled before I got into the car and then waved as I pulled out of the parking lot. It occurred to me that he was probably sleeping in the van, and a tinge of worry fizzed in my chest. He was young, and nineteen was the time to do that sort of thing, but I couldn't help the concern.

I didn't have much time to worry about Toby Lavery. Chester had been correct. The shop was packed with customers. Well, actually the shop had only a few customers, but one of them had filled the top of the middle stationery shelves with so many typewriters I wondered why I hadn't seen a truck or a van outside.

I shook off my snowy coat and got to work.

9

"Clare, this is Zeb Conner," Chester said. "He's here to talk about these typewriters. I'll let you answer his questions while I help the other customers. I've tried to track down Marion, but no luck yet."

"She'll be in soon," I said. I knew she was on one of the far slopes practicing some of her half-pipe moves today, but I didn't want to go into the details in front of Zeb. Besides, I could tell that Chester wasn't really concerned about Marion being late. He was simply not fond of this customer. I knew my grandfather well enough to read his tone.

"Terrific," Chester said, not meaning it. "You'll be in good hands, Zeb."

Zeb and I watched as Chester moved to a woman who was looking at the colorful rows of sealing wax along a back corner shelf. I noticed three other customers, but they seemed to be browsing more than anything. Chester or I would get to them as quickly as we could.

I turned to Zeb. "How can I help?"

Zeb wasn't like any Zeb I might have pictured. He wasn't an old guy in overalls, but a young guy with a seventies haircut, a thick mustache, and big metal-framed seventies glasses. I would have pegged him more for an Atari-collecting guy than someone who'd collected typewriters from that era.

"I need a typing class," he said as he pushed up his heavy glasses. I didn't know how his nose wasn't permanently marked with two indents from the nosepiece.

"Um," I said.

"I mean, I need to find a typing class somewhere that might be able to use these. They were gathering dust." Zeb sniffed enthusiastically and then pulled a handkerchief out of his back pocket. He proceeded to blow his nose, causing everyone else in the store to turn and see what was causing the noise. This sort of thing didn't get under my skin, but I knew how Chester felt about handkerchiefs and I suddenly understood why the two of them hadn't hit it off.

They are the most unsanitary items. They've bothered me ever since I can remember people using them. When I was a boy, I would have rather used a piece of sandpaper on my nose than a handkerchief that I put back into my pocket.

Though Chester wasn't a germophobe, he did have this one hang-up. Handkerchiefs never bothered me all that much, and to me, they, like all the shops on Bygone Alley, harkened back to a simpler time. But they were like nails on a chalkboard to Chester.

And Zeb's nose-blowing was particularly noisy, if kind of cute too.

"I see," I said.

He'd brought in twelve typewriters that were identical, at least when it came to their make and model. Their different colors made a fun rainbow: black, beige, red, and green. I thought they'd also come in blue and maybe orange back in their day, but I couldn't remember offhand. I was most familiar with the beige variety.

The Selectric had been made from the 1960s to the early 1980s, transitioning over three models: I, II, and III. Zeb had brought in a dozen of the II models, which immediately looked to be in terrific shape though slightly dusty.

Made as big, wide, heavy, utilitarian-looking creatures that took up a lot of space, they were one of the first typewriters that improved efficiency by using type balls instead of the more clumsy early typebars, which could, and frequently did, get jammed together and slow down the entire process, particularly if someone had speedy fingers. The type balls could also be changed out for different fonts. The Selectrics were actually one of my favorite old typewriters, specifically because of the changeable type balls. For usability, they were second in my heart only to the first typewriter with a correcting ribbon. Besides, even a grown, mature woman liked to giggle when the term "type balls" came into the conversation—with the appropriate crowd, of course.

"I'm not sure I know of any typing class that still uses typewriters, Zeb. Most typing classes are now called keyboard classes and they're for computer keyboards. I don't know of anyone who needs this many old Selectrics."

Zeb scrunched his mouth as he looked at me. His mustache wiggled. He couldn't have been very far into his thirties, but his fashion choices made me wonder if he'd just aged very well or practiced time travel. Between the glasses, the mustache, and the Selectrics, he struck me as someone stuck in the seventies, even though he looked as though he might have been born in the eighties. "Your grandfather said you wouldn't buy them from me."

"No, but we might consider keeping them on consignment for a short time. We could see if any of our customers are interested. We'd take a cut of whatever we sold them for. I'd turn them all on first and make sure they worked at least well enough."

"They work fine. What could I make?"

"Not much, I'm afraid. I wouldn't count on funding a retirement account or anything. You might get a nice dinner out of them."

"What about that polygamous group out in the valley over there?" He nodded to his right.

"I think polygamists also use computers, at least those polygamists."

"Yeah, but they have so many kids. Maybe they'd like to have the keyboards to pound around on." He typed in the air to illustrate.

I could not think of any reason why Zeb's idea might make sense, but something told me not to argue with him, that there was a small chance he might be onto something. It was either that or I was desperate to find a valid excuse to go see how my high school friend turned sister-wife

Linea was doing, and maybe ask her what in the world she'd been thinking.

"Tell you what," I said. "How about we keep them here for a week or so? I should know pretty quickly if anyone is interested. My niece has been working on a database with all the requests we receive. Maybe there is some interest that I just don't know about offhand."

"Give me any sort of deposit for them?" Zeb asked.

"No. You'll just have to trust me. We've been here a while, Zeb. I wouldn't steal your typewriters. But for the sake of both our security and peace of mind, I've got an agreement we can both sign."

His mouth scrunched again, but a moment later he said, "Well, all right, if that's the best you can do."

I assured him it was and led him to the back counter, where I found a copy of our consignment agreement. I filled in the blank spots and we both signed it. He left with a copy and a pep in his step. It was no wonder he was happier—leaving without having to carry them out with him had to be easier than the trip in.

"Consignment?" Chester sidled up next to me after he rang up the woman who'd purchased three colors of the sealing wax and two letter stamps, and answered the questions of the other customers before they left without purchasing anything.

"Yes. That okay?"

"Of course. I just couldn't continue on with him, Clare. The hankie was killing me."

"There has to be a phobia for that. We'll have to look it up."

"I can't fight it. I wish I could. I'm afraid I was rude."

"I think he's fine. We'll try to sell the typewriters, but he mentioned the polygamist group in the valley. He thought they might be interested."

"I think even some polygamists use computers."

"That's what I said, but I kind of wonder if he doesn't have a good idea. Or an idea to explore, at least."

"I can't imagine why. . . . Oh, you're just curious to see how Linea is doing."

"A little, but I'd like to talk to you about something else first."

"I'm all ears," Chester said. "And we have a surprise lull in business. Tell me before we get another rush."

It turned out I didn't need to make much of a case for needing help at the shop. Chester had thought we could use some assistance for a long time. He thought I hadn't wanted an outsider brought in. I realized he was kind of correct, and that I was overprotective of our Rescued Word world.

"But we do need help," I said. "I know that."

"Yes, but more than that, we need the right help. The right person or people. We'll find them."

"How?"

"Oh, they'll come into the shop now."

"They will?" I said.

"Yes, now that we've put that out in the universe, the connection will be made."

"We don't need to place an ad or anything?"

"Of course not. That would gum up the mechanism that is made of fate and destiny."

"I didn't realize you were so metaphysical," I said.

"It's good to be able to surprise you, but it's not that I'm metaphysical so much as it's that I'm old. I've seen this sort of thing happen again and again. Life experience will teach you to mostly be positive if you let it."

"Huh."

Chester laughed. "Well, we'll see. Oh, I went with Marion to buy the tickets for that movie star's serial killer film. I forgot to share with you that the only ones that were available are for tonight. Will that be all right with you and Seth?"

"I don't know. I'll talk to Seth when he gets back from his jaunt down south. He said it was just a quick day-trip. If either of us can't make it, I bet we can sell the tickets easily."

"Yes, the news about that poor girl is out. No big details are being released except that Mr. Bane was the person arrested for the murder. It's all bad business. Terrible."

"Yes, it is," I said. I almost spilled the beans about the party I was going to the next night, but then I remembered the secrecy and pinched my mouth closed.

"Ah, well. For now, I might have a valid reason, other than the typewriters, for you to go visit Linea if you really want to."

"You do?"

"Yes, well, you'll have to do a bit of work first, and then I'll tell you what it is."

"I can do that."

"Wait here." He turned and started toward the work-shop. "And see if you can find Marion. She should be here by now."

"She's on the slopes, but I'll text her to let her know you'd like her to come in when she's done."

"Thank you."

I texted my niece, knowing she wouldn't be able to answer right away but would when she had a moment.

Foot traffic outside the shop was steady, but it seemed the store rush was over for the time being. Places serving lunch would garner much more attention from visitors than we, or any other retailers, would for about an hour.

Baskerville joined me from his high perch as I grabbed the box of ribbon tins from the end of the counter and carefully dumped out the contents. Twenty-three tins, spread out in two lines, made a colorful collage. All their art had a distinct early-to-middle-twentieth-century feel. My eyes were immediately drawn to a few: a peachy orange round tin emblazoned with "Vogue Typewriter Ribbon," each of the words in a different font and color; a Carter's Midnight round tin dotted with white stars over a dark blue background; and another round one with only the picture of a colorful and evil-eyed dragon.

"These are wonderful," I muttered quietly to Baskerville. He sent them a semiapproving blink as he sat and observed.

I moved them around, placing them in order from my personal favorite to my least favorite, deciding that one of the larger, rectangular, upright tins should have the number one position.

My best guess was that the tin was created by a German company. *Gesetzlich geschützt* must be German. The mostly yellow tin's lid was stamped with those words, as well as the words "Hercynia Farbrand" and a red circle pattern. Inside the red circle was a picture of a winter mountain scene and an oversized bearded mountain man dressed only in his underwear. The whimsy of it struck a chord with me and made me smile.

As I moved it to the number one spot, I misjudged the available counter space and the tin slipped off the front edge and onto the floor.

I stepped around to gather it, but was momentarily halted in my tracks. The lid had come off the tin, exposing some surprise contents.

I crouched. Involuntarily I'd fallen into a slow-motion movement.

"What's that you've got, Clare?" Chester said from behind me.

I started at his voice. "Hey, Chester." I turned and looked back over my shoulder. "It looks like money. Old money. A lot of it."

"It does indeed," he said as we pushed up our glasses at the same time Baskerville meowed suspiciously.

10

"I didn't even know ten-thousand-dollar bills existed," I said.

"They're still considered legal tender, I think, but they haven't been printed in . . . oh, maybe over a hundred years. How many could possibly be left in the world?" Chester said.

"There are ten of them here. One hundred thousand dollars. I can only imagine what that amount of money was worth back when these bills must have been hidden in the tin. It's a fortune now. Then, it must have been a ridiculous fortune."

"I do believe so," Chester said.

Baskerville sat on the edge of my desk and eyed the money suspiciously. I thought I might have heard a low growl or two come from his throat as Chester and I had hurried to put the money and the rest of the tins back into the box before taking everything to the workshop. Once behind closed doors, we opened each tin but found no other money. In fact, we found nothing else, not even a piece of fuzz or a random paper clip.

We'd spread the money out on the desk. Ten ten-thousand-dollar bills, old obviously, but in good condition.

The man portrayed on the bills was Salmon P. Chase, who, I discovered after a quick Internet search, was Abraham Lincoln's U.S. Treasury secretary, at one time an Ohio governor, as well as a chief justice in the Supreme Court. He was also the man responsible for the introduction of paper currency in our country. I briefly pondered how someone so accomplished had never stuck in my memory banks, but I'd never heard of him until the quick search. Chester had, though.

I'd already called Seth, hoping he could tell me where in Salt Lake City I could find the man who'd given him the box of tins. I wanted to return the money as soon as possible. Today actually. It was a lot of someone else's money to be responsible for, and the sooner it was back in the rightful owner's hands, the better.

But Seth hadn't answered, so I left a message. I kept it pretty cryptic, because it felt like talking about the bills should be done in code or at least in hushed tones. He hadn't called back despite the numerous times I'd checked my phone.

"Should I call Jodie?" I asked Chester.

"No! I mean, not at the moment. Of course we need to return the money, Clare, but there's no reason to think there's anything illegal going on here. Let's not get the police involved—for a couple reasons. There's no need to waste their time right now. Also, *if* something illegal or unsavory happened regarding the money, well, I think perhaps enough time might have passed that it should be forgiven. These came from an old woman. What if she or her husband stole the money?"

"Then the police should know about it."

"Think about it. Isn't there something wonderful about the idea that they stole the money for their family, but they never needed it? Wouldn't it be great to follow through with their wishes now?"

"You just made up that story. You don't know what happened."

Chester shrugged. "Still. Not yet. I don't know. I guess I don't like to drudge up old business if we don't have to. Make sense?"

"Sort of."

"That's good enough for me. Now, we'll lock the money up for now, but I do have another task you could attend to, to keep your mind diverted."

Reluctantly, I redirected my attention, but checked my phone again before I said, "I'm listening."

"All right." Chester gathered the bills and put them in an envelope. He tucked it under the red Royal he'd been working on the day before. When he noticed my wide-eyed wonder at his idea of "locking up," he shrugged. "Who would ever look there?"

I was pretty sure Baskerville's eyes opened wide too before he blinked at me.

"Okay," I said doubtfully, hoping Seth would hurry and call back.

"Good. Well, this"—he scooted a book toward me and the corner of the desk—"is a book that I'm sure Duke Christiansen would love to have."

Out of habit, I took a good look at the book before I lifted it from the table. There are some books that shouldn't be touched any more than necessary. This wasn't one of those books.

"Laura Ingalls Wilder?" I said as I recognized the brown-haired girl holding a rag doll on the colorful dust jacket of *Little House in the Big Woods*. The cover was illustrated by Garth Williams, not the series' first cover artist, Helen Sewell. A quick look inside told me this was an old copy, but not extremely valuable. I looked at Chester. "I don't understand."

Chester shrugged. "I happen to know he likes to share the world of the Laura Ingalls Wilder books with all those children."

"They're a contemporary group. They dress modernly. They don't dress like the pioneers," I said.

"I'm aware of that, but apparently they still churn butter by hand and some other such old-fashioned techniques."

"Really? How do you know? And I thought you didn't like them."

"I'm not a fan of their practices, but they don't affect my life in any way. Besides, Duke did a favor for me not long ago. For us, really."

"What'd he do?" I said as I watched Chester squirm. He'd often made the comment that he thought the whole polygamy thing was weird. I didn't disagree, and I couldn't imagine what act might have been big enough for Chester to be subdued into shame because of a favor from Duke Christiansen.

"Remember that box of type we got a month or so ago?"

My eyes went to the shelf with the type box full of the letter pieces he was talking about. The box, full of a font of metal type that I had yet to pin down but was beyond thrilled to have in our collection, had been placed on my desk one morning to surprise me. Chester hadn't given me any details as to where it came from.

"Sure. You got that from him?"

"I did. He gave it to us. You were out of the shop, and he and Linea came in and said that there used to be a printing press in Duke's family, some such business about it traveling with them on their journey to Utah in a covered wagon. The press seems to have disappeared, but they thought we might use the box of type."

"Just gave it to us?"

"Yep. I offered to pay."

"Well. That's very kind of them. Goodness."

"And they didn't even try to convert me."

I smiled. "Right. I'm sure they know a hopeless cause when they see one."

Chester smiled too.

"I should thank them in person," I said.

"Yes, and you can take this book to them. One problem, though. One page is missing. Page twenty-five/ twenty-six. I would suggest a quick fix. It's not a valuable book. You could just insert a copy, let them know you'd print a page if they really wanted it. That would get you out there quickly and maybe give you a chance for a return trip later if you're really curious."

I looked at the book, at the Royal with the hidden treasure underneath it, at my silent phone, and said, "You're a little devious, Chester, but in the best way possible. I'll do the quick fix and run it out there, if you're okay with me leaving."

"If your niece gets here soon, I'd be fine with your leaving."

"Maybe our destiny will walk in the door."

"I am sure that will happen, but destiny usually keeps its own schedule."

"I should have this completed just in time for Marion to arrive."

"Excellent. I'll watch the front while you do your work."

In the world of book repairers and restorers, the quick fix I performed was simplistic and not really a repair at all. I pulled up the e-book on my computer, found the missing words, and printed out a copy. There was nothing about making a copy and slipping it in the middle of a book that would help improve a book's value—unless only readability was under consideration. Having the page in the book would help so the reader wouldn't be jolted out of the story somewhere in the middle. Considering the circumstances, I decided it was probably the exact fix Duke would want. They would want to read this book, probably, not just keep it safe on a shelf or sell it. I would print the page on the press and take it out to them later. I felt as if I was cheating the book and owed it at least that much. However,

Chester had been correct—now I'd have more than one reason to visit the polygamists' compound.

By the time I was done, Seth still hadn't called, but Marion had arrived, her cheeks and nose rosy more from her hard work than the cold.

"I did it, Clare. I landed the double shifty three times in a row. I think I've got it down."

"That's extraordinary," I said. I didn't know what a double shifty was, but I was sure she'd mentioned it before, and I knew it was an important trick to master.

I was ready for Marion to take on the Olympics, Chester was ready, and my parents were ready, but my brother, her father, Jimmy, might never be ready for the big deal his beautiful daughter might become. He'd be supportive, but his continual state of concern would somehow manage to make him always look less than so. We'd work it out.

I checked the phone yet again, I eyed the envelope under the red Royal, and I made sure Mr. Muir's book was tucked safely in my desk. I loaded my bag with Ms. Wilder's book, took some pictures on my phone of the Selectrics, and told my grandfather and niece I'd see them later. I was just about out the door, leaving the shop with only one customer who didn't seem to want any help as she perused, when someone came through the doors who was bound to stop my forward progress.

"Toby, hi," I said.

Baskerville had been hanging out by Marion, knowing he'd get her attention soon enough and she'd scratch behind his ears for as long as he wanted. But now he trotted up to the front of the store to greet the blog reporter. I knew something was up. Baskerville didn't willingly greet any-one unless he sensed that the person coming through the door was bringing something important. We were never immediately sure what the important component was, but it eventually became clear.

"Clare," he said. He rubbed his hands together and then blew on them. More snow had gathered on his hat, and it slipped off as he tilted his head down to smile at the cat. "I know it hasn't been that long, but I wondered if I could take you up on your offer of hot chocolate."

"Of course."

Baskerville jumped up on the pastel-paper shelves and sat. He meowed pleadingly toward Toby. I looked at the cat. I looked at Chester as he came from the back and seemed to also wonder what was going on.

"Can we help you?" he said to Toby as he kept an eye on the cat.

"Chester, this is Toby Lavery. He's a blog writer in town for the festival and I offered him some hot chocolate."

"Blog writer? I'm not sure I know what that is, but come in, young man. I make a wicked hot chocolate."

"Thank you," Toby said.

"We'll see you later, Clare," Chester said. "Baskerville, Marion, and I can take it from here."

"Thanks," Toby said over his shoulder at me as Chester guided him to the back. Baskerville hopped off the shelves and trotted behind them.

Perhaps it was as simple as the fact that I wasn't the only one to recognize that Toby needed some TLC. He didn't come off as pathetic, but there was a lost quality about him that made mothering gears kick in, even with grandfathers, and probably with young women and cranky male cats too.

I glanced back as Toby introduced himself to Marion, and quickly decided that Marion's instincts toward him might not be motherly. They looked at each other in that way. Of course, lots of young men looked at my niece that way; it was rare that she returned the gaze. I hadn't even noticed that Toby was cute, but he was, and in a way that I was sure Marion would find interesting.

Uh-oh, Jimmy would not be pleased, I thought as I pushed through the front doors.

11

Seth called just as I escaped the slow-moving festival traffic, which now had the added impediment of falling snow. I finally reached a speed close to the limit as I merged onto the two-lane road that would take me back behind a mountain and deposit me into Purple Springs Valley, where the Christiansen family lived. Others lived there too, though the valley and surrounding mountainsides were dotted with only a few homes. A monastery had also been a part of the valley for almost a hundred years. The monks didn't speak except for one hour a day, raised bees, and made wine, though not many people outside the county talked much about the wine. It was a Utah thing, staying hush-hush about alcohol, which we'd all come to accept. The clouds that dropped the snow must have covered only the Star City area, because it stopped falling just as my car dipped into the valley, and the sun's rays hit the front iron gate of the monastery.

Though the roads were clear, the entire valley was blanketed in snow that glittered when the sunlight skimmed over it. It was lovely.

"One hundred thousand dollars?" Seth said. "That's . . . unbelievable."

"I know. I want to get it back to him as soon as possible. Would you mind tracking him down?"

"Not a problem." He paused. "Well, I don't think it's a problem."

"What?"

"Daryl was in town to clean out his mom's house. I'm not sure where he went from there. I'll find him, though. I have his number. I'll let you know."

"Thanks. How's your assignment going?"

"Really well. I should be back soon. I'm on my way, but southern Utah is really nice this time of year."

"I know. Hey, do you have plans tonight and tomorrow night?"

"Let me think. Other than hoping to see you? No."

"You have any fancy dress-up clothes?"

"Something other than T-shirts and jeans? I just might."

"Tonight we have a movie and you can wear whatever you want, but I've also got tickets for a big festival event tomorrow, if you'd like to go."

"Love to."

"Great. Let me know what you find out about your friend."

"Will do. Love . . . I mean . . ." The pause was filled with a heavy sigh on Seth's part and the opposite on my part; I held my breath. "Clare, this isn't the best way to share feelings, but they're real and I guess they needed to be spoken at this moment. I'm sorry, but I do love you."

He was such a logical geologist-scientist.

I laughed and then breathed again. "Don't be sorry." I was a big believer in never, ever saying those words unless you were one hundred and fifty percent certain you felt them. "Guess what?"

"What?"

"I love you too."

"Well, that's a relief."

I laughed again. "We'll talk about this more later."

"Sounds good. Talk to you later."

We hung up. The words from Seth weren't a surprise, even if the moment of delivery was. Who liked predictable anyway?

The snowy postcard valley was as close to perfect as any winter scene could get. A white blanket covered the ground, and the accumulating snow along the sides of the roads hadn't become dirty yet. The blue sky and the bright sun warmed the cold air and made the perfect combination to give skiers sunburned cheeks and noses. Once the snow quit falling over town, our slopes would go crazy.

As I approached the high cinder block wall around the polygamist compound, I felt my nerve start to seep away. Though the wall wasn't that bad because there were also lots of snow-topped trees and shrubbery next to it to make the gray fortress somewhat welcoming—or at least less unwelcoming— I decided maybe I could have handled the question about the typewriters with just a phone call. Linea would know why I'd come out in person, to see if she'd become as odd as she guessed the rest of the world thought she was.

I pulled my car to the side of the narrow but not well-traveled road to think through what I was doing.

A flash of activity up ahead caught my attention. A group of people gathered at the end of a long curve that snaked around to the other side of the compound. There were no typical corners in the middle of the valley, but there were intersections, usually created to make transportation from the main road to someone's home easier than over the dirt roads. The group was small, maybe six people tops. They were all in winter wear and one of the members held a big camera on his shoulder.

The one person who wasn't wearing a coat suddenly stepped away from the group and faced the camera. Even if she had been in a coat, her tall stature and long blond braid would have told me who she was.

What in the world was Nell Sterling doing in the middle of Purple Springs Valley?

I didn't think twice as I pulled the car back out onto the road and drove slowly toward the actress and the film crew.

When they noticed me, the filming stopped. They turned toward my car and waited patiently for me to pass. I didn't pass, though. I stopped and rolled down my window.

I smiled and waved at Nell.

Her reaction caught me off guard. I didn't expect her to rush in my direction and I *was* interrupting her work, but I was not prepared for the play of the smile that began on her lips and then disappeared a second later. She didn't say anything to me, nor did she wave. In fact she turned her back to me as someone threw a coat over her shoulders. She wore a dress and apron similar to the one I'd seen Cassie Bane in only a short time before she was killed, but now it was covered by a big blue thing that looked like something for the shoulders of a football player on the sidelines.

"Can we help you?" Howie said as he approached my car.

"I'm . . . sorry. I met Nell yesterday and I was just saying hello. I realize now that I'm interrupting your work. I apologize."

"You're the woman from the paper and typewriter place," Howie said as he smiled.

"I am."

"Well, Nell's busy at the moment. I can give her a message."

"Just hello." I paused. I couldn't think of a worse time to share the secret word with Howie, but when was I going to have another chance? I looked toward the group. Everyone but Nell looked at me, and they were all close enough that I'd have to get Howie closer if I didn't want the others to hear what I said or read my lips. "Mind if I ask what you're filming?"

"Sure. Nell's got a part in an upcoming film about polygamy. The movie will be shot in a studio, but since we're here, we're filming an end credit—like an epilogue of a book—using the house as the background." He pointed. "Polygamists live there."

"Right. These women don't wear those clothes. I mean, some polygamist women do wear them, but these women are much more contemporary."

Howie shrugged. "Makes for a better story this way, darlin'."

I nodded, but my eyebrows came together and I pushed up my glasses in a disapproving manner. I wasn't overly sensitive about anyone's thoughts or criticisms of the Christiansens, but Howie's attitude and his patronizing use of "darlin'" got under my skin.

"How come you didn't go see Matt Bane when he was in the Star City jail?" I asked.

"Excuse me?"

"How come?"

Howie blinked at me. "I'm not sure my dealings with Matt Bane are any of your business. And how do you know I didn't visit him?"

"I know."

"Well, thanks for stopping by. We've got to get back to work. I'll let Nell know you send your regards." Howie turned and walked back to the group.

"You should make sure Matt has an attorney," I said to his back.

He didn't respond in any way as his attention was drawn completely back to his group.

I turned the car around in the road, using the three-point method, and slowly drove to the driveway of the big house. I didn't know why Nell had cold-shouldered me, but I was willing to chalk it up to something about my intruding. Movie stars acquire crazy stalker fans. Perhaps that's what she thought I was—why else would I be out in the middle of nowhere, but right where she happened to be?

I'd said my piece to Howie, and I hadn't even needed the

secret word to tell him to get Matt an attorney. I was glad I hadn't said it, in fact. I didn't want any sense of connection with him. Relief washed through me. I hadn't known that carrying the message around with me had been such a burden. I didn't know if Howie had done or would do anything to help Matt, but now I'd done my small part.

As I pulled into the long driveway, I could see the Hollywood group in my rearview mirror. Their activities came to a halt so they could watch me be admitted through the front gate after I said my name into a security speaker. Even Nell seemed curious.

I wasn't sure if making the movie crew jealous of my admittance was one for the polygamists' team or one for Clare's team, but I liked it.

I traversed the long driveway that led to the large, blocky two-story house. It seemed that design had been ignored and size had been made the priority. It wasn't an unattractive house, but its rectangular shape was plain.

I hesitated in the car only a moment after I parked it next to the shoveled walkway. I'd come this far, so I might as well go knock on the door.

"Clare, hello!" Linea said, and she opened the door wider. She smiled and didn't look polygamist-y at all, whatever that was.

"Hey, Linea, I hope I'm not intruding."

"Not at all. Come in. It's good to see you."

I followed her into a long hallway decorated with what had to be hundreds of framed photographs on both walls.

"We're baking bread. Come on back," she said.

I'd just told Howie that Nell hadn't been dressed

authentically to the Christiansen women. I'd been correct, mostly. But today, Linea did wear a simple apron over her jeans and sweatshirt, and her hair was pulled up into a bun, but it wasn't tight and long pieces had come loose around her face. She didn't ever wear much makeup and her olive skin and brown hair worked well together. She wore no makeup today. I always thought she was pretty. Jodie thought she was "okay."

"Duke and I stopped by the shop not too long ago. I was hoping to say hello, but we missed you. Talked to your grandfather," she said over her shoulder.

"Thanks so much for the type pieces. They are a wonderful and generous gift," I said. "Both Chester and I are very grateful."

"Glad we could do it."

The kitchen was ridiculous—vast and busy. The appliances were old and yellow. The cabinets with medium-toned wood and small iron handles and the blue countertops were old too, but everything was in great condition. The space was large enough to accommodate three butcher-block islands and a bunch of kids in the middle of making bread. I suddenly admired Linea simply for her ability to work with so much noise.

A quick glance over the group told me that most of the kids were under twelve, but one or two of the girls might have been teenagers. Those kids who looked at me smiled, but most of them ignored me and kept their attention on the dough in front of them, or chatted with the others around their butcher block. The smell of baked bread not only filled the air; it pleasantly consumed it. Six loaves were cooling on a wire rack against one wall, but there were many more loaves to come if I assessed correctly.

"Oh, dear, this is way too loud in here. Okay, everyone, keep working. I'm going to step out on the back porch with a friend for a minute," she said.

Murmurs of agreement spread through the room.

She continued to lead the way as we snaked around children dressed mostly in jeans and sweatshirts and pushed through some back doors, taking us out to a screened-in back porch that stretched the length of the house. It was well furnished with wicker chairs that had no cushions. I could see how appealing the space would be in the warmer months.

"Sorry about that," Linea said. "You do get used to it, but it can get crazy."

"No problem." I looked at her. She didn't seem the least bit hesitant about my being there. She wasn't trying to hide anything. She seemed so . . . normal. "How are you?"

She smiled knowingly. "I'm great. I'm happy about my lifestyle choice, Clare. I know it's not for everyone and it's certainly different from the norm, but I'm happy here. I know you and Jodie have wondered. I couldn't find a way to talk to you that didn't seem too weird, and the years have flown by."

"No, no, not at . . . well, yes, actually. You *were* the party girl. We've wondered." There was no point in lying.

Linea laughed. "I don't know if my desire to change my ways brought me here or if it was something else. I don't preach and I won't ever try to convince anyone that this is the way to go, but it's working well for me."

I inspected her. She did look happy. Some polygamist families made headlines when charges of abuse toward children and women were brought against them. There was no sense that was happening in this house, and I didn't think the Linea I knew would put up with such a thing, but I hoped she would feel comfortable enough to tell me if she needed any sort of help. "How many children do you have?"

"Three of my own, but there are fourteen in the family. I just saw your eyes get big. Don't run away screaming."

"I'm sorry." I tried to stop my eyes from bulging out of their sockets. "I'm glad you're happy. Can't let go of the . . . differentness of it all, but glad you're happy."

Linea laughed. "You look happy too. I see Jodie being all tough and coplike in town sometimes. She seems to be happy as well. Now, why have you come to see me?" She looked at the bag over my shoulder.

"Oh. Right. Well, first of all, this is for you and your . . . husband. And the kids of course. It can't begin to express our gratitude for your gift, but . . ." I handed her the copy of *Little House in the Big Woods.*

"Really?" She glanced up at me briefly before she smiled at the faded but colorful dust jacket. "It's one of our favorites around here. And it's a beautiful book. We'll take care of it."

"Well, I need to point out something. I'm going to bring you back an actual printed page, but Chester thought you might just like to have it to read, and I had one other thing to discuss today, so I brought it up."

I turned to and explained the missing page. Linea only seemed to hold the book closer afterward.

"This is an unbelievable gift, Clare. Thank you. I'm sure

the children and Duke will be thrilled. Please tell your grandfather thank you."

"I will." I didn't like the way her thoughts seemed to go to how her husband would feel more than how she felt, but maybe that was just my being too observant, too sensitive. Truly, what went on behind the tall gray cinder block walls was none of my business, as long as abuse wasn't a factor. "My other question." I grabbed my phone from my pocket and pulled up a picture of the Selectrics.

"Typewriters?"

"Old typewriters, but they're in good condition. We've taken them on consignment and the owner wanted to know if you all might be interested in them."

"Us? I don't think . . ." She laughed. "Well, I'm not sure. It's not something I would have ever thought about, but they might be something for the children."

"Think about it. Just let me know. I don't think there will be a big rush on them, but I'd like to let him know if you aren't interested."

"I will. Here, just message me the picture." Gingerly, she placed the book on a short side table that had at least six pairs of muddy boots underneath and pulled a cell phone out of her back pocket.

I didn't comment regarding how surprised I was by the fact that she had a modern cell phone. I shouldn't have been surprised, but it was difficult to change preconceived notions of simplicity and backwardness, even when I knew this was a contemporary group of people, and had just told a Hollywood guy as much.

Once the message dinged and she put the phone back

in her pocket, I said, "Do you know there are some Hollywood people out in front of your property?"

"I saw them." She rolled her eyes. "They're doing some movie based on us. Loosely based, I guess. We didn't give them permission, but we did receive a letter asking if we wanted to add input. They stopped by too. Duke told them no. It wouldn't matter what input we gave—they'd still just do whatever they wanted and make us look either bad or at least stupid."

"Probably. Do you go see any of the festival films?"

"No, not really. A night out at the movies for all of us would be a fortune and we'd take over a whole theater." She laughed. "Our movie nights are at home, with lots of animation. We churn our own butter for the popcorn, though."

"That's good to hear. I was beginning to really wonder where that party girl had gone."

"I was a wild kid. I don't think that's what led me here, Clare, but it is good to not be so wild anymore."

"I don't know, Linea—this is pretty wild."

"Well, the rebel stayed, but was tamed to steer her rebel ways in a different direction."

"Got it."

She led me through the kitchen again. I saw her hesitate briefly as if she was debating whether to introduce me to any of the kids, but she decided not to. There were no other sister-wives in the kitchen or in the house as far as I could tell, and I assumed Duke was at his job in Salt Lake City.

She gathered a mostly cooled loaf of the bread and slipped it into a brown grocery sack.

"Please enjoy," she said.

I didn't feel right about taking the bread, but I thought she might be offended if I didn't. Besides, it was homemade bread. Who in their right mind turns down homemade bread?

"Thank you," I said.

She saw me to the front door and we thanked each other again, but neither of us mentioned making plans for a future lunch date. There were just things that weren't ever going to happen, and Linea and I socializing together was probably one of them.

I glanced at the corner of the property the second I was outside the wall. Nell and her crew were gone, or had moved to somewhere I couldn't see.

My phone rang as I pulled onto the two-lane highway.

"Chester?"

"No, it's Marion, Aunt Clare. Can you come back to the store?"

"What's wrong, Marion?"

"We're okay, but there's a problem. Chester told me to tell you there's something wrong with the red Royal, but he wouldn't say what. He's also called Jodie. I have no idea what's going on, but there's a guy here who's really . . . adamant."

"Okay. I'll be there in fifteen tops."

At least everyone was okay, but I sped up as I wondered who the guy was and what he had to do with the fortune Chester had hidden under the Royal.

12

"Well, I'm his brother," the man said as he leaned against the back counter and crossed his arms in front of himself. He wore a bright white ski jacket, dark denim jeans, and a one-day beard that oddly made him seem too groomed.

"I don't understand," I said.

Chester, Marion, and Toby stood behind the counter. Coincidentally, they all had their arms crossed in front of themselves too. Baskerville alternately walked and sat around my feet. He hadn't meowed, but I could tell he was bothered by our well-dressed visitor.

"This man claims to be the brother of the man who gave us the tins," Chester said.

"Therefore, I should be able to retrieve the money," he said bitterly.

I had no idea how heated the words between everyone

must have gotten, but Marion wouldn't have called me if things hadn't seemed to be getting out of hand, and I sensed leftover heat in the room.

"Where's Jodie?" I said.

"Busy. Creighton's on his way," Marion said.

"Who are you? I mean, what's your name?" I said to the man.

"John Nelson. My brother's name is David. David told me to come get the money."

David? Was that the name Seth mentioned? It sounded familiar, but I couldn't be sure. We'd been telling each other the L word and that had seemed much more important than the name of the man who'd given Seth the tins. "Do you know how much there is?" I said.

"No. We weren't told. My brother told me to come up and get it."

"Up from Salt Lake City? That was quick," I said.

"I was already in Star City."

I looked at Chester. "There's no way they would have known unless they'd heard from Seth, but not knowing the amount . . ."

"Something doesn't feel right. We're going to call Seth and we're going to wait for Creighton," Chester said.

"This is ridiculous," John said.

"Not really," I said. "Surely you can wait a few more minutes. If the . . . contents are yours, then you should be grateful we're being careful."

John grumbled.

"All right, I'll call Seth," I said as I looked at Chester again.

John grumbled once more, something between a *tsk* and

a loud, heavy sigh. I looked at him and pushed up my glasses. Whatever wonky feeling Chester had been having about this guy just spread to me too. His frustration wasn't in line with the situation.

Unfortunately, I had to leave another message. There were some spotty cell coverage areas on Seth's route. I kept John in the corner of my vision and was almost certain he relaxed when I didn't receive an immediate answer. The wonky feeling grew.

Creighton walked through the door a second later. I met him at the front of the store and told him what was going on.

"You found a hundred thousand dollars and you didn't think to call the police?" he said with whispered perplexity.

"Correct."

"That was not very smart."

"As much as I'd like to argue with you, Creighton, I'm beginning to think you might be right."

"All right. Give me a minute with him," he said before he turned and walked toward John and the others. I followed behind.

"Sir, may I see some identification?" Creighton said.

"No, you may not. I don't have to show the police my identification."

"That is true. However, it might help to clear up the situation if we could confirm that you are who you say you are."

"I'm not showing you my ID."

"Maybe you should just leave," Toby interjected.

We all looked at him.

"Who are you?" Creighton asked.

"Uh. Toby Lavery. Here, I'll show you my ID." He reached for his back pocket.

"I don't need to see your ID," Creighton said. He looked at me.

"I met him this morning outside the police station. I offered him some hot chocolate," I said.

Creighton frowned and shook his head once. "Well, all right. Young man, I don't need to see your ID, but it would be helpful if I could see yours, sir."

"I'm serious. Maybe you should just leave," Toby said again.

I wondered if he was trying to impress Marion. Unfortunately, he didn't pick up on the fact that he was doing the opposite of impressing Creighton.

Creighton held his hand up. "I'll handle this." When Toby nodded, Creighton turned back to the man in the white coat.

"Look, this is ridiculous. I'll come back later, after you talk to that . . . Seth," John said, his words quick and, I thought, lined with concern.

He surprised us all by stepping around Creighton, who didn't make any effort to get out of his way, and marching quickly out of the shop.

"That was weird," I said.

"I didn't like him," Chester said.

"That was kind of scary," Marion said.

"He's gone," Toby said with a shy smile at Marion.

Oh dear, I thought.

"This whole situation baffles me," Creighton said. "Chester, Clare, we need to have a private discussion."

What we'd done—not call the police when we'd found the money—wasn't necessarily illegal, but it skirted along the edge of theft, even if the tins had been a gift and even if our plan was to return the money as soon as possible. If Creighton hadn't believed that we were attempting to contact the person who'd given us the tins, our irresponsible ways would have also seemed suspicious. A deceased woman in the mix didn't help with our seemingly naive maneuver. It didn't take long for Chester and me to answer Creighton's questions. He processed the tin and the money. I wasn't sad to see him bag up the hundred thousand dollars to take with him, but I was going to miss the cute German tin.

Just as he was about to leave, my phone rang. Seth.

"Hang on, Creighton. Maybe we can get this cleared up quickly," I said. I hit the answer button. "Hey, thanks for calling back. Quick question—what's the name of the guy who gave you the tins?"

"Daryl Brewsberry. I left a message, but I haven't heard back from him yet."

I was stunned momentarily speechless as I blinked a million times and felt the weight of the ramifications we would have faced if we'd given the money to the other man. We wouldn't have given him the money, but still, what if we had?

"Not David, but Daryl?" I said, enunciating the names slowly.

"Yes."

I was still stunned.

"Clare?" Seth said.

"Clare?" Creighton piped up.

"Clare?" Chester added.

I swallowed and told Seth I'd see him later. When I hung up the phone, I said to Chester and Creighton, "I think we have a problem."

13

"How in the world did he—I'll call him John, but I'm sure that's not his real name—even know about the tin?" Chester said.

Creighton hadn't left. He, Chester, and I were still in the workshop, all of us having been moved up to Creighton's intensity level. I'd told them the name Seth had given me and Creighton had stepped away from us for a moment and made two phone calls, neither of which I paid any attention to.

"Do you suppose we're being bugged or something?" I said at a normal volume with no regard to the idea that what I said might actually be a possibility.

"Why would anyone bug us?" Chester said, equally as clueless.

"Other than Seth, did either of you tell anyone about the money?" Creighton said when he rejoined us.

"No," I said.

"No," Chester said. "Wait."

"What?" Creighton said.

"I think I said something . . . like . . . oh dear," Chester said.

"What?" Creighton said again.

"I didn't know the young man was still in the store. I thought Marion was alone up front. I said something like . . . oh, goodness . . . something like 'Marion, your aunt found a wonderful surprise in one of the tins.'" Chester frowned and blinked at Creighton.

Creighton didn't waste a moment, but turned and marched to the front of the store. Chester and I followed behind.

"I've changed my mind, young man. I'd like to see some identification," he said to Toby.

Marion was behind the counter, Toby in front with his arms on it, leaning toward Marion. We'd interrupted a friendly moment, but both of their smiles disappeared with Creighton's tone.

"Sure," he said. He reached into his back pocket. "Oh. Uh, it's not in my pocket. It's just in my van." His face became shockingly pale. "It's parked not far from here."

"Let's go," Creighton said.

"All right." Toby sent Marion a quick smile that was probably meant to be reassuring but was more along the lines of scared-to-death.

We watched as they left the shop, all of us with wide, confused eyes.

"What's going on?" Marion asked when they were out of sight.

I gave Marion the details of the sequence of events as we knew them.

"But I didn't even hear Chester. I mean, I heard him, but I didn't understand him," Marion said. "And Toby was with me the whole time. He couldn't have heard either, and he never did anything to let someone else know there might be a treasure in the back of the shop. He just talked to me and then we went back and got some more hot chocolate. He was never on his phone or anything. Not even texting. He didn't even look at it, Aunt Clare. He had nothing to do with it. Why didn't Creighton just ask me those questions?"

"He will, I'm sure," I said. "One step at a time."

Marion blinked and sighed with the drama of an indignant teenager who was sure she'd just been wronged.

"It'll be okay, Marion. Creighton's a good cop," Chester said, but his eyes were focused toward the front of the store. He'd plunked his hands on his hips and chewed his bottom lip.

"What is it?" I said to him.

"Nothing. Just trying to understand. Nothing. Excuse me." Chester turned and went back to the workshop.

"Aunt Clare, do you think someone is listening to us, maybe somehow watching us?" Marion asked in an appropriately quiet tone.

"I don't. I think we're a little paranoid because we can't understand what happened. Once we know the specifics, things will become obvious and less weird. We'll figure it out. Don't worry about Toby. He'll check out fine and be back. The best thing to do is to get busy on something. That's the only thing to do really."

She wanted to protest, but she knew that I was still her boss. Kind of. At least when Chester wasn't around or if he felt like reading instead of paying attention to the store. Actually, her job was pretty secure. It would take a huge infraction to get her booted. We really could use some help.

Nevertheless, she forced a strained smile and moved to her computer just as the front door opened again.

"Need help, Clare?" Chester called from the back.

"Go tell Chester I'm fine," I said to Marion, who was relieved to put off getting to work a few minutes longer.

"Howie, good to see you again," I said as he approached.

"Hello." He flashed a quick, unfriendly smile.

"How can I help you?" I pushed up my glasses and forced my shoulders straight and tall. I wanted to put my hands on my hips to steel myself, but I resisted the urge.

"I need to know more about why you were talking to me about Matt."

"What do you need to know?"

"You talked to him, or at least that's how it seems. Could you please explain the circumstances of how you got to see Matt?"

Without a doubt, I didn't trust Howie, but I knew that there was no reason to trust any of these Hollywood people who'd come into my life.

I sighed and said, "Sundance."

"What?"

I looked around and then repeated the word.

"So, I can trust you," he said.

It wasn't a question, but I nodded just the same.

"That changes everything. Okay, what does he want you to tell me?"

"He wanted you to go see him. He wanted a lawyer."

"I see. That's it?" Howie didn't commit one way or another regarding whether he'd tried to visit Matt.

"Did you try to see him?" I asked.

He still didn't answer. Or if he did, it was with one quick shake of his head. Or was that a nod?

"He gave me his ticket to the party." I pulled it out of my pocket. "I visited him when he was in jail here in town. My friend is a police officer and I'd met Matt. Anyway, after he'd been in the store, I thought I felt a small kinship or maybe even friendship there. Admittedly, a little weird, but that's what happened."

"Why does he want you to go to the party?"

I shrugged. "Kindness of his heart, I guess. For talking to him, checking on him."

"He's in jail, arrested for possibly murdering his sister, and he gives you his party ticket. Doesn't jibe. What's really up?"

"I don't have any idea, Howie. It would be difficult to replay the moments with Matt in the jail, but it seemed like an easy transition. For whatever reason."

We fell into one of those quiet spells where it's clear that the first one who speaks loses the power in the conversation. I clenched my jaw and waited.

"Well, I suppose it's fine," Howie said a moment later. "I wish I knew what he wanted me to do."

"To go see him, to get him an attorney," I said, attempting not to punch him in the arm or say, *"For goodness' sake."*

"Has to be more than that."

I shrugged. This was getting old. "Did you try to see him?"

Howie just looked at me.

"Sundance, remember," I said.

"So, you know that polygamist group over there?" He nodded in the direction of the valley.

I couldn't help myself—I laughed. "Howie, you couldn't care less about Matt, could you? You just wanted to come in and talk to me about the Christiansens."

"No, that's not it," Howie said.

I put my hand on his arm. "I'm not going to ask anyone there to meet with you. I'm sorry, but I wouldn't do that no matter the circumstances. They will talk to you if they want to."

"Right. Well, I'll see you tomorrow night at the party, then." He turned to leave.

"Will you try to see Matt today?" I said as he walked away.

"I doubt I'll have time to run down to Salt Lake City today or even the next few days. Busy, busy, busy." He waved backward as he went through the front door.

"What a jerk," I muttered. The adrenaline that had shot through me because of our mystery visitor had now transformed into a sizzle of anger. Howie had been trying to play me, use me. He couldn't have cared less about his locked-away friend or associate or however they looked at their relationship. I didn't understand why anyone would want someone like Howie to assist with his career.

My phone buzzed across the back counter.

"Jodie?" I said as I answered it. "What's up?"

She whistled. "Good gravy on biscuits, girlfriend, you are in the middle of more messes than a platter of scrambled eggs. What's going on? Are the planets aligned funny? Or is that unaligned? Shoot, I have no idea. But I need to know what's going on. You and I will be going out for coffee in about thirty seconds."

I could already hear the siren.

"I'll be ready," I said before I hung up. Jodie's analogies were unlike her, but they made me hungry. I hoped for more than coffee. "Marion," I called toward the back of the store. "Need you up front."

~

"Toby seems fine. So far," Jodie said after she slurped a gulp from her hot chocolate. With the back of her hand she wiped off the whipped cream that had landed on her nose.

"That's a bigger relief than I thought it might be."

"Right. He's got a crush on your niece."

"How in the world did you figure that out?"

"He told Creighton. Folded like a cheap suit when Creighton gave him his evil eye." Jodie laughed. "Of course, for Toby, folding only meant telling the police about the fight he had with his mom before he left Los Angeles, his desire to become a famous gossip blogger, and his crush on Marion. That's as tainted as his young life might be. He spilled what he thought were his darkest secrets."

"Poor kid."

"Yeah." The humor left Jodie's eyes, slowly. "I did feel a little bad for him. As for this John fella, we have no idea who he was, but he isn't John Brewsberry, we're pretty sure."

"Did you find Daryl?"

"We did. He's on his way to town. He'd already made it up to the Utah-Idaho border. He lives in Boise and was on his way back there. He had no idea his mother stashed the money in the tin. He's in shock. What a surprise, you know. Mourning the passing of your mother and then discovering something that meant she had a secret of some sort."

"You'll give it to him?"

Jodie took another sip, this time without the whipped cream reaching her nose. "Not that easy at this point, though it's not too difficult. His mother died, which means there's an estate. Even though he had power of attorney over her, once she died, that was no longer in effect. We did a quick search and couldn't find anywhere else the money came from—you know, like if it had been stolen or something. There's some legal stuff to deal with now."

"Why's he coming back?"

"Got Judge Serus to see us. Daryl was an only child. It might be quicker if the judge wants it to be."

"You didn't want to just give it to him yourselves?"

"Nope. Don't want that kind of responsibility if there's some sort of problem. Though you should have called us sooner, good job turning it in at all."

I blinked. "I'm no saint, Jodie—you know that—but there's no way I would have kept that money. If it had been a ten-dollar bill, I might have, but even that would have bothered me. I couldn't sleep nights knowing I had one hundred thousand dollars that wasn't mine. Chester and I talked about calling you, but we didn't want to drudge up some old mystery that might have included Daryl's mother doing something illegal."

Jodie shrugged. "Might have been kind of fun to solve an old mystery. And you're a good person. There are plenty of people who aren't."

"It has nothing to do with that. It has to do with my peace of mind. And I'm sorry if we got in the way of you solving something."

"I'm busy enough. It all worked out okay."

I took a sip of my own hot chocolate and savored the warm liquid as it mixed with the cool cream. Neither of us had ordered anything to eat, but I was still thinking about it. We were at the diner across the street from The Rescued Word, so I could watch out the window and run over if Marion got swamped with customers.

Every shop on Bygone Alley was put together in the fashion of an older time. It hadn't been on purpose at first. After Chester opened The Rescued Word some sixty years earlier by converting an old mining-office building into the store, the diner moved in with pink vinyl upholstery and a filled jukebox. The upholstery had been redone a couple times, though it had remained pink, but the jukebox was still the original one. Elvis Presley was currently crooning in the background.

The cobblestone road, the old-fashioned streetlights disguised as gaslights, and the storefronts, most of them with wide front windows and carved wooden signage above, added appropriate charm. Dubbed Bygone Alley back in the day by someone I hadn't known, the side street had been given a perfect moniker, and when I wasn't going in thirty different directions with work projects or crowds of visitors, I could take a second or two and feel a real appreciation for where I lived and worked. Sitting in a pink booth with Jodie and enjoying some delicious hot chocolate was one of those times.

"Listen, I need to tell you something," Jodie said, threatening to ruin the moment.

"That's your serious face," I said. "That face worries me." I pushed my mug away.

"No need. It's not a big deal, but I just want you to know that . . . well, Creighton has started seeing someone. A woman. More than one date. More than two."

"That's good. Really good," I said.

"Really?"

"Yeah, have you somehow missed that I'm seeing someone too and I'm really happy with him? His name is Seth, just in case you haven't been paying attention." I pushed up my glasses and gathered the hot chocolate.

"I know, but, well, you and Creighton really had something."

"That was a while ago."

"I know, but he'll never get over you—you know that."

"Didn't seem to be on his mind much when he was with the other woman back then, while we were supposedly still together."

"He made a big mistake."

"One of the biggest."

"Right. But. Well."

"Jodie, I think it's great. Actually, I don't think that. I think it just is. My feelings for your brother left the building a long time ago. I'm including the bad feelings I had for him after he cheated on me. I had to let go of those too. Well, sometimes I remember them, but not often."

"He'd dump anyone to be with you again." She smacked her lips.

"That's not . . ." Actually I didn't know if it was true or not, but I didn't care. "Thanks for telling me, and I'm happy for your brother if you're happy for him. Now, can we talk about something else?"

"Wanna hear about me and Mutt?" she said with a wry smile.

"No details, but I'd love to know if it's going well."

"Great. Perfect." She reached into one of the pockets on her uniform shirt. "He gave me this."

Once I picked my jaw up from the table, I blinked a few times. "He proposed?"

"He did."

"What did you say?"

She handed me the solitaire diamond, which was at least a carat. It looked real. "I told him that a few months isn't enough to determine if we should spend the rest of our lives together, or at least be each other's first exes."

"You did?"

"I did."

"I don't know what to say. This isn't how I imagined you telling me you were getting married. I pictured a different scene."

"Like what? And you missed the part where I didn't tell him yes."

"I don't know. Something Victorian, traditional, I guess. Not over hot chocolate at the diner."

Jodie lifted one eyebrow.

"I know. Weird. Victorian's not you at all, but that's what I pictured. Oh, Jodie, this is a beautiful ring, and he's a good guy. You're really going to wait?"

"I think so. I think it's for the best. It's only been six months, Clare. Not long enough to know."

"It's not that I disagree or want to argue, but you two make a good match, and your family likes him."

"I know. Can you believe they like a long-haired motorcycle guy named Mutt? It's crazy, but I think we need more time."

"Just going to carry the ring in your pocket?" I handed it back to her.

"For now." She took it and stuck it back in the pocket, finishing with a quick pat.

"Something tells me there's more to this than you're saying."

"No."

"Okay. I'm happy for you, Jodie," I said. "We should have a party or something."

"Not yet. And it's nice to have people happy for me instead of wondering when in the world I was going to figure things out."

"That's not . . ."

She put her hand up and shook her head. I got the hint.

"Oh my gosh, I totally forgot. Guess who I visited today?" I said.

"Who?"

I told her about my visit with Linea. I tried not to be weird about all the kids, and shared her evident happiness and contentment with her choices. I also went so far as to tell her about running into Howie and Nell and the film crew, and how Nell gave me the cold shoulder and Howie came back to the shop and confronted me about the Christiansens.

I did not tell her about the secret word or that Matt wished Howie had gone to see him. In fact, at one point I quickly decided it was time to change the subject so I wouldn't slip up and reveal that I hadn't been completely truthful to her or Creighton about my visits with Matt.

My abrupt change of direction was interrupted by a woman's screech that came from the front door.

Jodie stood partway up in the booth and put her hand on her gun. I turned around to see what the commotion was about.

"Adele White!" The young woman dressed in Goth attire just like I'd seen on Adele stood inside the front door and pointed at me. No, not at me, at the person in the booth behind me.

We'd been sitting back-to-back, Adele and I, but this time she'd been dressed in pink Goth, blending her tiny self into the booth. She wore a bright pink hoodie over her black clothes with the hood pulled down enough to hide her face. Except from the woman who'd stepped into the diner.

"Adele, it's you! I'm your number one fan," the young girl gushed as she came over to the table.

I watched as Adele removed the hood and looked up at her fan before looking at me with a guilty smile.

How long had she been sitting behind me? Had I said anything that I shouldn't have?

As I waved and smiled uncomfortably at her, I was doubly glad I hadn't mentioned the secret word to Jodie.

14

"I wasn't eavesdropping," Adele said after the vapid fan left, Adele's autograph written with a pink Sharpie on the inside of her wrist.

"I saw you ask specifically for that booth. When you came in," Jodie said.

I looked at Jodie.

"I'm a cop. I notice everything," she said.

"So?" Adele said. "I'd met her." She nodded toward me. "It was good to see a familiar face."

"Why didn't you just come sit with us?" I said.

"I didn't want to intrude."

"Okay," I said.

Jodie had taken her seat again, but hadn't removed the scowl from her face. She and I didn't need to have a private conversation to know that both of us thought it was strange that Adele had requested to sit where she had. If she'd said hello, it wouldn't have been nearly as odd.

Adele had now twisted around, and so had I. We faced each other with only the backs of the two booths separating us. It was close quarters, but Adele's "biggest fan" had left and no one else in the crowded diner seemed all that interested in Adele. Jodie remained on her side of the booth and I wished she wouldn't scowl so deeply at the up-and-coming movie star.

"How's it going, Adele?" I said with so friendly a tone that it sounded phony. I cleared my throat.

"Horribly," she said with wide eyes.

"Cassie's murder. Matt's arrest. Yeah, it's been rough. I'm sorry," I said.

She looked at me as if she might have momentarily forgotten about the tragedies. "Right. And no one will talk to me. Howie's ignoring me."

I shared another quick look with Jodie before I turned back to Adele. "Who is he to you?"

"Matt's guy, his assistant, but he knows people and . . . well, he was going to help me get some meetings, sit-downs, this week. He has lots of connections."

"Maybe he's just busy," I said.

"He's always busy. He's like those movies that have the president of the United States in them. You have to take a minute or two when he can fit you in." Her voice was full of admiration.

"Really?" I said.

"Really?" Jodie said, her voice full of eye roll.

"Yeah, he knows everybody and everybody knows him."

She sighed. "I think he lied to me. I don't think he wants to do anything to help me."

"I'm sorry." I was pretty sure Howie was only out for Howie, but I didn't want to be the one to tell that to Adele. I hoped someone would tell her as much before she put too much stock in him, but it shouldn't be me.

She looked up at me as she bit her bottom lip. "I saw him go into your store just before you came over here. What did he want?"

"Oh. Um, nothing really. Just checking on the note cards that Matt ordered," I lied, thinking I must have kept my voice quiet enough that she really hadn't heard the conversation between me and Jodie.

"Oh. Did you tell him I picked them up?"

"Yes," I lied again.

"Any chance he said anything about me?"

I knew youth was all about self-involvement, but Adele took it to a new level. Maybe this was what happened when youth got mixed up with fame.

"I'm afraid not."

She nodded sadly. "That's what I thought. I tried to talk to him when he came out, but he wouldn't stop walking even for just a second. He said he had another meeting to get to."

"I'm sorry," I said, though the urge to take her by the arms and shake some sense into her was beginning to build inside me. "You should have just come into the store."

"Again, didn't want to disturb."

"Gotta depend on *you* only," Jodie contributed. "Your future is up to you. Don't wait for favors."

Her inspirational-poster comments caught me off guard, but the words were appropriate.

"Oh, I know. I've done all I can. I just need a break, one big break," Adele said.

"You got rave reviews with that movie you did last year," I said.

"That's old news. Now I need another break."

"It'll happen," I said.

"We'll see."

I'd never been more grateful to hear Jodie's radio fuzz followed by the pleasant-toned voice of the dispatcher.

"Jodie, you there?"

"Yeah," she said into the mouthpiece attached to her shoulder.

Sometimes the way they talked to each other seemed far too casual.

"You have a visitor. One Daryl Brewsberry. Want me to keep him here before Creighton runs him up to the judge?"

"I'll be right down," she said. "Ask him and Creighton to wait just a few." She looked at me. "Come with? It might be good to have you there too."

"All right," I said. I looked at Adele. "Hang in there."

"I will." She looked at me with a fearful determination; it was a strange combination. "I'll make it happen."

"Of course you will," Jodie said.

To counter Jodie's sarcasm, I smiled at Adele. She smiled back, kind of. She didn't make a move to get out of the booth, so I didn't think she would follow us, but I wondered about her sneaky ways.

There was something about her stalking that seemed to rattle another idea in my mind that wanted to make its way forward, wanted me to notice it. But it was like it was only on the tip of my tongue and wouldn't fully reveal itself.

"Clare, you coming with?" Jodie said from the door.

I'd stalled. "Sure. See you later, Adele," I said to the young woman, who now seemed like a tiny pink and black dot melting into the pink booth.

"Right," Adele said absently. She started chewing on an already short fingernail.

I wished I had her mother's phone number.

"Too much Hollywood, too young," Jodie said when we were in the police car.

I nodded.

Jodie flipped the lights and the siren on and the waves of visitors parted so we could make our way through. Today, I liked the rush of good adrenaline and wished to see someone I knew so I could wave, but no one familiar came into view.

Until we reached the police station parking lot.

"Is Toby still being held?" I said as I looked at his parked van.

"No, but he couldn't get the van to start. Creighton called a mechanic to stop by. It seems that since we are pretty sure that Toby is innocent, Creighton's taken the kid under his wing. He got him a sandwich too."

"Hope he really is innocent."

"Me too. If he has his way, he'll be marrying your niece soon, and none of us want a thief in the family. I think his plans were to head back to The Rescued Word when he was done here."

My first reaction was to say, *Over my dead body,* simply because I wanted Marion to do about a million more things before she got married. I didn't say the words out loud. Jimmy would faint if I told him all that had happened with his daughter and the wannabe blog writer.

I followed Jodie into the jail. Her heavy footfalls made me extra conscious of my own and sometimes I tiptoed behind when I was with her at work just to compensate.

She blew through the door to her office.

"Hey, thanks for waiting, Creighton," she said.

"Sure," he said, but he gave me a slanted look.

I wanted to explain that I'd been invited, but I didn't.

"So, you must be Daryl Brewsberry," Jodie said to the man sitting in the chair next to Creighton's desk. His back was to me as he stood.

He was tall, probably about six foot five, with wide, muscular shoulders. As I looked at his arms, I wondered when a busy geologist had time for such copious amounts of weight lifting.

"Yes, nice to meet you," he said. Jodie didn't extend her hand. These police officers didn't do that sort of thing. It had something to do with safety, so even in what might be considered the least threatening of situations, they didn't shake hands.

"This is Clare Henry. She's the one who found your money." Jodie signaled toward me.

Daryl turned to look at me. "You must be Seth's friend," he said as he smiled and shook my hand.

He was gorgeous, disturbingly so actually. I felt like I needed to look away from the penetrating brown eyes, the square jaw, and the dazzling teeth. He was almost more Hollywood than Matt Bane.

"Daryl. Thank you for the ribbon tins. They are extraordinary."

"My pleasure. I feel a bit wrong coming back for the contents of the one."

"I'm glad you were still close enough to come back."

"Actually," Creighton interjected, and looked at me, "you could come with us to talk to the judge. It might make this easier."

"That's what Jodie thought," I said.

"Let's vamoose," Jodie said.

Once again sirens and lights were involved, but that was only because the festival crowds had continued to grow. The snow had stopped, but the clouds hadn't dissipated. I wished for the sunny sky I'd been under in Purple Springs Valley.

The courthouse wasn't up the hill but farther down it, part of a cluster of the few government buildings needed to run the small town. It was rare that traffic was heavy in this direction, but anything was possible this time of year.

The offices had all been built to resemble ski chalets: sturdy pointy roofs and winter-ready siding that looked like clapboard but was made of a material that didn't allow moisture to seep in.

Creighton and Jodie sat in the front seat, and Daryl and I sat in the back.

"I heard about the murder. It's all over the news," Daryl said to me over the siren noise.

"I haven't paid attention to the news, but yeah, it's been bad."

"Matt Bane, a killer? Wow, you just can't predict something like that would happen. I don't know, though—we only know his superhero image. He must be more a bad guy than a good guy."

I nodded. I wasn't going to tell Daryl that I didn't think Matt Bane was bad at all, that there must be some crazy misunderstanding, but that's exactly what I thought even if I hadn't quite admitted it to myself until that very second. I sighed inwardly. I might not trust any of these movie people, but at least now I understood my willingness to help Matt in the small ways he'd requested. I sensed he was innocent. I sensed it deeply, as if it were truth beyond all doubt.

"Jodie, Creighton, any evidence pointing to anyone other than Matt as a killer?" I said.

Creighton ignored me, but Jodie twisted her neck partway around and said, "We don't discuss police business with the public."

Of course. I'd gotten caught up in all the siren noise and my own self-realizations. I shrugged my shoulders at Daryl, who smiled perfectly with his big white teeth.

As the four of us paraded toward the front door of the small courthouse, we were met by a familiar figure leaving the building.

"Howie!" I said.

"Hello," he said with surprise and a nod. His eyes were pinched and he seemed more off-kilter than he'd been in the shop.

"You okay?" I couldn't help but ask.

He looked at the police officers and then at Daryl. I wasn't completely sure, but I wondered if he spent a moment assessing the man's good looks before his eyes came back to me. It seemed like a Hollywood-guy thing to do.

"Trying to get Matt out of jail. The judge here was no help."

"Maybe someone in Salt Lake City could help," I said.

"He was arrested here." Howie looked at Jodie. "The judge says there's no bail. It would sure help to have him out of jail. Help his career, I mean."

"If he's a killer, he won't have a movie career," Jodie said.

"But what if he isn't?" Howie said. "You are all ruining his career if he's innocent."

"The evidence we have at the moment points toward him being a killer, sir. We don't take careers into consideration when we're looking at something heinous," Jodie said so professionally that I was momentarily impressed.

"He's innocent," Howie said.

My opinion of his support of Matt was starting to change. Maybe Howie wasn't such a jerk.

Creighton had been quiet since we'd left the police station, but now he stepped toward Howie and said, "Do you have information that might lead us or the police in Salt Lake in a different direction?"

It was achingly quiet for the few beats it took Howie to answer. He seemed to assess Creighton with as much scrutiny as he had Daryl, and I wondered if he did that with everyone. Perhaps everyone was a potential star.

"No, sir, I do not. I assure you that I would come to you

if I did. But I'm certain that Matt is innocent, and that makes me think that someone isn't doing their job correctly." The dig, if that's what it was, was definitely aimed directly at Creighton.

Creighton leveled his eyes at Howie. I'd never once seen him or Jodie become affected by vocal criticism. Complaints came with the job. As expected, Creighton didn't react inappropriately, not even with a sneer. He sniffed and rubbed his finger under his nose and said, "Thank you for your time."

He turned and moved toward the courthouse doors. Jodie followed behind. Nervously, I straightened my glasses and gave Howie a semi-friendly smile, but he didn't smile back. The entire confab was strange, and Daryl was the only one who seemed to enjoy himself. His smile grew wide as Howie walked away.

"That guy has something to do with Matt Bane?" he asked.

"Yep," I said.

"Cool."

"Clare, Mr. Brewsberry," Jodie said from the door. "Coming in?"

Reluctantly, even though there was probably a hundred thousand dollars at the end of the trip, Daryl pulled his attention away from Howie and followed Jodie and me into the courthouse.

❧

"You found the money?" Judge Serus said as she looked over the reading glasses perched on the end of her nose. She was young, maybe in her early thirties, and I wondered if she really needed the reading glasses or if they just appealed to her fashion sense. The pair she wore sported multicolored rhinestones along the top, over a green plastic frame.

"I did. In the tin," I said.

"The ribbon tin that Mr. Brewsberry gave to you?"

"Yes."

"Well, I gave it to her boyfriend to give to her. He'd told me about the shop she and her grandfather run," Daryl added.

"The Rescued Word?" Judge Serus smiled. I loved it when people did that after they spoke the name of the shop. I'd run into a few scowls over the years, but mostly there'd been smiles.

"Yes."

"I see. Where is this wayward boyfriend of yours?" Judge Serus asked.

"Well. He's not wayward. He's at work. He's on his way back to town, though," I said, not liking her as much as I had a second ago.

"I see. Well, it does seem simple considering there are no other heirs to the estate, and the police have done a thorough search regarding any other possible claimants to the money." Jodie and Creighton nodded confidently. "The copy of the will and the previous directives look to be in order, but I'd need to speak to the person—the boyfriend—who might have touched the tin in between its leaving Mr. Brewsberry's mother's house and arriving at The Rescued Word. I'm assuming that the box with all the tins might have been left unattended in the shop at least briefly."

I thought. "Yes. There weren't eyes on it all the time, but it wasn't necessarily left unattended."

"Well, I'll let that go because I can't imagine someone would suddenly and randomly decide to put the money in the tin just because, and if they were dumb enough to do so, I guess they lose, then. I just need to speak to the boyfriend."

"His name is Seth Cassidy," I said. "May I call to see where he is?"

"Sure. We'll take five. Bailiff."

Court, such as it was—a small room with a two-bench gallery, a bull pen made up of two small tables, and a separate and more highly set desk for the judge—was adjourned briefly.

I hurried out to the hallway—it wasn't wide and stately, but cute and cozy instead—and called Seth.

"I'm almost in town. Maybe ten minutes," he said as he answered.

"Stop by the courthouse. The judge wants to talk to you about the tin."

"Okay. No problem."

"Daryl's here."

"Great. That should make things move along quickly."

"See you in a few."

We disconnected and I hurried to the front doors to watch for Seth as well as find Jodie and Creighton. They'd both gone in this direction. I hadn't seen Daryl leave the courtroom.

Though the building was small, it was big enough to have more than one hallway. The bathrooms were located next to the main doors, and another hallway jutted off from there, at a right angle to the one with the courtroom. I knew there were attorneys' offices in that direction. I'd heard a world-famous novelist also leased a small space so she'd have a place to escape the crowds and write when she was in town, but I wondered if that was only a rumor.

I was just about to peer around the corner when two voices stopped me. I knew those voices. Creighton and Jodie often argued, but it was rare that I heard such venomous tones from either of them.

I couldn't help myself. I stayed hidden and listened hard.

15

"Do you have any idea what you did?" Jodie said.

"I didn't do anything wrong," Creighton said.

"What do you mean, you didn't do anything wrong? Everything you did was wrong. Why didn't you tell me about this before?"

"Not true. Not really wrong," Creighton said. "Considering the circumstances."

His tone belied his words. He knew he'd done something wrong, but didn't want to admit it. I'd heard that tone. I'd even been on the receiving end of those same words, though I doubted they were about the same sort of misstep.

Creighton's personality traits were bound to cause him some lifelong battles, both internal and external. He had a deep-seated sense of right and wrong—at least what he considered right and wrong. That probably came from his cop family. But he was also all about control. There were moments when his controlling behavior would jump in the middle of his personally defined morality and . . . fix things.

When he'd cheated on me, his first reaction had been to somehow justify his actions by making his betrayal something that would prove to be good for our future together. He couldn't get to the apology without first going through the motions of making himself feel better because what he'd done was somehow "right." It hadn't worked, of course, and by the time he apologized, it was far too late to salvage any sort of relationship.

"Yes, totally wrong. You're a cop, Creighton, not supreme ruler of the universe."

"Jodie. Enough."

"Right. You're the boss now. Now you get to do whatever you want. I don't think so."

"It's fine, Jodie."

"Clare?" a voice said from behind me.

I jumped but caught any noise of surprise before it came out of my mouth.

"Hey," I said to Seth as I hurried next to him, to a spot that wouldn't seem like I'd just been craning my neck toward the other hallway.

As casually as possible, I staged the best scene I could and moved up to my tiptoes for a quick kiss. To his credit, the moment Seth saw Creighton and Jodie come around the corner, he figured out what I'd been doing, and he played along perfectly.

"I got back as fast as I could," he said to me. He glanced quickly and casually at Jodie and Creighton. "Hey."

"Seth, you just get here?" Creighton said.

"Just walked in." He held out his hands and looked at them. "I'm a mess. Sorry."

Seth was covered in dust. I wasn't sure exactly what he'd been doing, but the activity had made his dark hair look like it had frosted tips along one side. His sweatshirt and jeans were also dotted and streaked in the gray dirt. He hadn't taken the time to put a coat on, but I imagined it was dirty too.

"No problem," Creighton said. "We'd better get back to the courtroom."

He led the way, but Jodie followed behind him, shooting both Seth and me suspicious sidelong glances. I hoped my neutral expression didn't give anything away.

"Seth," she said.

"Jodie," he said.

I was sure she and I would discuss this later.

The first thing Seth did was apologize to the judge for his appearance. This made her strangely happy and much less sarcastic, and she didn't mention his "waywardness" once. In fact, if I hadn't added the "boyfriend" part, I thought she might ask for his number.

From there the proceeding moved quickly. Seth hadn't even stopped to fill up with gas on the way back up to Star City after he'd helped Daryl with his mom's house. The tins had gone directly from a shelf in Mrs. Brewsberry's basement to Seth's car, to The Rescued Word. None of us claimed the money was ours, so after a bunch of legalese was printed and signed, the judge told Creighton he could hand the money over to Daryl. She wasn't even going to rule that the money be put into a separate account until any other avenues could be explored. The judge didn't sense there were any further necessary steps to take. Once court was adjourned, we all made our way back to the police station parking lot.

"Here, I'd like to give you a reward," Daryl said to me. After Creighton had excused himself and gone inside, Daryl pulled out one of the ten-thousand-dollar bills.

"No way," I said as I looked around, hoping we weren't being watched. Jodie did the same but much more dubiously. I swallowed hard. "Not necessary at all. Thank you, though."

"I insist," Daryl said.

"I don't care," I said. "Donate it to a children's charity or something. That's your mother's money, however she accumulated it, Daryl. She would want you to have it. I seriously could not sleep at night if I took any of it."

Daryl looked at Seth for some sort of help, but he only shrugged.

"Can I take the two of you out to dinner sometime?" Daryl said.

"That would be great. Next time you're in town," Seth said.

The next few moments might have been as surprising as overhearing Jodie and Creighton's argument.

Daryl turned toward Jodie and said, "It would be perfect if you would join us."

The silence that followed was rude, but also genuine. Was he asking Jodie out?

"Oh," she said a second later as she looked up at his overly handsome face and rode her eyes over those ridiculously wide shoulders. "Well, I have a boyfriend."

The regretful tone she infused into the words might have been her attempt at acting or not, but it was just the thing to ease Daryl's ego.

He shrugged. "Had to try. It's not often I meet someone like you."

"Well, thanks," she said so girlishly that I smiled.

Jodie was a pretty woman, but also one who took her cop role seriously. She came off tough and no-nonsense. More often than not, she stood with her thumbs in her belt and her feet firm and even on the ground. There was nothing supermodel about the pose. It was rare that men weren't intimidated or put off by her, but Daryl saw through her well-practiced exterior. It was fun to see her on the receiving end of such admiration.

"All right. Well, I guess I'm out of here. A police escort wouldn't be a bad idea." He winked at Jodie. "Just kidding. I'll be fine. Good to meet you and see you again, Seth. Thank you all for being so honest."

The good thing about the flirtatious moment was that Jodie either forgot about what might have happened in the courthouse hallway or just didn't want to bring it up. She excused herself a moment later.

"So, how's everything?" Seth said to me when we were alone in the parking lot full of cars and Toby's van.

"Oh, boy, do I have a lot to tell you. Have time for dinner before we go see a movie?"

"Absolutely. Let me get cleaned up."

"You can do that at my house."

"Works for me."

16

It was cold. The clouds were gone, having moved on, and we had a clear view of the sky and the blanket of stars that had been instrumental in naming our small piece of the mountainside.

The movie, *Kill Night*, had been the creepiest thing I'd ever seen. But it had been good, really good. Compelling to the point that I'd held my breath a couple times, and I forgot all about the popcorn Seth had bought for us to share. We'd all enjoyed it—Chester, Ramona, Seth, Marion, myself, and even Toby, who'd taken Jimmy's ticket when Marion decided to forget to tell her father about the movie and give the ticket to her new friend. The movie was so good that about five minutes in, I stopped watching Marion and Toby to make sure they were behaving. I was sure they had, though. No one could have easily given his or her attention to anything but the screen as Matt Bane took on the role of cop / serial killer like a pro. He was an extraordinarily good actor.

I let the story take me away, but once the end credits rolled, I couldn't help but look deeply into myself and see if I really did believe that Matt was innocent of killing his sister or if I'd been well convinced. Despite his flawless acting skills, I still sensed that he was not a real-life killer. I wondered if I'd ever be able to help prove it.

After the movie we all went our own ways. Toby wandered back to his newly repaired van and I watched Jimmy pick up Marion at the bottom of Main Street. Chester and Ramona went back to Chester's apartment, where they planned on some binge reading. They'd named the activity such after I told them all about the popular binge watching of television shows. They read aloud to each other. Currently they were binge reading some mysteries set around the goings-on in a farmers' market. It wasn't heavy reading, but they enjoyed the escapism of their bingeing and they both preferred whiling away the hours with books rather than with anything on a screen of any kind.

The festival turned Star City into an open-all-the-time town. Though most of the local businesses kept their typical hours, a couple of small restaurants and a few food or hot chocolate carts stayed open. The hill of Main Street saw foot traffic all through the night. Tonight Seth and I joined the visitors and probably some well-disguised movie stars as we ventured down the hill, bidding farewell to our group of movie watchers, and then back up again toward my small house.

Our dinner before the movie had been quick, sandwiches at my house as I told him all that had happened since the murder.

I wondered what he made of everything, including what I'd overheard in the hallway. Unfortunately, like me, he had no idea.

What did Creighton do that he deemed acceptable but his sister thought was wrong? The list was probably endless, but at least Seth and I agreed that the offending action must have had something to do with the murder, or with Matt Bane. But we came to that conclusion only because we couldn't come up with anything else. Of course, we weren't privy to all police investigations, though.

We wondered briefly if Jodie might have been angry about something Creighton had done regarding the money in the tin, but from everything I could see, Creighton had behaved like a perfect police officer on that one. Other than the mystery man who'd claimed to be the brother of the original owner, the rest of the transfer of the money went smoothly. If Seth hadn't confirmed that Daryl was exactly who he said he was, I might have had some doubts and more questions. And the money would never have left police custody if that had been the case.

"Are you sure you didn't mention the tins to anyone else?" I said. "I know you weren't aware of the money inside the one, but did you show the box to anyone else or tell anyone else about them?"

"Not a soul, Clare. There was no one to tell. I did exactly as I told Judge Serus. I put the box in my car and then drove up to . . . well . . ."

"What?"

"I did do that. But I guess I ran back inside the house to let Daryl know that I was taking off. It was maybe half a minute, but I guess I should have remembered that my eyes were off my car for that brief time."

"Was the car locked?"

"Absolutely. I didn't know a thing about the tins. Daryl claimed not to know or care if they were worth anything, but I didn't want to take any chances." He stopped walking and looked toward the other side of the road, though I didn't think he was looking at anything in particular. "The house was up a small slope. There's a set of stairs leading up to the front door. I ran up those and into the house. I called for Daryl, but he didn't answer. I specifically remember looking back down at the car, assessing that it would be fine for a second, and then went farther into the house, still calling for Daryl. He finally answered when I was at the back, at the bottom of a staircase. He'd gone back upstairs."

"Any sign of your car being disturbed when you went back out?" I said.

"None. I glanced in the backseat and confirmed that the box was still there. The doors were still locked. I think."

"Think?"

"Pretty sure. I don't remember the specific moment of unlocking them, but I'm sure I would have thought it odd if I hadn't needed to."

"But you're really not one hundred percent sure?"

"Maybe ninety-nine percent. No, I'm sure. There couldn't have been enough time for someone to do something with the tins. And why would someone have put one hundred thousand dollars in one of them anyway?"

"I can't think of any reason why, but it's strange."

"It is. I'll give Jodie the details of being away from the car for a second, but I don't think anything weird happened."

"Me either."

We started walking again, but just as we reached The Fountain, I peeked in the front window and saw someone at the front counter. Maybe the reception desk was manned only late at night.

"Seth, I'd like to go inside and talk to him," I said.

"Why?"

"I'm not exactly sure yet."

"Good enough. There's a nice fire in there. I'm game."

He held open the door and I led the way into the warmth. My nose stung pleasantly with the temperature change, and my glasses fogged up, unpleasantly. I took them off and tried not to squint as I approached the counter. Seth took off his glasses too and went in the other direction, toward the fire.

"We don't have any rooms," the clerk said with a decidedly bored tone.

The twenty-something man wore a striking peach-colored suit and kept his hair slickly combed over to one side. The look didn't fit with either the historic hotel or the typical festival attire, which was somewhat grungy, particularly this time of night, so I thought he must be trying to make his own original statement. I immediately liked that about him.

"Oh, not here for a room, but it looks like a great place.

I actually live here in town. My grandfather owns The Rescued Word. I work for him. I'm Clare Henry."

"Good to meet you. I'm Jacob. I love that place. You guys have a printing press in the back, right?"

"We do. It's a replica of a Gutenberg. My grandfather built it years ago."

"I would love to see it."

"Anytime. Stop by and I'll show you." I smiled. It had been a calculated move on my part to bring The Rescued Word into the conversation. Though not everyone knew me and my connection to the shop, everyone knew Chester, and everyone seemed to love something about the place. Either the paper, the pens, the old typewriters, or the printing press. Though it was definitely a needy play, it was my go-to method of introducing myself when I wanted to grease the wheels. I was pleased it had worked this time. "Could I ask you a couple questions?"

"Sure, that's why I'm here, I think. I get more questions than Google."

"Really?"

"Yeah. Must have something to do with the location of the hotel. People see me through the window and come in to ask all sorts of things. You know, 'Where's the best pizza place?' 'Have you seen any movie stars today?' 'Where's the secret places where the stars go?'"

I hesitated. It wouldn't hurt to know the secret places, but I had to keep on task.

"My question has to do with the murder that occurred here."

"Oh." Jacob's expression sobered. "Yes, that was terrible."

I sensed he also thought it was old news, but I trudged forward.

"Were you here or do you just work at night?"

"I was here, just covering a coworker for a couple hours while she ran to a doctor's appointment. I usually only work at night."

"Where were you when the police took Matt out of here?" I asked, remembering Omar's frustration at not having someone close by who worked at the hotel.

"Just back there." He signaled behind him. "After all the uproar, I ran to the office to call the owners of the hotel to let them know what was going on."

"Did you hear anything earlier than that? Yelling, a struggle of any sort?"

"Oh yeah. I'm the one who called 911. Before that I heard one door slam and a scream," he said before he pursed his lips into an authoritative pucker.

"That's it? When did you hear the door slam?"

"About thirty seconds or so before I heard a scream."

"What did you do when you heard the scream? Who screamed?"

"Called 911 right away and then ran upstairs. And I'm not sure who screamed. Maybe the police know."

I thought back to the moment that Matt was being escorted out of the hotel. Jodie had been the only female in the group, but the scream could have come from Cassie, or a man could have screamed too, particularly upon finding a dead body.

"Then what happened?"

"All hell broke loose, I suppose. It was crazy upstairs."

"Who was up there?"

"Well, Matt Bane was in the room with the body. He was frozen in place. His assistant—I think his name is Howie—and the other hotel occupant who comes here every year from San Diego."

"Did you think Matt was the killer?"

Jacob thought a moment as he tapped his fingers on his lips. "Well, Howie was in there with him, asking Matt what he'd done. And Matt was holding the bloody weapon."

"Weapon?"

"The knife."

"Right," I said.

"Excuse me." Seth moved next to me. He reached over the counter and extended a hand toward Jacob. "I'm Seth Cassidy, a friend of Clare's. Do you mind if I ask a couple questions?"

"Sure," Jacob said. Clearly he didn't mind being more popular than Google.

"You said you don't know who screamed?" he said.

"Correct."

"What did you tell the police?" Seth asked.

Jacob thought again as more tapping ensued. "I told 911 that I heard the scream; that's all."

"Did they ask you who you thought it came from?" I said.

"No, they never talked to me after that call. But I imagine the others already told the police the sequence of events," Jacob said.

Seth and I looked at each other. Whatever information the police had gleaned, they obviously hadn't asked for Jacob's complete version of the story. It might not matter, but it was difficult not to wonder about that scream.

"Jacob, I'm sorry if this is obvious, but was the scream from a male or a female?" I asked.

"Female, without a doubt."

Now it was even more difficult not to wonder.

"You found the body shortly after the scream?" I said.

"Yeah, I hurried up there and then saw what I saw," he said, but I could tell he was getting tired of the questions.

"This is weird, but do you think it was the victim who screamed?" I asked.

"Oh." Jacob thought. "No, actually I don't. There was too much . . . Well, it seemed she'd been dead for more than half a minute or so when I looked in that room."

"Did you tell that to 911?"

"Not specifically like that."

I wondered whether someone else had explained those details to the police.

"Is there a back exit out of here, from the second floor?" I asked the same question Omar had, but at least I got a hotel employee.

"Just the fire escape out the back window, but it's old and rickety and the window's hard to open."

And I'd received a much better answer than Omar had. The man in the robe told Omar there was no back door, but hadn't mentioned the fire escape or the window. Maybe he just didn't know about them.

"Did anyone ask you about the exit?"

"I don't think so."

"Do you have any idea if the police checked the window or the escape or the space behind the building?"

Jacob shrugged. "I have no idea."

"Is there any chance we could take a look at it?" I asked.

"Probably not. No, I don't think so. It doesn't seem like the smartest move. I think I could get in trouble."

"Of course," I said. "Sorry. But what if we were very quiet and just toured the upstairs level?"

Jacob looked up at the landing and then shook his head. "This is the one time of the year we're not allowed to do that. The people who stay here pay lots for their privacy."

"Makes sense," Seth said. "Thank you for your time."

"Yes, definitely. And come by the shop whenever you'd like to see the press," I said.

"I will. I can't wait," Jacob said with a smile. He leveled his gaze at me. "And go around the north side of the building. The south is blocked. The north side isn't easy, but the south side is impossible."

"What?" I said.

"You're going to look at the back of the building, aren't you?"

"Well . . ."

"Right. I'm just telling you. Go around the north side." Jacob smiled and then turned his attention to something on the counter in front of him.

Seth held the door and I led the way again. We beelined our way to the north side of the building.

"That's dark," Seth said. He turned on the flashlight app on his phone, still not making the narrow space appealing.

The corridor wasn't big enough to walk through even if it hadn't been filled with dirty snow that had somehow drifted into a slope up the side of the hotel building. It looked like it served as a depository for smoked cigarettes and empty coffee cups. I had the thought that I couldn't remember the last time I'd seen anyone smoking anywhere, let alone on Main Street.

"I can only imagine how bad the south side must be," Seth said.

"We're not going back there," I said.

"Nope. But I think you should call Jodie and tell her."

"Tell her the police might have missed something crucial?"

"Well"—Seth flipped off the flashlight app—"maybe not those exact words, but I bet if you take her out for breakfast tomorrow, you can find a softer segue into the conversation. And she might even tell you about what you overheard between Creighton and her."

"You think so?" I said as we reluctantly pulled ourselves away from where we stood and started back up the hill.

Seth shrugged. "If she's going to tell anyone, it would be you."

"True."

"Are we done being detectives tonight?" Seth asked.

"I think so."

"We can always begin again tomorrow."

"Deal."

17

The approach was tough. Though Jodie had little ego around me, she didn't like hearing from anyone that perhaps she or another police officer might have missed something.

But, to her credit, she rebounded okay.

She chewed a bite of her syrup-drenched pancake for too many chews, and with more vigor than necessary, and squinted at me. I waited silently for her brain to line everything up. She was highly intelligent, but she was also cursed with a short, overly reactive fuse. I could see her rein in the sparks from the ignition I'd lit.

"We talked to the person we *thought* found the body and the person who found the person who found the body. We thought Matt found the body. Howie came in next. I know Omar confirmed there isn't a back door," she said.

"Well, mostly that's correct. Jacob came upon Matt and Howie with the body, but a scream had prompted him to run upstairs. He was pretty sure the scream hadn't come from Cassie. She was in a state . . . Well, it looked like there was enough blood that she couldn't have been screaming so recently before he ran up the steps. I don't know—maybe all the logistics are off, but he's the one who called 911. And there isn't a back door, but the fire escape outside the window might have been another way out. But it would be tough, Jodie. I doubt anyone could have gotten around the building and out to the street easily. Do you know who screamed?"

"I didn't know there was a scream, but that doesn't mean that Omar didn't know, or another officer. Maybe the crime scene guys."

"I'm sorry."

"We didn't check the fire escape for evidence. I don't even think any of us looked out that back window."

"So you never talked to Jacob, the hotel clerk?"

"I didn't, no. And Omar said he couldn't find anyone. Maybe someone did later. I don't know if anyone tracked down who exactly the call came from. You say he thought the scream belonged to a woman, and he was pretty sure it couldn't have come from Cassie? Are you sure that's what he said?"

"Yes."

A string of profanity flung from her mouth as she set her fork down with more vehemence than necessary. A speck of syrup flew up from it and landed on her collar. She wasn't in uniform, so I let it pass without comment.

We were in a pink booth at the diner again, and I could see the elderly woman sitting behind Jodie bristle with her harsh words. She didn't turn around, though.

"I'm sorry," I said again. "It might not mean much. If there was another female in the vicinity, you can figure out who it was. It might have just been a man screaming. You've told me many times how recall can be sketchy."

"It could mean a lot or it could mean nothing. At the very least, it could give a good defense attorney some perfect ammunition for reasonable doubt. It's hard enough to convict a movie star. Shoddy police work, no matter what it truly means, is always a win for the other side." She shook her head. "This case has been one misstep after another."

"What do you mean?"

She shook her head again and wouldn't look at me. She tried to make it seem as though she were distracted, not ignoring my question, but I knew her too well.

"Such a waste of good pancakes," she finally said. Her appetite always disappeared when she was upset. "I'm going over to the hotel. Want to come with?"

"Yes. Of course." My appetite wasn't gone, but I tried to hide my disappointment over not getting to finish my own pancakes. I loved doing police stuff with Jodie, but only the safe stuff. I'd learned that it wasn't nearly as much fun when someone was shooting a gun in your direction.

I grabbed one more bite as we stood. Jodie paid by putting some bills on the table and making eye contact with our server. Even though she wasn't dressed like one this morning, everyone who worked at the diner knew she was a cop, and her method of paying was perfectly acceptable.

"I got this one," she said as I reached for my wallet so I could contribute my share to the pile.

"Thanks," I said.

We marched down Bygone Alley and across the street to the hotel. I tried to match my steps with hers. Even when she didn't have her uniform on, people seemed to understand that getting out of her way was the best option.

I said a few "excuse me's," but she didn't. I expected some "get out of the way's" from her, but she kept quiet.

Jacob was off duty, but another young person was behind the counter. Her eyes got big when she saw the attitude that came through the door. I wasn't sure she noticed me.

"I'm with the police." Jodie flashed her identification. "I need to have full access to the upstairs."

The girl was blond and pretty, petite with a tiny nose but big green eyes that seemed incapable of hiding emotions. She was stunned, unsure, and somewhat scared. Fortunately, Jodie picked up on these things and toned it down.

"There was a murder here, and it's important that I have an unencumbered look around up there. I'll tell your boss I pushed past you if they ask you any questions. They'll understand," she said with practiced gentle tones.

The girl nodded. She was maybe seventeen and her ponytail was perfect. If she was local, she might have known Marion, but I didn't bring up my niece's name.

"All right," she finally said. She reached under the counter and fished out a key that was attached to a paddle that had once been part of a Ping-Pong set. "This is a master key."

Jodie took it from her but not without raising an eyebrow. Even I knew a master key shouldn't be on something so big and obvious.

"Thanks," she said as she took the key. She'd save her admonishment for the owners.

We hurried up the stairs. At the top of the landing, I sent a fleeting glance toward the plant I'd hidden behind. It was hard to believe that Nell hadn't seen me there. The hallway didn't appear to have been part of a murder. The room where Cassie had been killed might currently be empty of hotel guests, but the door wasn't blocked off. The light behind an old-fashioned sconce flickered just like the one I'd seen on the first floor.

Jodie didn't rush to get to the window. She put her hand on my arm.

"We're just taking a cursory look," she said. "I need the crime scene techs here to do a thorough job. Not that it matters much at this point, but don't touch anything. Just let me."

"Got it," I said.

Jodie pulled a pen from her pocket and we closed the distance between us and the window. With the pen, she lifted back one curtain panel and leaned over to look out the window and at the sill. I stayed back a half step, but I raised myself up to my toes and looked where she looked.

The back of the building wasn't far from the side of a mountain. There wasn't a lot of space back there. Nothing that could ever serve as parking for anything bigger than a bicycle or two. There had never been and would never be a patio. Nevertheless, the fire escape landing, stairs, and ladder all led to a space where someone could escape from the building if there was a fire. Of course, after that, the person's options would be to climb the mountain or try to forge a path along one of the tight side spaces.

"Are there regulations that would deem this building unsafe?" I said.

"Probably. But the title of 'historic' goes a long way," Jodie said. "It snowed after the murder, right?"

I thought a minute. "Yes, for sure."

"The snow down there could have a footprint or two, but it's hard to tell."

I craned my neck. There was snow there. Dirty snow. And she was correct—it would be hard to tell if there were any footprints. Nothing was set on an even plane.

"The ladder's down," I said. The rusty extension ladder was, indeed, extended to the ground.

"Saw that, but we don't know how long it's been that way. How else could someone have escaped from up here?"

I looked around. "Out a room window, but the spaces on each side of the building are not easy to maneuver."

"Then there's only one other way," Jodie said. I looked at her as she pointed. "Up."

"How?" I asked. I didn't see a panel that led to an attic or the roof.

"Again, through a window. Maybe." She turned back to the window and moved the other curtain panel open with her pen. "Yep, there's another ladder attached to the side of the building, going up. There's a possibility someone hid up there, maybe leaving through the hotel later. Not sure."

"Should we go up there?" I asked.

"As much as I would like to do that, I'd better call this in now. Sorry to spoil your fun."

"What else can we do while we're here? Can we shove our way into a room or something?" Even caught up in the investigation, I was momentarily excited that I might finally get to see the inside of a room.

"I could, yes, but I don't really have probable cause at this point and I don't want to do anything to jeopardize this mess any more than we already have."

"That's too bad."

"You have to get to work, don't you?"

"I suppose."

"I'll come see you right after."

I looked at her a long moment. It suddenly seemed important to confess. "I overheard you yesterday."

"Excuse me?"

"When you were mad at Creighton at the courthouse. I overheard you both."

"Oh. Well, you shouldn't have. No one should have."

"Wanna tell me what it was about?"

"Nope, but thanks for asking."

"Jodie."

"Clare. There are certain things I can't tell even you. At least not yet. Maybe later."

"Like today later?"

"Clare."

"Got it."

"Go to work. I'll come talk to you."

"Okay," I said with an exaggerated sigh.

Reluctantly I left the hotel. As I stepped outside and accidentally into the middle of a passing crowd, I excused myself and moved to the edge of the sidewalk. I turned and faced the hotel, wondering if Howie had been in his room and if Jodie was going to knock on doors and ask more questions.

And where was Nell? And Adele?

Was I just putting those people and Matt in a group together because I'd come to meet them all on the same day or were they really a package deal? Did they have a connection other than just the romantic and business relationships? I suddenly thought I understood why Matt wanted me to observe them at the party. Perhaps the murder was something they or at least a couple of them had in common.

I'd have to find out later. For now, I had to get to work.

18

There were five of them and except for the one I could communicate with, they were old men, as old as Chester maybe but in much worse shape—hunched, bony shouldered—even under their shabby jackets and sweaters I could see their shoulder bones—and all four of them walked with canes that weren't just for show.

The younger one was probably close to my age, but he already had gray hair at his temples. I'd known people from Germany, but they'd never seemed as if they'd aged long before their time like these men did. Two men in the group wore sweaters with patches over their elbows; the other three seemed just as ragged with an array of frayed collars and shiny knees on their pants. I couldn't help but wonder how they'd afforded their journey across the ocean.

I didn't have to wonder long about their reason for coming

to Star City, though. Chester greeted me when I came through the front door and told me where they were from and about their small publishing house, which was more than a hundred years old, in Berlin. They wanted to learn how to restore books. Some books their company had published years ago were suddenly seeing a resurgence and becoming desired items throughout Europe. Along with their publishing skills, they wanted to learn restoration so they could bring the books back to pristine condition before selling them.

"There are no book restorers in Germany? Or perhaps France?" I said to Chester.

"They don't want to go to their competition, and they were coming to Star City anyway."

"Not to ski, I take it?"

"No, one of their brothers . . . Did I mention that all the elderly gentlemen are brothers?" I shook my head. "They are. Anyway, one of the brothers who isn't here with them is a producer on one of the films up for an award at the festival. He's out and about doing festival things."

"Which film?"

"*Statisch*. It means 'Static.'"

"Don't know that one. How did they hear about us?"

Chester shrugged. "We're a worldwide company, Clare."

"I suppose."

I introduced myself and shook all their hands, and didn't catch even one name. I was still trying to process the news regarding why they were here.

"Will you show us what to do?" the younger one asked with a slight German accent after I'd made the rounds.

"I'd be happy to, but it's not a quick or easy lesson. It

will take time," I said, not wanting to add that perhaps the older men didn't have the time available to them. The younger one did. "I'm sorry, I was trying hard to listen, but I didn't catch your name."

"Adalwulf. Please call me Adal."

"Adalwulf. That's a wonderful name. Well, we can come up with some sort of schedule, maybe Skype. How long are you in Star City?"

"I'm here until the task is done. My uncles will set me up a place to live."

I blinked.

"Would you like an apprentice, Clare?" Chester said as he moved next to me.

"Adal, will you excuse us a minute?" I said. Of course he knew what Chester and I were going to discuss, but I felt I had no choice but to have the conversation.

"Of course." He smiled at me and then at Chester as we turned to walk toward the workshop. We'd leave the door open in case any other customers came in.

"See? Fate, destiny," Chester said when we were in the back and beside my desk.

"Shouldn't an apprentice be younger, someone to take over the duties someday?"

"You're far too young to worry about that. Plenty of time. For now, you could teach our new German friend and spread some international goodwill. There are more apprentices in your future."

I inspected Chester. "What's going on?"

"I think this was your idea, Clare."

"No. There's more."

He shrugged again and frowned under his bushy mustache. "When you mentioned hiring someone, you got me thinking, and I might want to take a vacation or two. I'm not saying I planned and plotted for a group of German men to come in wanting to acquire our skills, but perhaps I'm making the addition of an apprentice too convenient. Nevertheless, some time away might not be terrible for me."

"Oh, I see. Perhaps there is a girlfriend involved? Does Ramona want to do some traveling?"

Chester sighed. "We're old, Clare. There are a few places we want to see before we die. And I bet he'll work for free!"

"We can't do that. We'll need to pay him something."

"You're teaching him some valuable skills. They have money."

"They don't look like they have money."

"They do. I talked to one of the guys earlier."

"You speak German?"

"No, they speak English, but the older guys just don't want to. The young guy will be great to work with."

"He seems nice enough," I said. "But . . . Chester, we don't know these people. And we *will* pay him."

"Work with him today and decide. You're the one who told me that Marion will not have one thing to do with this shop when she becomes famous."

"I think she'll come back eventually."

"I would not count on it. She's going to be a star. I wish we could put it off, but soon it will just be you and me and an employee or two. Or an interesting young man from Germany with 'wulf' in his name. How could this be wrong?"

He made a good case.

"Um, well, I guess it should be okay. Wait—let me get some references and make some calls just to make sure."

"Fine." He turned to go back to the front of the shop. "And remember that old Groma you fixed?"

It had been a Groma Bakelite, a portable typewriter made in Germany back in the 1940s. I'd fallen in love with its Art Deco styling and was sad to send it back, but that wasn't unusual; I became attached to most of the typewriters I worked on.

"Of course."

"That was Adalwulf's. He and his family were so impressed with your typewriter-fixing skills that they researched us and found all our other offerings too. When they decided to come to the festival, they put us at the top of their list to visit. They planned to ask if Adal could learn from you, but they didn't want to prepare us, give us a chance to say no to them, because they were so far away."

I remembered packing up the Groma to send to Germany. The shipping costs had been ridiculous. "Why in the world is this so important to them?"

"I'm not exactly sure. There are other ways to go about what they want to accomplish, but it seems they've latched on to us. I think it's a good thing. Maybe they're believers in fate and destiny too."

I blinked. "Did you know about this before?"

"Nope. Cross my heart, I didn't. I could feel something in the air, though."

"Hmmm."

"Really, Clare, how could anyone dislike someone who owns a Groma and is named Adalwulf?"

"I don't know, but I want to make sure, that's all."

"Of course. I'll go ask Adal for a list of references. Wait here."

I took a seat at my desk after Chester left the room. I had a stack of work that had been neglected for a few days, but fortunately nothing that needed immediate attention. Nevertheless, I was anxious to get back to it. Fixing an old typewriter didn't sound like much on the surface, but it was a real task with a satisfactory ending. I also still needed to research Mr. Muir's book, as well as whatever other smaller tasks I could fit in.

But what did I truly think about hiring an apprentice? I hadn't taken the time to think about it much at all. It was just recently that Jodie had planted the seed in my mind.

It wouldn't hurt. If he was a hard worker and a good learner, it couldn't possibly hurt to have him around.

I scooted away from the desk and rejoined everyone out front. Adal was writing something on a piece of paper with one of the shamrock pens. I looked at the worn-thin sweaters and the elbow patches and wondered if they'd really been able to easily afford the trip. I hoped so.

"Adal, if your references check out, we'd love to have you aboard. It won't all be fun work—you need to know that."

"I understand," Adal said.

His uncles had smiles as big as he did. They said things too, but I couldn't understand them, even though I figured they understood me.

Chester smiled the biggest of all.

19

I opened the door with a dramatic flourish. I was dressed to the nines. Drama was necessary.

"Holy moley," Seth said. "I've never . . . You look . . . wow!"

I laughed. "That was the right response."

"Seriously, you are stunning."

"Thank you. So are you actually."

Seth wore a black tuxedo with a crisp white shirt and a dapper black bow tie. He swung his hand from behind his back and flipped a fedora up and around before it landed on his head with a sideways tilt. He didn't look the least bit nerdy.

I clapped. "Nice."

"I've been practicing for an hour."

"It was worth the effort."

He brought his other hand around and handed me a single red rose.

"Oh, that's perfect."

"It might die soon. It's cold out here and the walk from my car up to your doorway might have killed it."

"I'll put it in some water. We'll leave it here. Come in."

I admired the perfect rose as I carried it back to the kitchen. I filled a glass with water, because I had no idea where any vases were, settled the rose into it, and took a picture on my phone. I wasn't one to post much of anything anywhere, but I wanted a picture before it did die. It was the first rose Seth had ever given me, and though I wished taking it with me were a viable option, and though I might not show my sentimental side very often, I would be glad I had the picture to look back on.

"I think we'll make a fine-looking couple," Seth said as I came back around and into the front room. He had that look in his eyes that made me smile goofily. Oh, the blush of a new romance.

"Me too. I guess we're ready. I'd ask you to sit down for a social minute or two, but I can't sit in this dress, so we'd just have to stand and look at each other. We might as well do that at the party. I have no idea how I'm going to sit in the car. You might have to strap me on the top."

My long, light blue, shimmery dress fit snugly everywhere. It had to be tight. It didn't have straps and would fall down if it wasn't molded to me. It made me more hourglass shaped than I actually was, and the side slit from the hem up to directly above my knee gave me no choice but to wear heels to keep the glamour going.

I threw on a faux-fur shawl that didn't go with the dress, but it was better than my ski jacket and it was too cold outside to go without anything. I hoped for a coat check before we made our way into the main party. And something I could lean against if I got tired or if my feet started protesting the heels.

Once in Seth's car, seated, but in a strange stretched-out, ironing-board-ish pose, I recited an address that was located high up a mountain slope, if I knew my hidden mountain roads well. If it were snowing, I would think it might be unsafe, but I suspected the route had been well cleared and the place we were going would be impressive. It was all too secretive and mysterious not to be.

I relayed my conversation and the events that had occurred with Jodie—who had not stopped by the shop as she'd promised she'd do. I would wait until the morning to call her. It was not my business anyway, but I couldn't help but wish she'd followed through with the promise to come talk to me, and I'd been vacillating between being hurt and a little angry that she hadn't. I didn't tell Seth about that part.

When I told him about Adal and the other German tourists, he said, "That can't be a real story. It couldn't have happened that way. It sounds too . . . scripted, I guess."

"According to Chester, that was the sequence of events that led to my having a real-life apprentice. I wondered if he'd somehow intervened with fate and destiny, but he promises he didn't."

"It sounds great, really. You could use the help, and someone from Germany? It will be fun to get to know him."

"I know. I was thrown by the whole idea at first, but it's starting to sound more appealing. I've never shown anyone how to do what I do. Well, I've tried with Marion, but she's been too busy to do much more than just pretend to care and pick up a few of the basics."

"Have you and Chester ever talked about future plans for the shop?"

"Not really. I think we both thought I'd just handle things after he's gone—but I can't bear to think about that—and by the time I'm gone, if I'm lucky to have a long life, I suppose, either the world will have no idea what typewriters and printing presses are or we will have unplugged and they will both become popular again. As long as I'm alive, I'll be at the shop, that's for sure."

Seth nodded, but there was something about his moonlit profile that made me do a double take. "Wait, you're not leaving, are you?"

He smiled at me quickly before turning his attention back to the winding mountain road ahead. "No, not for a very long time. I just signed a two-year contract for my Star City job."

"Two years isn't that long," I said.

"No, but there will be more years offered. That's just how it works with the projects I'm doing. Funding isn't always a sure thing, particularly more than a couple years into the future. I was offered this contract and something in New Mexico. I took this one."

"I didn't know you had the other offer."

He waved it away, but then put his hand back onto the steering wheel. "I didn't even think about taking it. I like

Star City much better than I would New Mexico, even though it's a pretty enchanted state."

I wanted to ask if part of the reason he signed the local contract had anything to do with me, but the question seemed way too needy. I didn't have to ask.

"I couldn't leave now even if I didn't like my cute apartment and the great mountain views. There's this girl . . . ," he said.

"Wow, that made my night even more than the rose and this fancy Hollywood party we're going to."

"Well, we'll see," Seth said.

After the next curve in the road we were transported into a world of bigness. It was a word I frequently used to describe the expensive and expansive places and things around Star City. It was no secret that the town was a mountain haven, a getaway for a number of the rich and famous. Mountain houses, grand hotels built with ski-slope accessibility right outside back doors or off multileveled and heated decks. Bigness wasn't everywhere in Star City, but it could easily be found.

A house directly from the world of bigness loomed above us, built into and onto the side of a mountain and certainly requiring some engineering logistics I would never comprehend. The moon and stars had been hung perfectly in the cloudless dark sky and they illuminated the wide multi-chalet-peaked dark structure as if a lighting designer had been involved. It was amazing what money could do.

"Is that one house?" Seth asked.

"I think so," I said.

"Whose is it?"

"I'm not sure. There are a number of big names with places around here. I'm just not one to ever be invited over to get to know them."

"Magic ticket tonight, I guess," Seth said.

He pulled the car onto a wide cobblestoned half-circle driveway in front of the house.

"Welcome," a gentleman dressed in a tuxedo said as he peered into Seth's open window. "We'll be happy to take care of your vehicle."

"Where do you park the cars?" I said as I looked around. There was only one other car in sight. A Rolls-Royce was parked along the far curve of the driveway. I wondered if it was just there for show. Its wide body seemed old in the moonlight, a shout-out to a time when lots of famous people rode in the back of their Rolls-Royces, their drivers a bigger part of their lives than they were these days.

"We have parking underneath." He smiled and nodded to the open mouth of space behind him.

"There's a parking garage built into the mountain and under the house?"

"Yes, miss. A big one." The shine in one of his moonlit eyes dimmed briefly as he winked.

"I see," I said.

He opened Seth's door as mine swung open too. Another man in a tuxedo held it wide and extended his hand.

I looked at him. "I'm a little wedged in. The dress is tight."

"Not to worry," my tuxedo man said. "I've got plenty of experience. If I hold your hand right here, you'll be able to swing your ankles. There you go. Now, I'll take both your hands and you'll be able to stand up easily."

His instructions were spot-on, and a second later I'd been successfully plucked out of the car.

"Thank you," I said.

"My pleasure." He swept his hand toward a space to the side of the garage. "The entrance is over there. You'll come upon an elevator that will take you up to the party."

"Thank you."

I slipped my arm through Seth's after he handed over his car keys and we moved toward the elevator. The clear sky and the higher altitude made the temperature up here even more icy frigid than what it was in town. We made foggy clouds with our breath and echoes as our fancy shoes clacked along the stones. The tip of my nose tingled with the exposure. Both of our glasses would need some adjustment time.

"Welcome," another man in a tuxedo said as he held the elevator door open. "Climb aboard."

"Where is everybody?" I said. I'd looked into the depths of the parking area, but it was too dark to see anything but more dark.

"People will come and go all night. I just dropped off a party of five above. I'm sure there will be more when I come back down."

I nodded, noticing that neither Seth's nor my glasses had fogged. Impressive. Either we hadn't been outside long enough or the magic of the night had sprinkled some extra dust on us.

The plush elevator, decked out in red velvet and faux

gold trimmings, took off smoothly. Each of the side walls was made of mirrors, and the back wall was a collage of movie posters. As I glanced over them, I began to think I knew just whom this elevator, house, and parking garage, and all these tuxedo people, belonged to.

However, I thought it would be terrible form to ask where we were. I nudged Seth so he'd look at the posters too. The elevator man pretended not to notice.

"Oh," Seth said a moment later. "Oh?"

I nodded.

The elevator man smiled. "Yes, it's his house. He's a terrific fellow, though I'm not sure I agree with all his politics."

"I didn't know he came to the festival. I've never heard about his attendance."

He laughed. "No, he doesn't attend many of the festival events. He'd be too much of a distraction. He lives here. You'll find his helicopter pad just on the other side of the mountain-top. He works in California, but is here more than not."

"I had no idea," I said.

"This is exactly how you learn about all this. You get invited to the party."

"I've never heard about the party," I said.

"There's a reason for that. You'll find out momentarily."

The elevator stopped without a jolt and the doors opened, bringing a tidal wave of noises and scents that were so intimidating that I took an extra second to step out.

"I think we found the party," Seth said above the music and chatter.

A woman appeared in front of us. She was dressed in a

black dress that fit her petite frame as though it were made for her. Her regal but friendly attitude belied her size, and her long brown ponytail was smooth, her makeup perfect.

"Come on in," she said with a wave of bright red polish on short manicured nails. "We're happy to have you here. I'll take your wrap if you'd like."

I swung the wrap off my shoulders and handed it to her. She put it over her arm.

"May I have your invitation and your names?"

I handed her the piece of paper Matt had given me, and she smiled when we told her our names. She neither wrote them down nor looked them up on any list, but nodded as if she'd successfully saved the information in her memory bank.

"Ms. Henry, Mr. Cassidy, welcome to the party. We ask that you enjoy yourselves, stay the night, or let one of our staff drive you home if you have too much fun. Do not take any pictures. We cherish the secrecy of these parties. Please don't later tell anyone you attended or the location of the house. You will be invited every year from here on out if you keep your attendance to yourselves, and believe me, we know when our party attendees don't."

Seth and I nodded in agreement.

"Excellent. Then, by all means, have a great time. Don't be afraid to approach anyone. Though we don't allow pictures, only those who are willing to mingle are invited back."

"Thank you."

She nodded and walked toward a space I assumed was the coat check.

"Wow," Seth said.

"I know. Wow."

"This is Flint Magnum's house?" Seth said.

"It appears that way."

"He has some of the best movie lines of all time."

"I know."

I didn't know if Flint Magnum was his real name or not, but it didn't seem likely. He'd been a leading man for four decades, if I was calculating correctly, starring mostly in action movies and Westerns. He was a tough guy, handsome, and he usually seemed to be carrying some sort of firearm. And frequently shooting it at bad guys.

I had no idea he had a secret mansion in the hills above Star City, but I knew of his reputation as a real-life good guy who put his money into conservative politicians as well as liberal causes. He was one of the founders of a big organization that took medical supplies to remote and violent places in Africa. I didn't know if it had been done strictly for PR, but I remembered seeing pictures of him there amid the violence, helping as he saw fit.

Flint Magnum. No one could possibly be immune to his celebrity, could they? Including myself.

We stepped into a large hall decorated with crystal chandeliers, an ice-cream-swirl patterned marble floor, and a few well-placed white pillars, oddly harkening back to Greek and Roman times but somehow fitting in with the other lush details. Tiered buffet tables lined the right wall, and a band reminding me of the Beatles took up space along the left wall.

The big crowd wasn't unmanageable, but my eyes were

so busy trying to take everything in at once that at first I missed details. I knew all the attendees were dressed nicely, but I didn't catch exactly who everyone was.

Until my eyes landed on one very familiar figure.

"No way," I said.

"What?" Seth said as he followed my glance.

"Look who's here," I said.

Seth looked where I was looking. "Chester?"

"Yep."

I didn't mean to abandon Seth, but my duty became singular. I wanted to find out what my grandfather was doing at the secret party, and why he'd kept the secret from even me.

20

"Clare! Hello, my dear. I wondered if you'd ever receive an invitation."

"Hi, Chester. Ramona," I said.

"Hi, darlin'," she said with her thick Southern drawl.

"You look gorgeous," I said.

"Oh, this old thing." She laughed as she took on a quick model pose, showing off her slightly curvy figure, which was cloaked in a conservative but somehow sexy red dress. The dress stopped just above her knees and she'd managed to find flat shoes that were perfect for it. Her sharp features—nose, chin, cheeks—combined well with her head of long dark hair, which was currently piled atop her head. She was lovely. And the more you talked to her, the more beautiful she became. Her kind heart showed through all the time. She was just the woman my grandma would have wanted Chester to find.

She and my grandfather made a great couple, in the way that opposites attract. They were both widowed, but that's about where their commonalities ended. Ramona was from Georgia and Chester from Star City. He'd thought he'd never find another love after my grandmother died ten years earlier. But Ramona and he had clicked and seemed to be surprised by how different they were, so much so that they were fascinated with each other and wanted to see what they might discover next.

"You are as lovely as a bluebell dipped in snow," Ramona said after she gave me a quick once-over.

I didn't think I'd ever heard a cooler compliment. "Thank you."

"And, Seth, gracious, you would never know how completely nerdy you can be." She whistled. "Handsome devil."

"Thank you, Ramona." Seth laughed too and winked at me.

"Chester, how long have you been coming to these parties?" I asked.

"About six years," he said. "Flint came into the shop one day and asked me about some old Underwood he had. He wore a hat and sunglasses, but I knew who he was. Years ago he did that movie about Wyatt Earp. I started to bring up some facts from Earp's day that I knew, and we talked for about an hour. Surprised as could be when I got the invitation. Been wanting to tell you about it for years, but the whole secrecy thing can't be ignored."

"I guess not," I said.

"I got my own invitation, if you're wondering," Ramona said. "My dead husband had all kinds of connections. Chester's my date. I had to ask him. His ticket was so old that it didn't have a 'plus-one' part. I just got my ticket, because I moved to town within the last year."

"Look, there's Flint," Seth said as casually as possible.

Flint Magnum walked directly toward us. He wore a black cowboy hat, a denim shirt, white jeans, and white cowboy boots with gold toes. And he wore it all well. He was probably the only person in the universe who could.

"Chester Henry, always good to see you," he said as he pulled Chester into a genuine hug.

My eyes were big as I watched the scene. Flint even knew who Chester was. How was that possible?

"Thanks for the party invite, Flint. It's always great to see you. This is my lady, Ramona, my granddaughter, Clare, and her date, Seth."

"Ramona, I knew your late husband. Fine man."

"Thank you."

"Good to have you here."

Flint shook my hand and Seth's, giving us each a moment of eye contact (his were such a pretty blue), looking at us like he was memorizing our names.

"Welcome to the party," Flint said to us all with a dazzling smile that couldn't possibly have been natural even though it didn't look the least bit phony. "Make yourself at home. Eat. Drink. Be merry." He looked at me again. "You work with Chester?"

"I do."

"I thought you looked familiar."

"You've been in the store recently?" I said, but then I realized my faux pas. If Flint had come into the store, I would have remembered him. I should have. Anyone would have.

"You wouldn't have recognized me, but, yes, I've been in. I'm a master of disguise. You've always been friendly. Thank you."

"Thank you! I mean, good. I mean . . ."

Flint laughed. "Are you the one working on my book?"

I blinked.

"The Muir book, dear," Chester said with a wink.

"Yes! I am. It's a wonderful project."

"Ah! Good to hear. We'll talk soon, but I'm off to greet others. Have a fun night."

And then he walked away. My imagination concocted dust flying up from the heels of his boots, but those boots had probably never seen and never would see a speck of dust.

"Nice young man," Ramona said, with an eyebrow lift in my direction. Flint wasn't young, but I got what she was saying.

We might both be with our cherished menfolk, but there was just something about Flint that would always be cause for raised eyebrows.

"I couldn't agree more," Seth said, giving us all a chuckle.

"Y'all should check out the buffet," Ramona said. "There's food there I don't even know how to pronounce, but there's also some that's familiar and delicious. I swear, I grabbed one of those mini weenies and another one appeared in its place before I could even finish chewing. They won't let anyone go home hungry or thirsty around this place. Signs of a good host."

"Sounds like a good idea," Seth said as he swung his arm around me. "Hungry?"

"I am. We'll talk to you later," I said to Chester and Ramona, sending Chester my own wink. We'd talk more about the Muir book.

The crowd had grown, so we carefully wove our way over to the buffet table. On the way, I saw three young actresses I recognized but couldn't attach names to. It would come to me at some point, but I knew that one was typically well behaved, while the other two had taken their celebrity in the predictable direction and were always portrayed as big partyers with the desire to wear less and less clothing as their fame grew. I watched them walk by and thought they all seemed perfectly lovely, sober enough, and dressed so that they were mostly covered up. I made a mental note to look for them later, more toward the end of the evening.

Just before we reached the buffet tables, a body nudged me as we passed.

"Excuse me," we both said.

"Adele!" I said. "Hello."

She blinked at me as if she was trying to place me. Her black dress was without sleeves and would have reminded me of the Roaring Twenties if she hadn't also worn heavy black work boots. Her hair was spiky and her makeup thick with eyeliner. Honestly, she didn't look terrible. She pulled it off well, but the look screamed so loudly with her ever apparent angst that I stifled a frustrated sigh.

"Hello," she said a second later and with an abbreviated smile. "Hello," she said to Seth with the same smile.

"You doing okay?" I said.

"I'm fine. Thanks for asking. See you later."

As she walked away, I wondered if she had a twin. Had the woman I'd seen at the diner, the one who seemed to want to listen in on my conversation with Jodie and then talk to me, not been Adele? If she didn't have a twin, were her personality differences part of her youthful angst? Who knew what really went on with anyone?

As Seth and I moved down the buffet table, I mentally noted that I was placing far too much on my plate considering the dress's lack of elastic, but I couldn't help myself. Normal buffet food like shrimp, cheese, and crackers were all there, but they were somehow better than normal, beautifully presented and richly flavored. Maybe it was the mountain air, or the same magic that had kept our glasses clear.

Along with the normal stuff, there were many other items. Prime rib, barbecue ribs, potatoes with every sort of imaginable topping, pastry puffs with a variety of different fillings—some with things like seafood and others with more dessert-type fillings like chocolate and pastry cream.

"I guess we can come back," Seth said as he looked at his full plate and then longingly at the buffet table and the items that couldn't fit.

"I'm sure we can come back as often as we like," I said.

A woman in a black dress and conservative white apron leaned toward us from the other side of the tables. "Of course, feel free to come back as much as you'd like. It's even acceptable to take some home. If you don't want to sneak it away in a napkin, we have take-home containers. No one is shy. You shouldn't be either."

"Thank you," I said. I hadn't even noticed her watching us.

"Thank you," Seth said, his tone infused with glee. I couldn't help but smile at him.

Tall tables had been set up to the side of the buffet. Chairs were available, but I, like a few others I saw, could only stand. I was only one of the chocolate-pudding pastries down when I saw someone I wanted to talk to. It was more that I wanted to see if she would talk to me, but either way, I patted the corners of my mouth with a white linen napkin and told Seth I'd be right back.

I beelined my way to Nell Sterling. She was even more stunning than usual in a shortish, strapless, sequined black dress that wouldn't allow her to sit either. Heads turned as she moved through the crowd, but since it was the kind of party that promoted communication, the attention wasn't distant. Friendly greetings were sent in her direction. She returned them with equally friendly waves and smiles, but she didn't stop to talk to anyone. Until I got directly in her way.

"Nell! Hello," I said. "Remember me?"

"I do. Yes, hello, Clare," she said with an icy tone that I thought broke the rules of the party.

I didn't much care if Nell Sterling and I ended up friends, but I really despised phoniness, and if that's what I'd come across when she was in the store, I just wanted to know. No, I needed to know.

"It's good to see you," I said.

"Right. Excuse me," she said as she turned to walk away.

I reached out to touch her arm, but she'd stepped away from me far too quickly.

I thought back over our brief interaction and there was nothing that would be cause for her cold shoulder. Unless, maybe, she thought I was friends with Adele. I'd given no indication that I even knew Adele when she'd come into the shop. However, if that was the reason, Nell must be stereotypically Hollywood shallow and I didn't need to waste any more of my time wondering if I'd offended her.

I wove my way through a group of thirty-something actors who'd all been in a movie that had been a big part of my teenage years. I smiled shyly at each of them, and they smiled at me, saying hello when I could barely look up at their famous and friendly eyes.

I remembered what the woman at the elevator had said about the requirement that everyone be approachable, but I still couldn't bring myself to tell these actors how pivotal they'd been to my life, how they'd set up expectations regarding what college would be like, and how it hadn't turned out that way, but thankfully I would always have those experiences from their movie. I'd work on it and hopefully get better as the evening wore on.

"She didn't want to talk to you?" Seth said as I rejoined him at the table.

"No, not at all."

"Sorry. From here she looked pretty rude."

"Unfriendly for sure. I might have done something to offend her, but I have no idea what it was."

"Can't worry about it."

"Nope, not at all."

"Clare, Seth." Another voice pulled me away from the pastry puff I'd taken from my plate.

"Creighton! Hello," I said.

"Evening," he said.

"Hi, Creighton," Seth said. "You got an invite too?"

"I did," he said with less enthusiasm than probably everyone else at the party.

"Not your thing?" I said.

"Not really." He tugged at the tight white collar of his dress shirt. I had to admit that he looked great in the black suit and tie, all of which stopped just short of being as formal as a tuxedo.

"How long have you been coming to these?" I asked. "I mean . . ."

Creighton smiled and waved away the awkward question that I kept forgetting was somehow a secret. "This is my first year. You?"

"Our first year too," I said. Seth smiled and then found a piece of cheese from his plate.

It was weird whenever Creighton, Seth, and I were in the same square footage. I didn't want it to be and I wanted us all to be grown-ups, but it was still weird and sometimes uncomfortable, though we all tried hard for it not to be.

Sometimes I tried too hard, catching myself doing things like making comments that cemented the fact that Seth and I were a couple. It was a childish behavior but it sometimes happened involuntarily.

It wasn't that the two men didn't get along. They did— well, it was more like they didn't "not" get along. They tolerated each other just fine, but they weren't going to do much hanging out together. My role in their lives hadn't been the reason those chances were thwarted. They were just two very different people with totally different interests.

Mostly, probably, I just needed to mellow.

"You look lovely," Creighton said. Then he cleared his throat. "You both look lovely."

"Thanks!" Seth said with a big smile. "You're not so bad yourself."

We all chuckled, hopefully ridding the moment of any further tension.

"Excuse me," Creighton said a moment later. "I'm sure we'll run into each other again."

I watched him walk away and wondered a few things. Where was his date? Where was the girl Jodie had mentioned? And what had the argument with Jodie been about?

Creighton didn't strike a lonely man's pose, but moved with confidence and authority even when he wasn't on duty. I knew he was searching the crowd and on alert even in the midst of the frivolity of a party. Except . . .

"Seth, something's weird," I said.

"It all tasted great to me," he said.

"No, not the food. But Creighton's being here."

"Why is that weird?"

"He doesn't have a date."

"Doesn't need one."

"No, but something else is going on."

"Why do you think that?"

"He would have a date."

"Maybe his date is in the ladies' room."

"No, there's something else." I wiped my fingers on the napkin. "You ready to mingle some?"

"Sure. I saw two movie stars I hoped to meet. They acted in one of those old Western television shows. My parents had a black-and-white television and we only had a few channels. For the longest time I thought Ponderosa still existed in some remote Western part of the country."

"Let's go find them."

Everyone obeyed the instructions and was friendly and welcoming. Seth and I didn't ask for autographs, but lots of other people did. Seth met one of his childhood heroes, and I found a couple of people from the group I'd been too starstruck to talk to earlier and told them how much they'd meant to me. They seemed to genuinely appreciate my mushy, almost incoherent gratitude.

As we mingled and then became separated, I kept part of my attention on the entryway. I was looking for someone specific and I knew when it was just about time for that someone to make her arrival.

I wasn't disappointed and I wasn't surprised by the new party attendee. I knew she'd be there, and I knew she would arrive at the top of an hour, just like she always did.

I'd grabbed a lemonade from the bar a few minutes earlier. When I saw Jodie, I gulped down the last swig, set the glass on the corner of the bar, and made my way to my best friend.

21

"Clare! What are you doing here?"

"Matt Bane gave me his invitation. You?"

Jodie blinked. She wore black silky pants and a pink silky top. She looked girly and pretty. Her hair wasn't pasted to her head, but fluffy and wavy almost down to her shoulders. It was always a surprise to find it out of tight confines.

"Where's Mutt?" I said.

"Couldn't make it."

"Right."

"Clare?"

I grabbed her arm and pulled her back, toward a space to the side of the party entrance.

"Something's going on here tonight, right? Or going down? What's the term?" I said.

Jodie laughed. "Neither is transpiring, at least that I'm aware

of. I have my small pistol at my ankle, though, just in case."
She lifted her pants leg to show me the tiny gun tucked and
locked into a tiny black holster that blended with her black hose.
"I'd like to know more about this invitation from Matt Bane,
though. I thought you guys didn't talk about much."

"Right. Well, he did give me the invite, but we didn't
talk about much. Jodie, Mutt would be here if this was just
for fun. Creighton would have a date too. I saw him."

"Where's your date?"

"Seth is in there."

"Are you worried you're missing out on something or
are you concerned for your safety?" Jodie asked, her mouth
moving to a straight, serious line.

"I'm . . . I'm not worried. I think . . . well, you didn't
stop by to tell me what you found at the hotel."

"Oh. Sorry, Officer Henry. My bad."

"You said you would." It was impossible to sound anything but petulant with those words. I rolled my eyes. She
knew I was rolling them at myself.

"Truly sorry," Jodie said as she put her hand on my arm.
"You're right. I did say I would, but I'm afraid what we
found was something I'm not at liberty to discuss. I should
have just called you and told you the police were on the
case and all was well."

"But all isn't well, right?"

"Clare, there's been a murder. Of course, something's
wrong."

"You're here because of something you found?"

"Not totally. I'm here because it's a party I was secretly
invited to, and Creighton's friend was busy. We decided to find

each other once I got off duty and be each other's plus-one. And there's been a murder, so both of us decided that it wouldn't hurt to attend and be observant. Is the food good?"

"Delicious."

"Good. Take me to the buffet?" Jodie rubbed her hands together.

"Secretly?"

"What?"

"You were secretly invited?"

"Yes."

"How?"

She bit her bottom lip and threw her hands up to her hips. Her girly left the party and she became the tough officer she was. She looked at me a long time before she answered. I knew she would answer, though. She always answered if she had to think about it. She'd just say no immediately if she wasn't going to share.

"Well, an invitation was mailed to me at the police station. One was mailed to Creighton too. Before you ask, yes, we're having them checked for prints, but there's not a lot we can do with anonymous mail."

"That is secretive. No note or anything?"

"Just our names on the envelopes."

"Who would have done that? Would Flint have been that secretive?"

Jodie looked out toward the party. "I may never know if you won't let me go in."

"Oh, right. Let's go. I'll show you the food."

I led her directly to the buffet table, where her anticipation was well met and her expectations exceeded.

I knew she'd be busy with the food for a while and she didn't need me hurrying her along, so I excused myself and told her I'd find her later.

The party space was big and wide even though it was a space made for a house, not a hotel or resort. I tried to imagine what it was used for when there wasn't a party in it, and the only thing I could come up with was that it would be cleaned and prepared for the next party. I was surprised I couldn't spot Seth or Chester as my eyes scanned the crowd twice. I saw Creighton as he moved toward the buffet table, but he didn't see me watching him, so I didn't wave.

I was about to set off to make my way down the middle of the big room again when a flash out of the corner of my eye captured my attention.

There were hallways leading out from four different directions, two on each side of the big room. I was certain I'd seen something blond at this end of one of the hallways to my right, as if a long trail of blond hair had been disrupted and then the body attached to it yanked into the hallway.

I immediately thought of one person: Nell Sterling.

I didn't hesitate as I took off for the hallway. I didn't proceed cautiously, but with tight-dressed short steps as I hustled around the corner and into the space.

And no one was there.

The hallway jutted to the right about ten feet ahead and though the party behind me was noisy, I thought I might be hearing something coming from the deeper nook. I continued the stutter steps, but this time I slowed before I could be seen.

I looked around; no one was paying me any attention

and most people were busy having too much fun to look down this hallway anyway. I positioned myself so my back was up against the wall and I listened hard. There were definitely two voices around the corner, both female.

"I can't believe you came to this party," one voice said.

"Why wouldn't I?" another said.

"The man you claim to love has been arrested for the murder of his sister."

"Right, and you're out of love with him. You're the ridiculous one, with your bleached blond hair and all that makeup. Everyone knows you still love Matt. And you're losing the aging battle, Nell. You know it and everyone else knows it."

I didn't need to peek around the corner to know that the two voices belonged to Adele and Nell. I did, however, have the fleeting urge to voice my opinion about Nell actually looking spectacular, no matter what her age was. I kept hidden and listened.

"You don't have one clue, Adele. You have no idea what you've gotten yourself into. You're a child and one without a sense of direction. Take advice from this old woman— either get out of this business or get someone in your life you can trust. You're going to sink. The sharks won't even need to help. You'll do it to yourself."

"Matt was on my side. Howie will help me."

"Oh, Adele, you just don't get it. Howie is all about Matt. He's only on your side if Matt is on your side. Howie will drop you so quickly he will forget your name. And if he forgets it, so will everyone else. If you haven't figured out the other part yet, let me explain—Matt's career and reputation are

damaged. He's damaged goods when it comes to helping anyone with their career. Murder convictions will do that."

I also wanted to point out that Matt hadn't been convicted quite yet, but I continued to hold my tongue.

"What if he didn't do it?" Adele said.

"I don't think the police even suspect anyone else," Nell
said, with more confidence to her voice than I thought was
appropriate.

I listened harder.

"But there's at least a chance. I mean, what if it was
Howie who killed Cassie?"

"What? What are you talking about?" Nell said. She
might have been a good actress, but I heard the waver of
uncertainty and perhaps some fear in her voice. I was sure
Adele did too.

"Listen to me, Nell. Howie's up to something. I think
he might have had something to do with Cassie's death."

"Do you have some sort of proof?" Nell said.

"Not yet, but that's why I'm here. I wanted to see what
Howie did tonight, who he talked to. He hasn't done anything
to help Matt. He didn't even seem all that upset by his arrest.
He's continued to work, like he's not bothered at all."

"Right. So have you."

"I'm shook-up, Nell. Howie isn't at all."

Nell was silent a long time before she continued. "You
know we have to get the location shots finished. We had
to get them done."

"So, the show must go on, right? No one cares about
Matt! I don't understand."

"Adele, lots of people care about Matt. We all do."

"Then why isn't anyone upset?"

"Everyone is upset, but there's something to what you said—the show going on. It does. We have to do what we have to do."

"I think you're all terrible, horrible people!" she yelled, tears and emotion lining her voice. I didn't hear her foot stomp, but I imagined it.

I knew Adele was coming in my direction, but I didn't see an out. If I tried to get ahead of her, I knew I'd just get in her way. I disengaged my back from the wall and tried to look casual. I had zero acting ability and was sure to be caught.

But Adele didn't even notice me. She blew right past me in a flurry of head-down huff and anger. The next person coming around should be Nell. I took a deep breath and worked harder to look casual.

The clack of her heals preceded her appearance. She didn't miss me.

"Clare, what are you doing?" she said.

"Eavesdropping," I said with a shrug.

A smile pulled at her lips, but then they straightened again as if she remembered she didn't like me.

"I'm afraid we weren't very interesting." She smoothed an imaginary wrinkle on the front of her dress.

"You were. You think Adele's right about Howie?"

"I doubt it," she said with her own shrug.

I inspected her for signs of lying, or extremely good acting. I saw neither, but that might not mean much.

"You think Matt really killed his sister?" I said.

Nell lifted one eyebrow. "I would never have guessed that Matt Bane could kill anyone, Clare, but this Hollywood world is full of made-up stories. We think the ones we care about are letting their guards down when we're with them and the cameras aren't, and we're getting a chance to know the real people, but maybe not. Maybe Matt's just a really, really good actor. I've been fooled before."

"You don't trust anyone?"

"Not a smart move, trusting anyone." She shook her head and leveled her gaze.

"Really?" I cleared my throat. "I mean, okay."

Nell smiled. "However, in regard to Howie, you probably don't think he should be trusted, but he's about the only one you can trust if he's on your side. If he's not on your side, then watch out. Or at least that's what I thought. I'm not sure now."

"How in the world do you know if he's on your side?"

"That's just it, Clare. That's the reason I thought he could be trusted. He tells you—good or bad, he's up-front. If he doesn't like you, he'll just come out and say it. His track record is good and all about honesty, even if it is brutal."

"Up until now maybe?"

"I can't accept that yet."

"You might want to consider it," I said, knowing full well that Nell Sterling didn't need my advice. Nevertheless.

"Right."

"Were you mad at me?" I said.

"Oh. Yes, I suppose I was. I might still be."

"What did I do?"

"I saw you following me up Main Street two nights ago. You watched as I went into the place I'm renting and then you looked out what I presume is your window up at me.

I thought we'd jumped right over the stalking part after I came into your shop. I was disappointed."

Of course her declaration begged the question, *"So you didn't see me in the hotel?"* I didn't ask it aloud, though. That small difference might mean everything, including learning something about someone's involvement in Cassie's murder. I thought she'd mention it if she'd seen me there.

A surge of adrenaline zipped through me. I was about to do something I hadn't predicted I would want to do. But the time seemed strangely right, and my next question fit with the reason Matt had wanted me to go to the party.

"What was on the iPad I saw you carrying?"

Nell blinked hard and I could tell this probably wasn't going to go well. But then her surprised eyes softened.

"Nothing earth-shattering," she said with a sigh.

"Obviously there's something on it you don't want people to see."

"No, Clare. Not people. Just one person."

"Who?"

She shook her head and wouldn't look at me.

"What if it has a clue to the killer, be it Matt or someone else, on it?" I said.

"The police cleared the room. I didn't think I was taking something with evidence of a murder. I wouldn't have."

"I don't understand."

"You don't need to. Now, please, Clare, don't stalk me." She started to walk away.

"I'm sorry," I said quickly. "You're beautiful, Nell. That's old news, but I didn't want to bother you at the time. It's difficult to think of you as just a person. It was stalkerish. I'll never do it again. I promise. I wasn't trying to find out where you were staying. I was just curious. When I saw you were staying so close to my house, I became strangely intrigued. Then I saw Howie, and . . . well, I was just intrigued. I'm very sorry."

She started slightly when I mentioned Howie, as if I'd hit a nerve. But she normalized quickly.

"Just say hello next time," she said.

"I will. For sure."

"Good. Now, I've got to go out there and be pretty and witty. Flint wants us all on our best behavior and he sticks to his word about not inviting people back if they misbehave. I like it when I make friends I can just be normal around, Clare. I'm glad for this little conversation. I feel like we might have moved back to normal. Oh, and I think I'll have you clean off only a little of the chocolate from *Barnaby Rudge*, the part that's illegible. Other than that, I think it's a good idea to keep it as it is."

"Well, I'll have to get over the fact that I think you just maybe called us friends, but, yes, I'm not going to send any pictures to the tabloids or anything. And I'd be happy to clean the book. Bring it back in any time." As I'd said "tabloids," Toby popped into my mind. He'd probably sacrifice a toe or two to talk to Nell Sterling. I wondered how far off normal it would be for me to ask her to grant him an interview. I'd think about it.

"Good. Well, we'll talk later." She stepped toward the party but then turned around again. "I saw you with a tall guy, glasses, curly hair. Is he someone more serious than a date?"

"He's my boyfriend. I'm sure he'd dump me for you, though, if you're interested."

She laughed. "No, he wouldn't. He's interesting-looking. Is he smart too?"

"Nerdishly so."

"Lucky girl. See you later, Clare."

I watched her melt back into the crowd. She was good at it, obviously practiced enough that she didn't look practiced. I didn't envy her one bit. Our brief conversation told me lots about Nell Sterling.

She lived a famous but probably lonely life. She might have placed her trust in the wrong people a time or two. And trusting her might not be the smartest move either. Was it simply the pictures of her and Matt on the iPad that had led her to taking it? She'd said "one person." Was she trying to protect Adele's feelings? That was hard to believe, but it was possible.

I'd eavesdropped on two hallway conversations now. It wasn't my style and I didn't like the questions that my actions had left me with, not to mention the sense of guilt. Maybe it was time to just mind my own business.

As I looked out toward the party, I spotted Jodie and Creighton standing along the perimeter of the room. They weren't just enjoying the party. They were looking for something, or someone.

I'd have to start minding my own business tomorrow.

22

By the time I made it to the spot I'd seen Jodie and Creighton, they were gone. I didn't even catch which direction they went and I didn't see them for the rest of the night. I thought I saw Howie once, but I couldn't track him down. I was there with Matt's ticket and his request that I observe the people in his life, but ultimately I didn't do as much as I'd hoped. However, Seth and I enjoyed the party, leaving only when we were too tired to stand and too full to eat another puff pastry. The Hollywood stars we mingled with left us both with a funny sense of the surreal. Had we really talked to him? Had we danced with them? The absence of pictures would probably always make me wonder if it had been as incredible as we thought it had been. Maybe there was a hallucinogenic in the pastry and the night hadn't been the most spectacular time ever after all.

The next morning I was jolted awake by my phone buzzing across my nightstand. I was so discombobulated by the early hour and the caller ID that I wasn't immediately aware of the fact that the sun hadn't risen yet.

My phone read SALT LAKE CITY DEPARTMENT OF CORRECTIONS.

Since Jodie was an officer and I'd also dated one, I'd received a few calls from police stations over the years, but not from the big city, and not from a prison, certainly nothing with "Department of Corrections" in the name.

I hit answer.

"This is the Salt Lake City Department of Corrections prison system. You have a collect call from a prisoner. If you accept, please push one. If you don't accept, please hang up."

Against my better, albeit sluggish, judgment, I pushed one.

"Hello?" I said.

"Clare? This is Matt Bane."

I held back the anxiety-induced sarcasm of "No kidding" and said, "Hey, Matt. How are you doing?"

"As well as can be expected. Listen, I know it's early, but this is when they said I could use the phone. How was the party?"

"Fun. Thanks." This was weird. "I appreciate the ticket. I saw a couple of your friends, but not Howie. No one was arrested or admitted to killing your sister. I'm sorry."

"It's okay. Hey, is there any chance you could come down to Salt Lake to see me today?"

"Um. Well."

"It's important, and I don't want to talk about it over the phone."

The fact that a scary state prison had now been inserted in the mix toned down the connection I felt to Matt a bit. However, I couldn't deny that it was still there. "Okay. When?"

"As soon as possible. Early visiting hours are in one hour."

The pause went on long enough that the silence was impolite, but a moment later I said, "I'll be there."

I debated calling Jodie to let her know my plans, but I didn't. What did it matter that I was going to visit him? She would tell me I was being starstruck and I still wasn't sure that was completely incorrect. However, I might be able to wrangle out of her what she and Creighton had been looking for at the party. I decided to take the easy and quieter route and not call.

I didn't call Seth either, because I knew that he had to get up extra early for a meeting. But someone needed to know what I was up to, so earlier than any human should be awake during the festival, I steered my car down Main Street toward Bygone Alley.

The sun had just started peeking over the mountainous horizon as I parked on the street in front of the shop. I noticed a figure in the shadowed doorway and grabbed my phone to call either Chester in his apartment above the shop or the police, but the figure emerged and my concerns turned into less worrisome questions.

"Adal?" I said quietly to myself.

He wore faded tan pants, big clunky boots, and a sweater too thin for the frigid temperatures. He lifted one hand, covered in a glove without fingertips, away from an item he held and waved and smiled. I imagined I could hear his teeth chattering.

"Hello," I said when I got out of the car. "It's good to see you. Are you okay?"

"I wasn't sure what time I was to arrive."

"Oh. Sorry about that. Well, come on in and we'll put a plan together."

I'd spent two hours working with Adal the day before, but it had taken only about five minutes to realize that I'd found the perfect apprentice. Before we'd started on a simple printing project I ad-libbed, I hadn't realized exactly what I'd look for when it came to evaluating an apprentice's skills. But I soon knew there were two important tells. The eyes and the hands. To restore books, hands could be neither impatient nor ungainly and eyes could neither be dull nor scared. Adal had confident, strong, and relaxed hands, and eyes that, even when they were full of question, were bright and ready for answers.

When I first started working with Chester, he said that I'd been made to do the tasks that went along with my job. He said I was even more qualified than he was, but I didn't understand how he could "see" such a thing. As I watched Adal the day before, I finally understood what Chester meant, and I realized that Adal was probably even better suited for my jobs than I was.

It would be good to work with him, see my world and my work through someone else's eyes. It would be a true honor to teach him, and I had no doubt I'd learn plenty too, about him and myself.

I unlocked the front door and flipped on the lights and then moved the temperature up on the ancient thermostat on the wall above a display of parchment. I had to tap the thermostat twice to get it to kick in.

Once I heard the distant revving of the furnace, I said, "It'll warm right up. Chester likes to sleep in the cold and Baskerville likes to curl up in his armpit at night. Chester's apartment is above the store. He usually comes down about ten. I'm early today, but most days I'm here about eight thirty. Come on to the back and I'll make you some coffee."

"Thank you."

"Do you have any idea of the hours you'd like to work?" I said as we went through the door and into the workshop.

Before Adal could answer, our attention was directed toward the bottom of the stairway that led up to the apartment. Baskerville stood at the bottom and looked at us with sleepy, critical eyes.

"Hey, Baskerville. All is well. We're just early," I said.

"Hello," Adal said with a big smile toward the tired cat.

Baskerville meowed reproachfully.

"Ah, here, kitty. Come see me." Adal crouched.

Baskerville lifted his head higher and looked at Adal suspiciously. I was about to say something like "He won't come to you" when the cat trotted toward Adal.

"Sweet boy," Adal said as he scratched behind Baskerville's ears.

"Uh-huh. Also a traitor, but we don't need to dwell on that at the moment."

Baskerville meowed again.

I moved to the coffee machine next to the back wall. Chester always prepared the water and the grounds the night before so all I had to do was push start. I glanced inside the few mugs we'd accumulated and decided the most sanitary choice would be to give Adal his coffee in a foam cup. I'd get the other mugs cleaned up or buy him one of his own later.

"What do you have?" I nodded toward the item resting on Adal's knee as he continued to pet the now smitten cat.

"A book. I thought we could work on it at some point. It's missing four pages."

"All from one sheet of paper?"

"Yes."

"May I see it?"

"Of course."

Adal stood and met me at my desk, where he handed me the book, sending a whiff of something that smelled like lemons and roses toward my nose. It was an odd combination but pleasant. I wondered what soap he used.

"It's beautiful," I said as I ran my finger along the spine of a copy of Friedrich Nietzsche's *Twilight of the Idols*. It wasn't a first edition from the late nineteenth century, but a copy from the first half of the twentieth century. Old but not monetarily valuable. It was in great condition, only worn at one corner. "Nietzsche, huh? Heavy stuff?"

"Yes." Adal smiled. "Thank you. It was my grandfather's." He reached into his sweater pocket. "I made copies of the missing pages long ago. I found a copy in a library in Düsseldorf."

"That's perfect. I'm sure we have the font. We can re-create the pages if you'd like. Is it something you're keeping or do you want to sell it?"

"Oh, no. It is one of my treasures."

I smiled at my new apprentice. "I understand. All right, we'll do it in the next couple of days. Unfortunately, I have an errand to run in Salt Lake City this morning."

"Would you like me to watch . . . watch the shop?"

"Only if you want to. It's early and you can keep the front doors locked and explore back here if you'd like. There's nothing that's too fragile and we don't have any secrets." I glanced toward the red Royal and realized that we had, in fact, had a big secret recently, but it was back where it belonged now. "If we get any valuable books in, we lock them up or take them home. We need to work out a salary. I promise we'll do that later today."

"No need. Mr. Chester took care of it, and it's more than fair."

"Okay. That's good." I'd discuss the amount with Chester later.

"I'm so happy to be here. Thank you for the opportunity."

"You're welcome. And I'm glad you're here. I think I'll enjoy teaching this stuff and it will be fun to have someone other than Chester and my niece to talk to about it all."

Adal told me he'd let Chester know about my errand as he walked me to the front of the shop. The box of ribbon tins had been placed on the counter, and the one that had held the money, the one presumably from Germany, was out of the box and next to it. I didn't know when the police had returned it.

The tin was German. So was Adal. Was there some connection there that might have something to do with the money? I stopped at the counter and pondered the possibilities, but truthfully no overlapping seemed to exist. There was no way the two of them could be tied together, or the three of them if you took into consideration the impostor who'd said the money was his. Still, though, the German coincidence was strange.

"Clare?" Adal said.

"Do you know what these are?" I said.

Adal looked at the tin on the counter and then peered over the top of the box.

"No."

"They're typewriter ribbon tins."

"I should have known. Yes, I've seen something like these before."

I got no sense that Adal was lying about his knowledge about the tins. He seemed pleasantly and gently honest.

"Right. Okay, I'll be back as soon as I can. Thanks for watching things. My niece will be here in a couple hours. She knows what she's supposed to do. Just tell her I said to get to work. You can stay or go when she gets here. If you leave, I'll call you if I make it back so we can get started on something." I frowned. "I'm sorry. We're not very well prepared, but I promise that we're glad to have you here. Please be patient and I'll get things worked out better."

"I am fine. You didn't expect me to come into town and ask for a job. I'm happy to be here."

I left, closing and locking the door behind me. The German connections I'd tried to make had distracted me. That uneasy sense that I was missing something came back too. My head was in another world entirely and I almost stumbled off the curb.

I shook myself out of it and decided to think about it all later. The roads were clear and there wasn't a cloud in sight, and I had a potential killer / Hollywood superhero to visit. I pulled onto the freeway toward Salt Lake City as the sun arrived full up over the mountain slopes.

23

The Utah State Prison sat at the south end of the Salt Lake Valley, just on the west side of Interstate 15 and not far from newer neighborhoods that spread all the way to the Oquirrh mountain range on the west and the Wasatch range on the east. There'd been talk about moving the prison, but I wasn't sure whether any decisions as to where had been made yet.

The list of infamous people incarcerated at the facility wasn't long, but it was definitely creepy. A few of the more notable inmates were killer Gary Gilmore and killer Mark Hacking, who had shot his wife in the head and thrown her body in a Dumpster because he didn't want to face his lies about being admitted to medical school—he was still there; Ted Bundy, whom everyone seemed to remember, had been there in the 1970s before being extradited to

Colorado. And on the uglier side of polygamy, Warren Jeffs, president of his own goofy church, had also spent some time there. Not a good guy at all.

Killer and Mormon-document forger Mark Hofmann was also still imprisoned there, serving a life sentence. Chester had known one of his victims and we weren't allowed to discuss that particular evil guy around him because it brought back too many bad memories.

The sky was as blue in the Salt Lake Valley as it had been up the canyon and the roads were perfectly clear; only a low ledge of snow had accumulated next to the roads or at the ends of parking lots. I found a spot in the prison's main lot, not far from the guard tower, and went through the visitors' door. The experience was nothing like my visit to the Star City jail cells.

Obediently, I showed my identification, signed a sheet of paper guaranteeing that I was who I said I was, and that I was there to see who I said I was there to see. I also agreed to a pat down. The female officer didn't smile, but she was gentle and didn't get too touchy-feely.

I left my bag with the front guard before I went through the metal detector, thankfully not setting off any alarms.

"This way," another officer said.

He held open a door and told me to have a seat in the third chair in the line of five in an otherwise empty room. He said I wasn't to touch the glass between the prisoner and me and that I was only to talk through the handset that looked like a phone handpiece.

The gray walls and the old linoleum were beyond stark. The thick, cold glass that would separate me from Matt was almost too big a reminder that I was in a prison with violent criminals.

The mere idea of the crimes that had been committed to put the people inside the bowels of this building left me second-guessing my decision to make the trip.

I was further bothered a moment later when Matt Bane came through the door on the other side of the glass. A guard guided him to the chair across from me and said things I couldn't hear. Matt nodded, his messed-up and dirty hair bouncing with his agreement.

After the officer left, Matt picked up the handpiece. I did the same on my side.

"Thank you for coming," he said, tinny and distant. He looked horrible, but not injured.

"Sure. You okay?" I said.

"I'm hanging in there," he said, the tone of his voice telling me differently.

"Good."

"How was the party?"

"Fine, Matt, but that feels lousy to say. Nonetheless, thank you for the ticket."

"You're welcome. Did anything strange happen?"

"Not that I noticed. Not really."

On the drive down the canyon, I'd thought about telling Matt that Adele suspected Howie might have had something to do with Cassie's murder, but I'd decided against it. It was time for me to tell the police things, not these people who had come into my life only recently and whom I strangely seemed to trust, or feel connected to like I did with Matt.

The hour or so on the road had given me some

appropriate moments of introspection and I'd realized that I wasn't necessarily starstruck. It was that these people were familiar to me. That's what fame and celebrity did—took strangers and made them seem like your friends, or your enemies. Matt's superhero image had automatically made me see him as a friend. I only truly realized this when, after seeing him play a heinous killer in *Kill Night*, I'd started to think of him differently, and definitely not so much as a friend, though still so familiar.

He nodded. "It was a long shot."

"What was a long shot?"

"I thought maybe the killer would be exposed. Did anyone say anything to you?"

"Why did you think the killer would be exposed there of all places?"

Matt shrugged. "Long story. But that might not matter at this point. Flint Magnum is a friend, though. I thought maybe . . ."

"Has he visited you?"

"No. Long shot, like I said. Anyway, I actually had another reason for asking you to come see me. Remember when I came into the shop to order the note cards?"

"Of course."

"Remember the pen you gave me?"

"The shamrock one? Sure."

"I think the killer took it."

"I don't understand."

"It's another long shot, but I just remembered something last night. When I found my sister . . . well, she was dead by then. But that pen you gave me. I gave it to her right after you gave it to me. She was bugging me as we were walking back to the hotel. I gave it to her as a good-luck thing for some meeting she was going to. She thought it was cute. She put it down the front of her shirt."

"Like in her cleavage or something?"

"Yes. Well, sort of. She was wearing a high-necked dress. She unbuttoned one of the top buttons and slipped it through the buttonhole." He touched the middle of his chest. "It was just there. She liked it. She said she wouldn't take it out until the meeting was over."

"What was the meeting?"

"That's the big mystery. I think the police are trying to find out where she went too."

"No one knew?"

"Only Cassie and whoever she was having the meeting with."

I thought back to something Jodie had told me. "And you thought she came back from the meeting with someone else. That's what you told the police."

"I did. I thought I heard voices, more than just Cassie's."

"Male or female?"

"Female."

"Huh," I said, thinking about the scream. "So, you don't think the pen was still on your sister."

"I know it wasn't. Well, I didn't see it, don't remember seeing it. It was a terrible moment, though. I could have missed it."

"She might have given it to someone else, or it might have fallen out of the dress."

He shook his head. "I really don't think she gave it to

anyone. She was very superstitious. She loved that kind of stuff."

"Maybe it was in the room somewhere."

"It's possible. But no one is listening to me. I'm finally meeting with an attorney later today, but I wondered if you'd ask the police in Star City to check it out."

I looked at Matt through the thick, extremely clean glass. Was he onto something or was he just grasping at straws?

"I can do that."

"Thank you." The relief that relaxed his features made me want to cry.

"Did Howie come see you?" I asked.

"No, but he got a message to me that an attorney was on the way. The message said that he wasn't allowed to come see me in Star City. You mentioned that might have been a rule or something. You must have talked to him."

"Only briefly." I wondered if Howie had been subject to Creighton's rule or if he'd just been making an excuse to not see Matt.

I couldn't stop myself. I cleared my throat. "I think Adele thinks Howie might have killed your sister."

A half smile pulled at his mouth. "So something did happen at the party?"

"Not really. Kind of. Well, just that."

"Did she confront Howie?"

"Not that I saw. I overheard her telling Nell."

Matt frowned. "I see."

"What?"

"It's pretty childish, but I was hoping to get a visit from

Nell at some point too. Hasn't happened. Maybe she tried and wasn't allowed in either."

"You really care for her?"

"Yep. A lot of good that's going to do me." He ran his hand through his hair. "I'm sorry. That's a stupid thing to think about, but maybe thinking about Nell is just something I do to forget where I am."

"Maybe. Nell doesn't think Howie's a killer. What do you think?"

"I have no idea what to think, Clare. I can't believe I'm in here. This isn't a role I ever hoped for."

"No one does. If you're innocent, you'll be released."

"I am innocent. I don't think I'm being framed, but I think the killer got away with murder and I was in the wrong place at the wrong time."

I thought a minute. "So you don't think someone is trying to make you look guilty?"

"Just wrong place, wrong time. I mean, really, if I'd come upon someone with blood and the murder weapon on them, my automatic thought would have been that they were the killer, or *might* have been at least. There was no other evidence, I guess. That's why I wonder about the pen. It might be evidence, but the police might not realize it."

"Do you think the killer is worried about your freedom?"

"Doubtful. They're probably happy because at least someone else looks guilty."

"Is it really possible to act that well?"

"I don't know what you mean."

"Are there good enough actors to fool everyone into thinking they were innocent of murder?" A bad trick question, I knew, but I watched him closely to see if I could discover anything, even if I wasn't sure exactly what it was.

He thought a moment. I was surprised his answer wasn't automatic. "A good actor has to convince him- or herself of the role first. Then it's easier. I'm not sure someone could fully accept killing someone else unless they were a complete sociopath. And that happens, of course. Acting the role of a killer would have to be much different from acting like you weren't one."

"Which might be the case here."

"Of course."

Dammit, I thought. I still wanted to trust that Matt Bane was telling the truth.

"I'll talk to the police about the pen. Today."

"Thank you. That would be helpful. I'll tell my attorney too. At least it's better than nothing." He tried to smile, but it was such a sad expression on his already sad face that he quickly gave up trying.

There wasn't much else to talk about, so when the guard came over and told Matt his time was up, we both hung up our handsets and left our plastic chairs with very little ceremony.

I glanced at my watch as I made it back out to the parking lot. I had plenty of time to stop and talk to Jodie. I couldn't help but take a minute to look up at the clear blue sky and notice that the sun had taken a modicum of chill off the winter air. It was going to be a beautiful day and I was eternally grateful I would get to enjoy it from this side of the prison walls.

24

"A pen, huh? A shamrock pen." Jodie put the end of her own cheap pen in her mouth and chewed.

"Yes, you know like the ones on our counter. We got them in early for Saint Patrick's Day. Shamrocks on the top. Chester thought they were atrocious, but Marion likes them. We're giving them away."

"I didn't notice the shamrock pens in the store."

"Did you find any in the room? Have you seen anyone in Matt's circle with one?"

"No, regarding finding one in the room. I haven't been looking otherwise, so I can't be totally sure, but I don't think so. They probably won't be a popular item until March."

"I doubt they'll ever be completely popular, but you're right about March being a better time to spot them."

"Besides, that's not necessarily an indication of a killer. There are too many other variables involved."

"Right, but maybe."

"I'll keep my eyes open."

I looked at her as she chewed. I didn't think I'd told her something that would catch a killer necessarily, but I knew she'd put a little muscle behind it.

She hadn't been bothered that I'd gone to visit Matt. She thought it was bizarre that I cared so much that I'd even take a call from him, let alone hop in my car and take a trip to the prison, but she wasn't angry about it.

"Want to tell me what you found in the hotel room?" I said.

"No."

"Please. A hint?"

Jodie released the pen from its torture. It had already been deformed, but it was worse now. She leaned her elbows on the desk and moved closer to me. I leaned closer to her.

"Beads," she whispered.

"Beads?" I whispered back.

"Yep, from some sort of fancy-schmancy piece of jewelry. We think either a necklace or a bracelet."

"Where did you find them?"

"On the ground underneath the window of the room that held the murder victim. And—" She stopped abruptly.

"You can't stop now!" I said, still keeping my voice quiet.

Jodie's eyebrows came together, but after a pause she continued. "Some fabric. A piece was stuck on the outside of the window frame. Something got torn."

"Color?"

"Brown."

"Not helpful."

"It would have only been less helpful if it had been black. That's everyone's favorite color around here during the festival."

"Somebody did go out the window, then?"

"Best guess is yes."

"Where did they go after they went out the window?"

Jodie shrugged. "We don't know. There are remnants of footprints in the snow and mud, but we can't get anything from them and they might be too old anyway. The people at the hotel don't man the front desk very well and they have no inside security cameras, just ones outside. We think the person went up to the roof and then came down later, out through the main doors, when the coast became clear again. We don't think anyone got in between the buildings to leave. Too tight of a space."

"What was on the cameras outside?"

"There's one from the downslope angle, but not one from the upslope. We're going over them, but we can't see anyone leaving the hotel soon after the murder."

"Entering before, maybe with Cassie?"

"Good question, Clare, but not entering either. Unfortunately, there's that missing-camera-from-the-upslope problem. Not a good view."

I thought a little longer. "You were looking for something at the party. Were you looking for torn clothing?"

"No." Jodie smiled. "But we would have been all over it if we'd seen any torn brown clothing." She lifted her head and looked around. No one was paying attention to us. "We were checking jewelry. It was a huge long shot that we'd see something that matched the beads we found or were a similar style or something, but it was worth the effort, we thought. And the party was fun."

"It was," I said distractedly.

"What?"

"I can't think of one person I've seen in the last five days who wore beaded jewelry."

"Expensive beaded jewelry."

"Expensive or cheap. I'll keep my eyes open too."

"Right. Clare, that's fine, but your first move is to call me if you have any suspicions about anyone. Got it?"

"Of course." I took a pen out of her pen cup, checked that it hadn't been masticated, and then spun it back and forth in between my finger and thumb. "Adele thinks Howie might have been the killer."

Jodie blinked. "Okay. Well, so much for calling me first. How do you know this?"

I explained the other of my hallway eavesdropping excursions and my conversation with Nell. Jodie wasn't impressed.

"He's under no suspicion at all," Jodie said.

"Why? He was there."

"Still. No indication he was the killer. We checked into things. You'll have to trust us on that one."

"I do."

Jodie smiled. "I have a little good news, though."

"I'm listening."

"We have a line on the guy who claimed to be John Nelson, mystery thief of money in ribbon tins."

"Tell me."

"If we've got the right intel, he's a grifter, a con artist. He scammed three local businesses before he even visited The Rescued Word. He's really good."

"He must be. He must be psychic too. To know there was money in the tin."

"Yeah, that one's got us baffled, but we'll ask him when we catch him, and we'll catch him."

"What makes you so sure?"

"He's arrogant and getting careless. The festival is a great chance to take advantage of people and businesses. He won't leave until it's over."

The phone on Jodie's desk rang. The noise was so loud and we'd been speaking so quietly that I jolted. Jodie smiled again.

"Yep," she said when she picked up the handset. "Okay. Well, sure. Give me a minute and then send her back." She hung up the phone.

"You gotta skedaddle. I have work to do," she said to me.

She stood and let me lead the way out of her office. As we entered the hallway, I saw a familiar figure enter from the other end. Linea walked toward us, her steps quick and sure, the look on her face beyond exasperated.

There wasn't time to elbow Jodie before Linea was upon us.

"Jodie," Linea said. "Clare, it's good you're here too. You can help me explain all this to Jodie."

"Sure," I said, having no idea what was on her mind.

Jodie looked back and forth between Linea and me. She sighed.

"All right. Let's go to an interview room. Clare, you can stay until I tell you to leave."

We followed Jodie into the interview room I was becoming very familiar with.

Linea didn't wear a ski coat, but something closer to a peacoat, navy blue and worn slightly at the elbows. Her rosy cheeks didn't do much to alleviate the stress showing with the frown of her mouth.

Jodie closed the door to the interview room after Linea and I sat.

"What's going on, Linea?" Jodie said after she sat down too and placed a notebook on the table in front of her. We'd automatically taken the seats that seemed most appropriate: Linea and I on one side and Jodie on the other side in the position of power.

"That man, Howard something-or-other, will not leave us alone," she said. "He keeps knocking on our door and asking to come in. He wants to film the inside of our house, Jodie! I don't understand why he won't take no for an answer."

"How many times has he asked to come in?" Jodie asked.

"Does it matter?" Linea said.

"Legally, not really. I'm just trying to get a feel for this," Jodie said.

"Well, three, I guess. The last one just about half an hour ago and I came right in to see you."

"Why didn't you call?"

"I worry the police won't take our complaints seriously. I wanted to talk to you and I wanted to do it in person."

"We would take anyone's complaints seriously, but I understand your concern. All right, Linea, tell me what he said."

"He said they're working on something that is mostly fiction, but based on my family. He heard about us from some big-time director who has a house in Star City, and was told we're so *normal*." She paused, either to catch her breath or calm down. "He said they'd like to get some of the details as close to real as possible. I told him we weren't interested in being a part of his project and that he needs to go away. The first two times Duke told him nicely. This time I wasn't so nice."

"I see. How many times, this time, did you tell him to go away? Did he try to force his way in? Did he put his foot in the doorway or anything?"

She shook her head. "He wasn't forceful, but I had to tell him no a few times. He . . . worries me, though."

Jodie cocked her head. "Does he worry you or just bother you?"

"He worries me," she said. "Since that woman who came out with him the first time was murdered. I'm worried. I know you arrested the killer, but still."

"Cassie Bane came to your house with Howie?" Jodie said.

Surely Jodie found this as interesting as I did, but she kept her demeanor stoic, as her eyes focused in a curious slant. I sat up straighter and leaned a little closer to Linea.

"Yes, I think she was going to be a part of the project

too. I think she was going to portray Duke's second wife. She was more forceful than Howie, but his persistence is still bothersome."

"Who was going to portray you?" I said before I could stop myself. I looked at Jodie apologetically, but her focus was still on Linea.

"Someone named Adele something, but I didn't know who she was," Linea said, her surprise at my curiosity obvious.

So, Howie, Adele, Cassie, and Nell were all involved. I remembered the film crew as I looked at Jodie again, but she still seemed to have forgotten that I was in the room. The actors and Howie were, as I'd sensed, a group together, perhaps because of the project.

Jodie said, "Linea, do you know of any other actors or actresses who were involved in the project?"

"Sure. Nell Sterling—I know exactly who she is—is going to portray Patrice, Duke's first wife."

Jodie nodded once. "All right. I will talk to Howie and tell him to back off, but I'd really like to know if there's anything else you could tell me about the project."

Linea nodded and sat up straighter.

"I guess I don't know much. Duke told me that Howard and Cassie Bane stopped by the first time and he told them that we wouldn't be interested in helping them with the project. He must have told them no because he knows how our type of lifestyle can be put in such a bad light. He wouldn't want any part of it."

"Okay," Jodie said with a prompting tone.

"I don't think I know any more than that," Linea said.

"I saw Howie and Nell Sterling on the corner of their property the other day when I was up there," I added. "They had a small camera crew and they were filming."

"Directly on the property or next to it?" Jodie asked.

I looked at Linea. "Does your property line extend over to the side street?"

"Yes."

"On the property, then."

"Trespassing," Jodie said.

"You can arrest him for that?" Linea asked.

"I could, but I'll probably just threaten him with the arrest if that's okay with you. Despite the murder that has occurred, I don't think Howie has any intent to harm you. I think he's just an annoying human being whose life is all Hollywood. I'll be annoying to him and see if that gets him to stop."

"Okay. Thanks," Linea said doubtfully.

"You're welcome." Jodie blinked and she seemed to fall out of cop mode. The features on her face softened and she smiled slightly. "It's good to see you're happy."

"I am. Thanks."

"Don't know how you changed from crazy party girl to what you've become, but each to his or her own, I say."

Linea laughed, and the stress in the room that I hadn't realized was so palpable dissipated a little bit. "Oh, I'm sure you've wondered, but, yes, it's a life I enjoy. And, no, I don't want even a little part of any attempt to portray it in a movie or series or whatever."

"I don't blame you. You never know what those movie folks will do to make money."

"It was great to see you the other day, Clare. Good to see you too, Jodie. I don't harbor any illusions that we'll hang out and be best buddies, but I wouldn't mind meeting for dinner sometime down the road."

"Sounds good to me," Jodie said.

"Me too," I said.

"Thanks for coming in. I'll take care of Howie," Jodie said before she flipped the notebook closed and stood.

"Clare, could I give you a ride back to your store? I'd like to take a look at those typewriters and talk to you about them," Linea said.

"Meet you there. I've got my car."

"All right."

Jodie walked us out, but waited for me inside the doorway as Linea pulled out of the parking lot first. I rolled down my window and stopped in front of the door when I noticed her. A snowflake landed on my nose, but I didn't notice any others coming down. I looked up at the unexpected thick clouds coming in. It was either the beginning of a big storm or just a few passing flurries.

"What's up?" I asked as she pushed open the station's door again and leaned out toward me.

"Stay away from those Hollywood people, Clare. I don't know what's up, but there's something more than Matt Bane just killing his sister. In fact, I'm finally beginning to believe he might not be the killer. They're a group that seems to be together too much. It sits like a bad piece of sushi with me."

"Okay." The visual made my stomach turn, but I was glad she sensed what I had.

"I mean it. Just stay away. I'm going to go track down Howie now and give him a piece or two of my perturbed mind. Just keep a distance."

"I will."

"Good deal. Now go talk to our polygamist friend about some typewriters. I bet no one in the history of the universe has ever said anything like that before."

I smiled and waved as I pulled out of the parking lot. I didn't have any desire to talk to the Hollywood people, but I wondered what in the heck was bothering Jodie so much. Were her cop bells ringing without any real provocation or had she and Creighton actually turned up more than she was telling me?

I was sure I'd find out. Eventually.

25

Linea waited for me outside the shop. A west wind had picked up and the temperature might have fallen twenty degrees since I'd first gone to talk to Jodie. There was no sign of the sunny blue sky I'd been under earlier. Another day of Utah weather.

"You could have gone in," I said to her as I turned my head against the wind.

Linea nodded and smiled weakly. "I don't want to bother Chester."

I opened the door and led us inside.

"Bother Chester?" I said after the door closed behind us, and wiped some hair away from my face.

Baskerville peered down from his high ledge and meowed cheerfully at our visitor. I wondered where our surly cat had gone.

"Hey, you." Linea smiled up at the cat. "Cute cat."

Baskerville circled twice, and then wound himself in a small, tight ball.

"Yeah, and surprisingly friendly lately," I said.

I looked toward the back of the shop. Toby and Marion were both behind the counter watching something on her computer screen. In tandem they looked up, smiled, and waved.

"Adal said he'd come back when you called him," Marion said. "He's a nice man. I'm going to like having him here."

"Thanks for letting me know." I turned to Linea as I loosened my coat collar. "Why would you bother Chester?"

"I'm not sure he approves of my lifestyle choices."

I smiled. "Chester's not judgmental. He's seen everything."

"I know, but lots of people from my past life prefer the party girl over the polygamist girl."

I laughed, though I wondered if she'd meant to be funny. "No worries."

As we approached the counter, I sent a furrowed brow toward Marion, but she didn't see me. She and Toby were totally taken with whatever they were looking at, making me think that any customer who might have come in would have felt as second fiddle as I currently did.

"Marion, could you turn that down, please?" I said.

"Oh, sure," she said with a weak smile.

"Toby," I said.

"Hi, Clare." He stood and smiled. "Sorry we're being too loud."

I glanced quickly at the computer screen, but it was difficult to distinguish what I saw other than a group of people outside what I thought was the festival's main theater. Before I could ask what they were doing, another thought occurred to me.

"Toby, could you stick around a little bit? I'd like to talk to you in a few minutes."

"Sure," he said.

He probably hadn't planned on leaving Marion's side any time soon, but I'd stopped him just in case.

I led Linea back to the workshop, to a low shelf where we'd placed the Selectrics.

"Coffee?" I said.

She smiled sheepishly. "No thanks."

"Oh. You know, I have lived in Utah all my life and I still forget that a large segment of the population doesn't drink coffee."

She laughed. "I understand. It's one of the things I miss."

I nodded and then turned toward the Selectrics. "Here they are. Do you really want them?"

"You don't sound like you're working hard to sell them."

"It's not that. They're great typewriters, but they're old and not many people would enjoy using them anymore."

"We have a lot of kids at our house. They look sturdy. Kids and sturdy make a good combination."

"True."

"And we only have one computer. There's no way the kids will get to work on it. We'll have to get another one if any of them leave our homeschooling situation and attend something more traditional, and typing is always a good skill to have."

"Well, this might work well, then," I said, realizing she was saying the things I should have been.

It seemed that Zeb Conner had been onto something. It would never have occurred to me on my own to talk to Linea or her family about them, but now the idea made perfect sense.

We completed the transaction and I recruited Toby and Marion to help transport the typewriters to Linea's car. I caught the moment that Toby got a good look at Linea before he flustered.

"You're . . . ," he began, but then stopped abruptly as his cheeks reddened.

"Toby," I said. "This is Linea Christiansen. She's a friend. Linea, Toby Lavery."

"Nice to meet you," he said as they shook hands. He couldn't rein in his curious stare.

"Yes, I'm one of the sister-wives," she said.

"I'm sorry, but I've been hearing so much about your family and the movie that is being produced. I'm sure the real story isn't as interesting as the gossip is making it out to be."

Linea shrugged. "I don't know. I suppose it depends upon your definition of interesting. For the most part, we're about cleaning up after a bunch of kids, but we do a number of things differently than what would be considered mainstream."

"I've heard some bad stories about polygamy, but none associated with your family," Toby said.

I blinked. I couldn't decide if he'd suddenly forgotten his manners or if he was fishing for a story. Either way, it was an interesting technique that I wouldn't have thought he had the maturity to pull off.

When he continued on, his motive became ultraclear. "I have a blog. I'd love to share the real story, the boring one, the one about cleaning up after a bunch of kids."

"I don't think so, but thanks for asking," Linea said with a wink in my direction.

After she drove away from the shop, down Bygone to Main Street, I put my hand on Toby's arm.

"Toby," I said.

"I know. You think I was too pushy," he said.

"Oh. None of my business, but I have a question. Let's go inside."

We reentered the store, this time without Baskerville bothering to glance in our direction.

"Do you know who all the actresses are who are set to play the wives in the series?" I asked. It had occurred to me that he might know.

"Sure. Nell Starling, Adele White, but the last one was up for grabs."

"Was the woman who was killed a possibility? Cassie Bane?"

"Oh, that rumor?" he said.

I nodded like I knew what he was talking about. I thought her going out to the Christiansen house with Howie made it more than a rumor.

"No, she wanted the role, but that would have been totally weird," he continued.

I looked at Marion, who seemed as perplexed as I felt. "Why?" I asked.

"Matt Bane was slated to play Duke. It would have been weird to have his real-life sister be one of his wives."

I felt my stomach drop. Did Jodie know that Matt was set to play Duke? We'd been talking about the sister-wives. Duke's character hadn't even come up until now. Did it matter?

"Yeah, that would have been even stranger than the whole multiple-wives thing," I said. "So the rumor was that she got the part?"

"No, the rumor was that Cassie was still trying to get the part, that some guy who works with Matt, Howard something-or-other, was still working to get her aboard."

"Why?"

Toby shrugged. "I have no real idea."

I fell into thought as the actors and their respective roles in the real-life drama and the Hollywooded-up drama lined up in my mind. How did all these people in the circle around Matt Bane become involved in the same project? The information that Toby gave me didn't shed much light on any valuable conclusion, but I suddenly realized that the common denominator wasn't Matt Bane as much as it was Howie. Did he work with or for everyone?

I also realized that everyone in the small circle—Nell, Adele, Howie, and maybe Matt too—might have had a reason to want Cassie dead.

Of course I knew that getting any sort of role in television or film was a difficult task, but could it be worth murder?

Maybe.

"Who else was up for the part?"

"Don't know. No one that I heard of. There's still some

time before the movie—though they might make it a series—goes into full production."

Howie and Nell had been taking advantage of their time in Star City for the festival to film the epilogue. They could have come back later, but I guess Nell might have a point—they were there, so why not?

Maybe, though, the better question was "why?"

I looked up at Toby and Marion, who were both looking at me with patient but expectant eyes.

"Will you watch the store? I need to call Jodie."

"Sure," Marion said.

I pulled my cell phone out of my pocket as I set off for the workshop, but was halted again as I glanced over at Marion's computer screen. The image on the screen was no longer the theater, but somewhere else in Star City, in front of a bar. And there were people walking by.

"What's that?" I said as I turned. "On the computer."

"It's a site for the festival. Anyone who's attending can upload pictures or video that they shoot. It's fun. Marion and I were just watching video of a comedian who'd had a little too much to drink and decided it was time to share some personal information to a crowd of onlookers."

"Anyone can put stuff up here?" I said.

"Sure," Marion said. "Why, do you want to put something up?"

"No, but is there any way to search for things by location or time?"

"Um, not by location, but things are up there in the order they're added," Toby said. "It's how lots of us writers look for things we might want to track down."

"So what's on there now is live?" I asked.

"Yep, and it will switch out if someone tries to upload something else," Toby said.

Just before I pulled my eyes away from the screen to call Jodie, I caught the image of someone who looked familiar. I returned my attention to the screen.

He wasn't wearing a white ski coat, but a black one this time. His facial features were fairly indistinct, except for some thick 1970s glasses that looked immediately familiar. Without the 1970s hair, he resembled the guy with the white ski coat more than the guy with the handkerchief, but his—their—features suddenly became obvious to me. I was seeing the man who'd claimed to be John Nelson *and* Zeb Conner. I had no idea how he'd done what he'd done or why, but there was no doubt in my mind they were the same person. I couldn't believe I hadn't seen it before, but the glasses and the wigs and the fake facial hair had made all the difference.

Not only had he not left town, but he was close by. The bar he emerged from was just across Main Street, not far from The Fountain.

"You want a story?" I said to Toby as I moved around him.

"Yeah."

"Come with me," I said. "Marion, you watch the shop."

"But . . . ," Marion said.

"Watch the shop, Marion," I said over my shoulder as Toby and I ran out through the front door.

26

"You're where?" Jodie said into the phone. I heard the muffled movements of her standing up and gathering her keys.

"We're walking down Main Street, from Bygone Alley, east side. He's looking in the window of the leather shop."

"Clare, just get back to The Rescued Word. I'll handle it from here."

"He hasn't even noticed us, Jodie. We're staying back far enough."

"Who's 'we'?"

"Toby and me. The blog writer."

"Oh, for Pete's sake. I'm on my way."

The call was disconnected. Toby and I were trailing behind John/Zeb by a few stores. He hadn't looked toward us once. Even with the cold wind and snow, the pedestrian traffic was thick enough that we could probably hide well enough, but the fog from our combined anxious breathing was a little bigger than everyone else's and I was afraid that might give us away.

"Look in the window," I said to Toby.

"Of the post office?" Toby said after he noticed which building we were next to.

"Whatever."

"Okay."

"All right, come on," I said a second later.

I tried to remain casual. I did my best to dodge the foot traffic while keeping my eyes on the prize, but we were going to have to get closer to make sure we didn't lose him.

"He is gutsy," I said.

"Who? What are we doing?" Toby asked as he kept up with my unpredictable footwork.

"Just stay with me and keep your eyes on that guy up there. The one with the black coat and thick glasses."

Toby craned his neck. "Okay, I think I got him."

A bunch of things happened at once just as we made a big forward move to close the gap between us and John/Zeb. Jodie's siren sounded loud and clear—the noise pealed up from the bottom of the hill; the crowd somehow parted so that the man we were following had a direct line of vision to us if he happened to turn around and look; and like I had experienced a few times in my life, his inner radar must have told him to do exactly that. He knew something was up and he somehow knew to look in our direction. Right at me, in fact.

I thought he might be surprised to see me, but there was

no sign of that. Instead, he smirked at me and then nodded as if to tell me, "Well played," before he turned again and started running down the hill.

I made some sort of disgusted and annoyed sound before I started to follow him.

"Wait. You want to chase him?" Toby said, keeping pace with me.

"Just watch where he goes. And look for the police car so we can show Jodie."

"Okay," Toby said.

"There's Jodie," I said. "You keep your eyes on that guy."

I darted to the curb and waved Jodie to a stop. Festival-goers hadn't been deterred by us, but the scene we were causing was annoying to some and curious to others, who probably thought it was some stunt for the festival.

"He's over there!" I pointed down the hill and searched for Toby. "Where is he?"

"He turned right at the bottom of the street," Toby said.

In quick maneuvers that included screeching tires and more sirens, Jodie had the police car turned around and zipping down the hill before I could try to jump in the car with her.

"I'm sorry. I didn't think that running down there would do much good," Toby said.

"It's okay," I said as I watched Jodie turn right. As I pulled my eyes away from the back of the car, I thought I caught a glimpse of the man, on the other side of the street as if he'd turned left, not right.

I craned my neck to get a better look, but by then and with the continuously dynamic crowd, I couldn't distinguish one person or one black winter coat from another. Had I imagined seeing him across the street? Had Toby really watched where he'd gone? I couldn't help but feel a small thread of suspicion about the blog writer. I shook it off.

"Come on, let's go back to the shop. I want to take another look at that Web site."

"Sure. Sorry," Toby said again.

"Don't worry about it. The police will get him."

"Yep." Toby rubbed his finger under his nose. And didn't look me in the eye.

e⁓

"I didn't see him anywhere," Jodie said as she walked through the shop's front door, peeling her coat off along the way. She was extra warm-blooded after a chase of any sort and always peeled immediately when coming in from the cold. "But I spread the word. Others will be looking for him."

"I wish we could have followed him better," I said. Out of the corner of my eye I thought I saw Toby's shoulders twitch with uncertainty.

"I'm glad you didn't. There's no need to put yourself in the way of potential danger. Now, what do you have for me?" She plopped her coat on the front counter. The small breeze the maneuver stirred up was scented with the Mexican food that she must have had for a meal recently.

"This site," I said as I signaled her around the counter. Toby and Marion moved behind us.

"That looks like the chairlift over by . . . that's it. That's the chairlift. This is live?" Jodie said.

"Yes, and it's mostly archived. Visitors to the festival

take their own pictures and videos and post them online for everyone to see," I said.

"And you think somewhere in there will be Cassie's killer?" Jodie said as she quickly picked up on where my mind had gone. She grabbed the mouse and scrutinized the screen.

"There's a chance that somewhere in there is a picture of Cassie walking into The Fountain after whatever meeting she had. Maybe someone was with her. Maybe you can see who, and maybe that will somehow help."

"Okay," Jodie said distractedly.

The rest of us remained silent as she worked through the site.

Finally, she said, "You might have something here. I'll get our tech geeks on it."

"Yeah?" I said.

Jodie laughed. "Yeah, you're too smart for your own good sometimes, Clare, but this is a good and safe way to contribute."

"Thanks. I wouldn't have known about it except for Toby and Marion."

"Right." Jodie didn't hide the suspicious glance she sent Toby. He looked momentarily uneasy, but Marion missed it.

Jodie didn't even have all the information I had, but she was suspicious of everyone, so I wasn't sure I should put any stock into it anyway.

"All righty, then. I'm getting back to work. Temperature's falling fast out there. We'll encounter too much inebriation this evening. But, Clare, know that we're on this. All of it."

"Thanks."

Jodie moved around the counter, picked up her coat, and left the store, having to work hard to close the door against the harsh wind.

Distractedly I followed behind and looked out the window. Dark clouds blanketed the sky; pedestrians leaned over, holding their collars closed and keeping their heads down. I looked up at Baskerville on the ledge. He looked down at me, obviously hoping I'd make the right decision.

I turned around again. "We're closing early. Let's all go home. Toby, where are you staying?"

"He can come over to my house," Marion said.

My brother's face flashed in my mind. It held a look of horror and it was aimed toward me when he learned that I was the one who let a boy go home with Marion while he was still at work.

"No. Toby, you're coming with me. Marion, we'll take you home first."

I turned to look out the window again. I made a few calls, confirming that Chester was safe at his girlfriend's, that Seth would come over to my house later—if he could make it home through the storm, which he was fairly certain he'd be able to handle. I also called Jimmy and told him the plans. He said he was already on his way home from a business trip in Ogden. I gathered Baskerville. He didn't come home with me often, but I didn't want him alone if Chester couldn't make it back to the shop and his apartment in a timely manner.

It was time to batten down the hatches.

27

"There's someone coming up your porch steps," Toby said. He'd been watching the storm outside my front windows.

"Probably Seth."

"I don't think so."

I came around the half wall that separated the kitchen from the front room.

"It's probably someone I know who needs to get in and out of the cold. Let them in."

Toby pulled the door open and a tall person clad in all-black winter gear, topped off with long blond hair, rode the cold inside.

"Nell?" I said when she unwrapped the scarf around her face.

"Hi, Clare," she said with a brief smile and rosy cheeks.

"Nell Sterling?" Toby said with a squeaky voice.

"Pleased to meet you." She extended her gloved hand, which he shook a long beat and a big gulp later.

"You . . . are stunning," he said.

"Thank you."

But Nell Sterling didn't have time to be stunning. She was there for something else.

"Clare. I hope you don't mind. Since I caught you spying on me, I knew where you lived. I tried to call the police, but no one answered. I don't quite understand how no one could answer, but it happened. I know one of your friends is an officer. I came over to see if you would try to call her cell phone for me."

"Sure, but why?"

"Adele is leaving town."

"Why would the police need to know that?"

"Because I think there's a chance she killed Cassie."

"What? Why?"

Nell frowned and blinked a couple of times. "I've been thinking about it. She was jealous of everyone in Matt's life, and she thought it was weird that Cassie wanted to be one of Matt's wives in that polygamy project we're working on."

"That *would* have been really weird," I said. "But murder?"

"Yeah. No doubt weird, but Adele took it . . . well, she took Cassie's ambition personally, I think."

"Wait. She thinks Howie had something to do with Cassie's murder. You don't think Howie had anything to do with it?" I said.

"The Howie I was talking about earlier?" Toby said. We ignored him.

Nell shook her head and sighed. "No, I don't. Howie and I are together. A couple. The world doesn't know. Matt doesn't know. We hoped to keep it quiet, but after what Adele said to me at the party last night, we decided to tell the police—soon. We didn't think Adele would leave today, and we just hadn't worked up the nerve. I know it's dumb—our relationship being front-page entertainment news is much less important than Matt's freedom, but . . . well, I don't want to be so caught up in all this gossip stuff, but I'm afraid I let it get to me. Against my better judgment. And Adele might be innocent, but she's leaving and I think the police need to know. And . . . I just think she might have. . . . Well, I don't think Matt could have."

"How do you know she's leaving? Where's Howie?"

"I don't know where Howie is, and I had someone at The Fountain watching Adele for me. I thought she might try to run before I could get the answers Howie and I have been searching for. The guy from The Fountain called me about fifteen minutes ago, but the phone went dead before we could disconnect. Adele might already be gone."

I didn't have time to think through anything Nell had just said. If her story was wonky, it was a risk I was willing to take. If she was setting Adele up to move suspicion away from herself or Howie, then I hoped the truth would eventually become clear. I pulled out my phone and hit Jodie's speed dial number. The tone went dead.

"Oh, no, the storm," I said. "The weather can take out phones—cell and landlines—up here if it gets bad. We're still just a small mountain town."

"Damn. All right, I'll go see if I can stop her," Nell said.

"We'll go with you," I said as I grabbed my coat and hoped Toby did the same. I glanced at Baskerville, who'd become lord and master of the couch by curling up on the top of one of the throw pillows. Without uncurling even a little, he eyed me with his own version of raised eyebrows. He couldn't believe anyone would go outside in the storm. It was difficult to disagree with him, but at least I was pretty sure he wouldn't mind the time alone.

Nell, Toby, and I were out the door and standing on the sidewalk in front of my house only a few seconds later. Actually, not standing as much as battling against the forces of the wind and blowing snow.

"It looks like the sidewalk and road are still kind of crowded with people, no matter how cold it is out here," Nell said from behind the scarf she'd rewound around her head. The wind took her voice up the hill.

I'd become used to the hardiness of our winter visitors.

"We'll be better off walking than driving. Quickly," I said.

"Do you want me to do something different? Try to get ahold of someone?" Toby said as we began our frozen trek down the slope of the sidewalk.

I looked at him. If he had some ulterior motive, I couldn't read what it was.

"No, just come with us."

I had no idea what we were going to do once we got to the hotel. We couldn't stop Adele from leaving if that's what she wanted to do.

As we moved around people and through small crowds, I couldn't help but wonder why staying inside by a roaring fire and with steaming mugs of something hadn't occurred to all these people.

We zigged and zagged, keeping our heads down so the wind wouldn't take the skin off the exposed parts of our faces.

When we were directly outside The Fountain, Adele, a taxicab driver, and three pieces of luggage burst through the front door.

"This way, miss," the driver said. He hadn't found a spot directly in front of the hotel, but about twenty feet down the hill.

"Adele! You're Adele White!" a voice called from a gathering of young people.

To her credit, Adele replaced the hurried, irritated look on her face with a friendly patience, or at least as friendly as it could be as she was being pelted by snow that had turned icy and wind that had only gotten brusquer.

"Hi," she said.

"Could we get pictures?" the same voice said. It belonged to a young woman who wore thick black eyeliner and short, spiky black hair—two of the spikes stuck out from the front of her knit hat, so I just assumed there were more under there.

The camera phones came out and got to work.

"How about an autograph? Here. Sign my arm." A boy who matched the girl when it came to makeup and hairstyle stuck out his arm and yanked up his sleeve, exposing his skin to the cold.

"Sure. You have a pen?" Adele said as she moved forward.

"Uh. Anyone have a pen?"

"It's okay. I do," Adele said. She reached into her front coat pocket and pulled out a pen.

"Uh-oh," I said.

"What's that?" Toby said.

The shamrock on the top of the pen was bent, but there was no question that it had come from The Rescued Word. I thought back to when she'd come into the store. I was certain I hadn't given her her own pen. Her eyes had moved over the counter, and maybe they'd even lingered on the cup that held the pens, but I knew I hadn't given her one and I knew I hadn't seen her take one. I suddenly had a crystal clear memory that she hadn't known about the note cards—I *had* planted that seed myself.

"Adele!" I said.

Adele hadn't noticed us before my exclamation. No one had. We were just background. But with my raised voice, she turned and found me in the crowd.

"The pen?" I said.

Adele looked at the pen, at me, at the pen again, and then at the ground. She didn't know how the pen gave her away, but she knew she was guilty of something, and the tone of my simple question had clued her in that I'd somehow figured her out. She looked up, scowled, and said, "Sorry, folks, I'm late for a plane. Gotta go."

As she stepped away from the extended arm, an enormous gust of wind blew up the mountain, taking with it a couple of hats, a scarf, and the pen she clutched in her exposed and probably cold hand. I watched as the shamrock lifted into the air and then got lost in the blinding glow of a streetlight pocked with falling snow. I would never be able to catch it.

"You can't go," I said as I barreled my way in between Adele and the cab. "Someone call the police."

"I can do whatever I want," Adele said.

I'd processed the fact that there were cameras rolling, even if they were attached to phones. The crowd watched, and silently, raptly recorded the scene.

I noticed that the one person I thought would be recording wasn't. Toby repositioned himself close to me so that he could lunge at Adele if she had a notion to do something similar in my direction.

"No, you can't," I stammered. "Because"—I looked around and raised my voice—"I think you killed Cassie Bane."

Gasps cut through the wind and cold, but I'd become so pumped with adrenaline that I was warmed through.

"I didn't kill anyone," Adele said.

"I think Clare is right. I think you killed her." Nell stepped next to Toby.

More gasps, particularly when Nell removed her scarf again. Even through the bizarre circumstances, I noticed that Nell's blond locks didn't whip around weirdly with the wind. They moved like waves of wheat. Some people just had it.

"Ha! What do you know? You were poison to Matt. You and your flirty smiles, leading him on like you did. I told Cassie she shouldn't fall for your act. I told her you and Howie were together. She didn't believe me."

Murmurs of "Who's Howie?" spread through the crowd.

"Why did you kill her, Adele? Why did you kill Cassie Bane?" I said, raising my voice even more. I really hoped those cameras were rolling and had strong microphones.

A long silence followed as Adele melded into her part. She liked being the center of attention. She liked the drama, the role. These things were much more important to her than the real-life risk of her freedom. She was suddenly the star, and she would play it up.

"Cassie was in the way. She was in my way and in Matt's way. I went with her to that stupid meeting. It was a final audition for the last sister-wife, and she got the part! Can you believe the director thought it would be okay for Matt's real-life sister to be one of his sister-wives in a series that was on track to be a big hit? Even Howie tried to argue that she shouldn't get the part. The director thought the angle of them being real-life siblings would sell more tickets. But we would have been a disgusting laughingstock. I was going to shine in my role. I was going to become a star. Cassie was going to ruin it for all of us."

It was difficult to argue with her conclusions, except she might not have become the big star she predicted, and she shouldn't have committed murder to solve the problem.

"You could have just quit," I said, more quietly now. I couldn't help but feel a tiny bit sorry for her. "You're young. There would have been other roles."

Adele shook her head. "No, you don't understand. These things don't come along all the time."

"But Matt? You let him take the fall?" I said.

"I didn't mean to," she said with emotion pulling at her

voice. "I didn't mean for that to happen, but . . . I left out the window. I didn't know he would do what he did. I didn't know he would come in the room."

"You screamed," I guessed. "What was he supposed to do?"

"I don't know why I screamed. I couldn't stop myself. After I stabbed her it all seemed so horrible!"

"Better you than him, huh?" Nell said.

Adele sighed. "Something like that." She added, "I tried to make people think Howie was the killer. It would have made sense."

Another moment of silence followed as Adele came out of her role, realizing what she'd just done and understanding how stupid it had been. Her eyes grew wide with fear and confusion. Perhaps her life in Hollywood had caused psychological problems that had brought her to this point. Or maybe she was off already. Maybe Hollywood had just made her worse.

"Adele, come on," I said. "Let's go inside and talk about this some more."

It was a stupid thing to say, but I couldn't think of anything else. She smirked and then reached for one of the pieces of luggage that she'd let fall to the sidewalk. The thin layer of snow that had already covered it slid off and onto the wet cement.

In a quick, agile move she grabbed the shoulder strap of the bag and swung hard, hitting Nell before the blond actress could step back. Between the slippery footing and the impact of the bag, Nell went down hard, smacking her head.

"Nell!" I said as I stepped around Adele. Toby and I crouched beside her.

"I'm okay," she said as she put her hand at her temple, but I could tell she was woozy.

"What's wrong with you?" I said toward Adele.

As I looked in her direction, I noticed the bag was coming my way and it was too late to do much about it. I tried to react by bringing my arm up to protect my own head, but I knew I wasn't going to manage it in time. I braced for impact.

But it never came.

I'd shut my eyes tight and when I opened them, I still saw Adele and her bag, but someone else had stopped them from hitting me. Someone had grabbed the strap before the bag had had a chance to come around all the way again.

Two actors, the bag, and the blowing snow were framed perfectly by the light from a nearby streetlamp. I could see Adele's shock and half of the face under the man's cowboy hat. He wasn't in a good mood.

"I don't think so," Flint Magnum said as he took the bag from Adele with one hand and held her arm in his grip with the other one. "Not today, little lady."

I didn't know if the onlookers thought they were witnessing something made up, an act, or if they knew it was real, but nevertheless a few of them applauded and I heard one "Bravo!"

And then I heard the peal of approaching sirens. I smiled, and knew Jodie was on her way.

It was great to have so many people around to save the day.

28

"Clare, I don't know about this. Jimmy might have a heart attack before the night is over," Chester said quietly as he leaned close to me.

"He'll be fine. Matt Bane will be gone soon," I said, but I wasn't so sure. Either the way he looked at my niece was something learned from being a leading man or he was totally taken by her beauty.

I had to admit she was stunning in the black dress that looked nothing like Goth on her. Toby thought she was beautiful too, but he didn't look quite as happy.

We were gathered in The Rescued Word, the place we'd decided to meet before going to the Star City Film Festival's final awards ceremony, where Matt Bane would probably win the best actor award for his portrayal of a serial killer in *Kill Night*.

He was mourning his sister, but the relief over being exonerated had overridden his sadness long enough that the second he'd walked out of the prison, he'd made his way to The Rescued Word. He'd thanked me and then asked if we all wanted to attend the awards ceremony as his guests. It had seemed somewhat spur-of-the-moment when he'd invited Marion to be his date, but I wondered if even that had been planned. He sure seemed to like her. But it was difficult to know what these actors' real motives were.

It had taken Jodie approximately thirty seconds to find a necklace in one of Adele's suitcases with beads matching those found at The Fountain. Adele told her the matching bracelet must have snapped off when she'd climbed out the window. Jodie also found a torn brown top, made of the same material as the piece the police had found on the window frame. Adele had also admitted to taking the shamrock pen from Cassie at the meeting with the director. It was a slam-dunk case once all the correct evidence had been gathered.

Chester and Ramona were with us and dressed up again; Seth was next to me, just as dapper as he'd been at the party. Jodie and Mutt had been invited and they looked downright awesome and not even slightly rough-and-tumble in their dress-up clothes. Toby had also been invited and given a special all-access press pass. I thought he would have rather just gone as Marion's date, but at least he was going to get his chance to make a mark in the blog world. Matt Bane also offered him an exclusive interview. Toby's world was about to change big-time.

Jimmy was coming to the awards ceremony too. He didn't have a date, but it was clear he didn't like Matt Bane. I wasn't sure the father of any young woman Matt took on a date could like or trust the extraordinarily handsome actor. But Jimmy would be fine. Eventually.

I'd never once before seen Flint Magnum on the streets of Star City, but Chester assured me that he frequently traveled them. I didn't think I would ever understand how he was so good at hiding himself. Chester shrugged it off.

In fact, Flint had just come from The Rescued Word when he'd saved me from Adele's bag. He'd hoped to come in and talk to me about the Muir book. When he found the shop was closed and since the snow was coming down so heavily, he thought he'd be able to walk up the street without garnering much attention. He didn't have the chance to do that very often.

After the police took Adele away, I told him I still hadn't finished my research on the book, but I promised I would get right on it. He thanked me and told me he could either send someone to pick it up when it was ready or I could bring it up to his house. He said he'd put my name on a "welcome list."

Jodie hadn't received any phone calls about the ruckus outside The Fountain. She and some of the officers had been monitoring the Web site with the live festival action. The feed had gone down with the phones, but when it came back up, I was the first person Jodie saw on the screen. She took only a second to figure out that the police were needed.

"Found him," Jodie said over my shoulder.

I turned. "Found who?"

"John/Zeb."

"Oh yeah?"

"Yep, arrested him too."

"That's a relief. How . . . I mean, I don't get it. How did he do what he did?"

"The luck of the criminally inclined." Jodie shrugged.

"I still don't get it."

"He'd stolen the Selectrics from some old office-supply warehouse. He thought he could get a little for them, so he brought them into the shop. Apparently, you weren't in yet and Chester was really busy. The box of tins was on the counter. He was looking through them and he saw the money. He wanted to pocket it right then, but another customer saw what he was doing. He put the tin back and came in later."

"You're kidding." I thought back to when I'd looked through the box on the counter after I'd helped Zeb. "But he even said Seth's name."

"He's a good con man. He was chatting up Chester apparently—had picked up on the hankie phobia, actually—but Chester mentioned you and, for whatever reason, your boyfriend, Seth. He picked up on that too and used it. It's how con men and psychics do their thing."

"Wow, he could have gotten away with that money."

"But he didn't. It went to the correct person. And we got the bad guy. He's been busy this festival season. He's in trouble, but I'm not sure how much we'll be able to pin on him. We're working on it. Actually, Creighton's working on this one big-time."

"Hey," I said, "what was the argument about? The thing Creighton did that I overheard?"

"Oh."

For a second I thought Jodie wouldn't tell me, but she soon continued, quietly, and after she made sure no one else was listening.

"Creighton wouldn't let an attorney go back and talk to Matt Bane. He's not a fan of these Hollywood folks and we've all seen too many of them not have to pay for their crimes. He wanted Matt Bane to sweat it out, so he lied to the attorney who showed up, told him that Matt already had one."

"That's being a bad police officer at best, and totally illegal at worst, Jodie. I can't believe he got away with it."

"I know."

"It's not good. And he's the boss now."

"I know. Could get bumpy ahead, but I'm working on him. What I just told you doesn't get past us. Justice has been served, but I'd rather Matt Bane didn't think he should sue the Star City Police Department. Even if maybe he should."

I swallowed. For her, I'd keep quiet, but I was also going to keep a watchful eye on her brother.

"Got it," I said.

"Ready, everyone?" Matt said. He smiled at Marion and held his arm out.

"Hey, Matt," I said as I remembered something. "What was that call? The one Howie came to tell you about when you first came into the store."

Matt thought a moment and said, "Oh! There's going to

be a *Kill Night* sequel." He smiled sadly, probably remembering how horrible that day had turned out to be. I wished I hadn't asked. He humbly added, "The first one got picked up worldwide."

"Congratulations," I said, though, again, I felt sorry for Matt Bane.

"Thank you," he said.

I saw something in his eyes: a shift, a change, as he put on a brave face. Had I just witnessed an actor acting or a young man being polite because he'd invited all of us to an event he might not be emotionally prepared to attend, but one that would probably be big for his career? Was I seeing an example of "the show must go on"? I was sure he'd be fine eventually, but Cassie's murder was going to haunt him for a long time.

He hadn't been upset in the least about Nell and Howie. In fact he'd suspected they were together. He'd wondered if it was their relationship that somehow led to his sister's murder, but he couldn't figure out how or why. It was the reason he'd sent me to the party. He thought Nell and Howie would come out as a couple and that would somehow lead to suspicion being cast on someone other than him.

It hadn't worked. At all.

Nell had later confided to me that she'd gone to pick up Matt's iPad to save Howie from seeing some pictures of her with Matt. She told me that her heart belonged to Howie, but she'd had a recent weak moment with Matt. She didn't want Howie to get to the iPad before she had a chance to remove the pictures. I had no idea how all of that would play out, but I hoped they'd figure it out okay.

Poor Toby. Marion couldn't help but be in a haze of romantic fairy-tale land. She smiled at Matt. I was pretty sure she'd forgotten about everyone else in the room.

Toby had told me that he'd been embarrassed he couldn't catch Zeb as he ran away from us. He hadn't lied about the direction he thought the con man had turned, but he just wished he could have helped more. I'd only thought I'd seen Zeb on the other side of the road.

Seth and I let everyone else go out the doors before us. I looked up at Baskerville on his shelf, and he gave a blink and a nod of approval—or was that relief to see us get out of there?—before he turned and curled into a circle.

After I closed and locked the door, relishing the cool but comfortable and non-stormy night we would walk through to get to the theater, Seth crooked his arm and smiled at me.

"You are ravishing," he said.

"You too." I smiled. "Ready?"

"Absolutely. What is it they say? Lights, camera, action."

I laughed, and for that night, we walked among the stars—those around us and those over our heads—in our perfect mountain town.

Our festival story was one for the books.

Turn the page for an exclusive preview
of the next Dangerous Type Mystery,

Comic Sans Murder

Coming soon from Berkley Prime Crime

1

Larry Gerald might not have thought it too odd to find an abandoned ski boot on the Star City Resort slopes, but it's what he found inside it that was most unexpected.

He spied the gray boot resting atop the still-solid snow base at the edge of a small copse of pine trees, their branches currently green and not powdered with the white stuff. It was his first day on a snowboard, which might have contributed to his piqued curiosity about the boot. He'd taken a lesson but had spent more time on his behind than upright on the board. He welcomed an excuse for a moment's rest as he came to an awkward stop next to the boot and sat back onto the snow.

"Ouch," he said, realizing that even sitting was going to cause some pain for a little while. At least he was out of the way for a minute or two, he thought as he looked toward the run. Most of the boarders were at least ten years his junior and moved down the mountain or through the half-pipe as if their snowboards were extensions of their legs, not something foreign buckled onto them.

He shook his head at himself and his inability to accept that even he, onetime star athlete, was destined to lose a little of his innate athletic abilities once he reached thirty, never mind thirty-five. Besides, he'd been a swimmer, not a snowboarder. Different muscles.

He smiled at himself. None of that mattered. He was having a great time in Star City, Utah, taking a well-deserved vacation and enjoying the sights, the sounds, and the greatest snow on earth. Even now he could look in one direction and see the valley that held charming Star City shops, and in the other direction at snow-covered slopes alive with the pulse of curving lines made by happy skiers and snowboarders. Life was good.

Mostly, at least. Law school had been rough, the divorce rougher. Still plenty of time to make a good go of it, though.

He reached over for the boot, thinking he could tuck it under one arm and drop it off at lost and found. He'd been so off-balance on the board that carrying a boot the rest of the way down couldn't possibly make the experience any worse.

Ski boots are naturally heavy, but there was something different about this one, something weirdly balanced, maybe. With the boot in his thick-gloved grip, he peered inside.

And then he screamed and flung the boot, sending it flying a short distance through the air, landing only a few feet away and on its side.

Though the inside of the boot had been filled mostly with what Larry would describe as "gore," he knew he'd seen the foot, ankle, and sock that had originally gone into the boot. When it had been attached to the rest of a body.

His breathing and heartbeat sped up immediately, and though he'd never had a panic attack or hyperventilated, he knew that something like that was about to happen.

He noticed a snowboarder making her way toward him. She'd either heard his scream or had noticed the flying ski boot and the drops of blood that now fell across a small patch of the whitest snow, making it not so much the greatest snow anymore.

"Hey," she said as she took off her helmet and goggles, strands of her curly blond hair escaping its ponytail. "You okay?"

"I know you," Larry said, oddly zoning in on the fact that he'd seen the girl before, rather than focusing on what had been in the boot.

"You might have come into my great-grandfather's shop, The Rescued Word. I work there sometimes. I'm Marion."

He nodded and wished he could just keep his attention on her and that wonderful shop rather than what he'd seen a few moments earlier.

"Are you hurt?" she asked again. "The blood?"

"It's not my foot," Larry said.

"What?" Marion asked, but realization came over her features quickly. "Oh. In the boot. There's a foot?"

"Yes."

"Well, that . . . that just sucks."

"Big-time."

She didn't look into the boot but she swooned for a beat or two. Larry tried to get up to help her, but his legs were spaghetti. Fortunately, she recovered quickly.

"I'm okay, and I can get help," she said as she held out her hand. He fell back onto his sore behind again.

Marion pulled out her phone and looked at the screen a moment before she pushed a button. She brought her eyebrows together as she inspected Larry. He was trying to look like he was okay, but he wasn't, not even close.

"Aunt Clare. Hey, will you call Jodie and tell her there's a problem up on Thor? Yeah, the half-pipe run. No, I'm not hurt. I'm up here with a man, though. Yeah, he found something that the police need to see. Okay, well, I'm not going to look in it but I think it's a ski boot with a foot still inside. Only the foot."

Larry didn't bother to add "ankle and sock too" but the words rattled through his shaken and muddled thoughts.

"Right," Marion said. She ended the call and smiled stiffly at Larry. "The police will be here quickly. You sure you're going to be okay?"

Larry nodded, thinking that maybe law school and even the divorce hadn't been all that bad after all.

2

"Yep, that's what it was," Jodie said as she sucked on her straw. She'd hit bottom two pulls ago, but she wasn't one to let any drops of pineapple shake go to waste.

I shook my head, having lost interest in my own hot fudge sundae. But Jodie was a cop; she was used to these sorts of things.

"Where was the rest of the body?" I asked.

"That's the million-dollar question."

"No clues at all?"

"None. Not much evidence either. It wasn't as . . . messy as you might think. Frozen for the most part. It was beginning to thaw."

"Oh, Jodie. I don't want to think about that." I pushed up my glasses.

"I understand. Let's just say there are no clues yet. We're hoping something turns up soon."

"Could the person still be alive?"

"It's a possibility, but we don't think it's likely. As of about thirty minutes ago, no one missing a foot has checked into any hospital in the western United States. Even someone trying to hide they were hurt would be hard-pressed to try to take care of that sort of wound on their own. Most people would seek help even if they were guilty of something and afraid of getting caught."

We were inside the diner across the street from The Rescued Word, sitting opposite each other in a booth composed of a Formica table and pink vinyl bench seats.

Shortly after I'd called Jodie to send out the troops for my niece Marion and the man on the Thor snowboard run, Marion had actually come into the shop with the tale of the afternoon's brief but jarring adventure.

She hadn't been too shaken up, but she'd been bothered in a wired sort of way. It had taken two hot chocolates and one of Chester's stories to get her back to her normal bubbly self. Chester, my grandfather and Marion's great-grandfather, was the original owner of The Rescued Word. He frequently made up stories—some of his most famous were about the carved wooden doors over the middle shelves of the shop, which was in a building that used to house the Star City Silver Mining Company. All of his stories were wild fabrications, but today he worked extra hard to distract Marion's thoughts from spooky ski boots by inserting whiskey-addled fairies and magic silver from the old mines. I think she was more perplexed than entertained, but before long she was smiling and questioning the plot's logic. Of course, Marion's father—my brother, Jimmy, a single parent—would probably want her to seek therapy just to make sure she was really okay. Jodie had said that Marion hadn't seen much and made the call to Clare based solely on what Mr. Gerald had said. Jodie also said that Marion would be fine. She was young and would move on soon enough—unless she'd been the one who'd separated the foot from the body, Jodie had added with a sly grin.

"What about a skiing accident? Maybe the body got flung to a place you guys couldn't spot right off," I said.

"We're looking. That's another possibility, but, again, it's unlikely. There are just too many weird things that would have had to happen for it to be something like that. Of course, weird things do happen, so we'll see."

"Foul play you think?"

"Probably. But it's all really strange."

"I'd say."

"So, other than the boot, how's Marion doing?" Jodie said.

I thought for a moment. "Oh, you mean the competition?"

"Yeah, sure. I'm worried about her."

"We all are, but she's moving past it."

Marion had been a part of the Olympic snowboard qualifying series of events. The events, the Grand Prix, had been held on our own Star City slopes. She'd aced the first two events, but then a heavy and sudden wave of self-doubt got into her head, and she couldn't finish, thus ending any chance of her being invited onto the team this time around. She was so young, still only seventeen, so she'd have another shot. But it had most definitely been a rough time for her. I'd tried to comfort her, and Chester had tried to explain that it was not a big deal, that her life would be long and she'd have lots more chances, and Jimmy had continually wondered how he'd failed his daughter.

"Good. She'll do great the next time around," Jodie said.

"I think so too. That is, if her family doesn't get in her head too much. We're trying to figure out the right balance. But she's still hitting the slopes every day and her coach says she's still improving, that she hasn't reached her peak. Maybe something deep inside her knew she wasn't ready yet. Hard to understand subconscious motivations."

"She's amazing."

"I agree."

Jodie gave up on the shake, moving the cup to the other side of her clean plate. We'd both ordered cheeseburgers and fries, but most of my food was still on my plate.

"How's it going with the visiting celebrity?" Jodie asked.

"Nathan is working hard and driving poor Adal crazy."

Nathan Grimes, world-famous horror author, had made The Rescued Word his temporary place of business. He'd enjoyed time in Star City before, working on a couple of his most popular and bestselling novels: *Jump* and *Spark*. All the titles of his books were one word. I hadn't had the chance to ask him how that had happened, but he'd been working with Adal for only a little over a week, and only part-time, as they planned and prepped to print a book of Grimes's poetry on the replica Gutenberg press that Chester had built in our workshop. It stood amid old typewriters, typewriter parts, tools, and typeface boxes. Nathan had heard about the press when he'd been in the middle of *Spark*, and he hadn't been able to shake the idea of self-publishing his poetry. I didn't know how well the book would sell, but anyone who'd read his horror novels was sure to be surprised by his romantic way with words.

Adal was my apprentice. He'd come from Germany with the hope that I would teach him everything I knew about rescuing words: fixing typewriters, operating an old Gutenberg printing press, repairing books, even where to find the best paper products throughout the world. He and many of his family members, the male ones, had shown up in January for the Star City Film Festival. They'd stopped at the shop, and before I could even understand most of their names, Chester had offered the apprenticeship position to Adal. It had turned into one of Chester's best decisions ever. Someday Adal would take his skills back to Germany, but he was ours for a while.

Adal had been a part of The Rescued Word family during the Grand Prix, which had taken place in February, and had become a surprising source of comfort for Marion. He was a stranger from another land who brought a perspective that she somehow tuned in to. He'd helped us all, but mostly Marion. It was time for Marion's job at the shop to take a backseat to her dreams. She could still work on personalizing stationery on her computer at home and at the shop when she wanted to, but Chester had made it clear that she had to choose the best way to follow her dreams. He'd quit complaining when she couldn't be found or was late because she was on the slopes. It would have been only me and Chester at the shop if Adal hadn't come along, and we all preferred the idea of an apprentice over an employee.

"Adal dealing with the famous author okay?" Jodie asked. "How's he doing?"

"He's a pro, but why do you ask?" I said, though I suspected I knew the answer.

Jodie shrugged. "He's taking Latin from Anorkory. You know that, don't you?"

I laughed about his lessons with our resident Latin teacher. "I do know that. German, French, Spanish, and English just weren't enough for him"

"He's very into languages."

"He's very into you," I said as I picked up my mug of hot chocolate. I took a sip and then looked at her over the top of the cup.

"It's hard to take your disapproval seriously when you have whipped cream on the tip of your nose," Jodie said.

I wiped off the cream.

"Better?" I said.

"A little, but I still don't understand your disapproval."

"Well, it isn't disapproval so much. It's concern."

"I'm listening." She took a drink of her water and kept her eyes wide, exaggerating her attentiveness.

But I still knew she was listening, so I took advantage of the moment.

"You and Mutt broke up only a couple of weeks ago, and I'm not really sure you broke up all the way."

"Oh, we broke up all the way. No worries there," Jodie said bitterly.

"Well, you haven't told me what happened. That's weird. You tell me everything."

"I do not tell you everything. You don't tell me everything either."

"Actually, I do," I said, a tinge of hurt in my voice. "What won't you tell me?"

Jodie cleared her throat. "I don't want to tell you the details of the breakup yet, Clare, just like you didn't want to tell me the details of your breakup with Creighton soon after that happened. My breakup with Mutt is a sore spot that needs to fester a bit before I start picking at it and then finally let it heal. This is how wounds work. They go through stages. Remember how you were with Creighton?"

"I do, but he's your brother. I was afraid . . . of your loyalty to him," I said.

Jodie laughed. "That's the most ridiculous thing I've ever heard. Not once since we were sixteen have I put my brother before you. I knew what he was when you started dating him. I wasn't surprised at all when he cheated on you. You needed time too."

"I'm sorry," I said. "I should have told you."

"No, that's not what I'm saying at all. I just want you to understand that I'm in no state to talk about my breakup with Mutt yet, even with you. But when I'm ready, you'll be the only one I'll want to talk to. I promise."

"Okay, but . . ."

"Right, it's too soon to start dating someone else. I've never had many dating options, and another one so soon after a pretty serious relationship is weird for me, but I like Adal. That's it—*like*. He likes me. We like each other and want to get to know each other. He invited me to take Latin with him. It's the weirdest thing anyone has ever asked me to do. I said yes, but I'm not going to fall in love so quickly this time. Okay?"

"Okay," I said quickly, but then paused a beat. "You do know he has plans to go back to Germany, right?"

"Yes, I'm aware."

I paused again. "And, Jodie, I'm sorry for what happened with you and Mutt, whatever it was."

"It's okay. Really okay." She forced a sad smile.

"Mutt and Adal. You sure pick guys with strange names," I said with a smile.

"I know. Elmo's probably next." She laughed.

A loud rumble pulled our attention toward The Rescued Word.

"Expecting anyone?" Jodie asked as a white panel truck came to a noisy stop and a young guy jumped out of the driver's side. He stood in front of the shop and took turns inspecting a clipboard he held and the front of the darkened windows.

"I'm not. I should check on Chester."

We got the bill taken care of quickly and by the time we were across the street, Chester was in front of the store with what appeared to be a delivery guy. Chester wore a red silk robe that I'd never seen before, and held a sleepy-eyed Baskerville, our cat (well, all of ours, but mostly his), in his arms. They were both in decidedly sour moods.

"What's up?" I said as we approached.

"This young man says we are expecting the items in his

truck. I have explained to him that we are not, no matter what they are."

"What's in there?" I asked.

"Typewriters, I think," he said. He was young and his face looked flustered and unsure in the glow of the old-fashioned streetlight.

"Little late for a delivery, don't you think?" Jodie said. I saw her hand go to the spot where her gun would be holstered if she were in uniform.

The kid shrugged. "Got caught in some snow up around Evanston. Sorry I'm late, but once I got here I wasn't sure what to do except see if I could get these delivered. I'd like to get back on the road and back to Evanston tonight. It's gonna storm in this direction tomorrow and I came all the way from Nebraska."

"Where in Nebraska?" Jodie asked as she inspected the back license plate.

"Lincoln."

"That's a long way to bring some typewriters," Jodie said.

"Yeah, I was supposed to meet Lloyd here this afternoon. I've been calling him for hours, leaving messages that I'd be late. He was here today, right?"

Chester and I looked at each other.

"No one named Lloyd was here today as far as we remember," I said.

"Oh man, I was worried when I couldn't get ahold of him. I'm sure he'll call me back, but he told me specifically to meet him here this afternoon. He'll call me when he can. Must have gotten busy or something. He said there was a small reunion too—some meetings, I think. Maybe you can talk to him tomorrow?"

"I can't even think of someone I know named Lloyd," Chester said.

"Yeah, he said he knew you guys. Lloyd Gavin?" the young man said.

"Lloyd Gavin?" Jodie and I said together.

"We went to high school with him," Jodie said to me as I nodded.

"Wait a second," Chester said. "A gentleman called last week and asked for you, Clare. He wouldn't give me his name, but he said you and he knew each other when you were kids. I said you weren't in. He said he had some typewriters we should look at, but I told him we weren't interested. He mentioned he was coming out for some meetings and would stop by. I reiterated that we didn't want to buy any typewriters, either for consignment or otherwise. He laughed. I remember being distinctly put off by his attitude. I told him to travel safely and that I had to go. Maybe that was him."

"That sounds like him," the kid said. "But they're not for sale. They're gifts."

"He was one of the really smart kids in school," Jodie said. "We always thought he'd go far, but Lincoln, Nebraska, wouldn't have been a destination I would have predicted."

"He did go far. He's a very successful businessman in Lincoln," the kid said.

"What's his business?" Jodie asked.

"Computer hardware and software development."

"Lloyd Gavin," I muttered, remembering his sweet and shy personality more than I remembered his smarts. He'd asked me to the junior high dance, but had broken out in hives right before the dance. His dad had come by my house to apologize for his son's nerves. I'd been heartbroken about missing all the fun, but I went back to Lloyd's house and we watched movies. He and I became friends after that. In fact, he'd been my best friend until Jodie had come into my life at sixteen.

When Jodie and I became close I'd tried to include Lloyd in our friendship, but he told me he could handle being friends with only one person at a time, that it was all just too much for him otherwise. He told me it would be better for me to hang out with Jodie than with him.

I'd thought that was pretty weird then and had no idea how to handle what at the time had seemed like an ultimatum, but now, years later, I knew that Lloyd was an introvert, perhaps as much of an introvert as someone could be; painfully shy. Somehow I'd managed to break into his world, and the ultimatum was actually an unusually mature kindness sent my way.

"Clare?" Jodie said. "You with us?"

"Oh, sorry. Yeah, I'm right here. I knew Lloyd in high school and we were pretty good friends when we were younger, but I don't understand what's going on with some typewriters that he wanted to give us."

"How about you open the back?" Jodie said to the delivery boy.

"Will do. Name's Dillon, by the way."

"Nice to meet you, Dillon," Jodie said, keeping a suspicious slant to her eyes. She placed herself in between me, Chester, Baskerville, and the back of the truck. Never such a thing as downtime for Jodie. "Open the back."

A few seconds later, Dillon raised the back door and then turned on his phone's flashlight.

"There ya go. They look like a cross between sewing machines and typewriters. Mr. Gavin said you'd know what they are, and he wanted you to have them. Made me promise not to wreck the truck."

We stepped closer and looked inside. Dillon had been correct—the three machines inside did look like sewing machine–typewriter hybrids.

"Oh my," Chester said.

In tandem he and I adjusted our glasses.

"Hoovens," Chester said with a breathy sigh. Baskerville, not interested in the items in the truck, jumped out of his arms and trotted back to the shop's stoop, sitting and wrapping his tail around himself. His patience wouldn't last long, but he'd sensed that Chester and I might need a moment.

"That something good?" Jodie said.

"Yes," I said. "Very good. Very rare."

"Awesome," Jodie said. "Alrighty, then. Can we get these unloaded so Dillon can hit the road? I can call for help."

"Jodie, we can't just take these," I said. "They're too valuable."

"Let's see if we can get ahold of Lloyd. What's his number? Do you know where he was staying?" Jodie asked Dillon.

"Sure, but I've been trying to call him since last night. No answer."

"As you said, maybe he's just been busy. Tell me the hotel too. We'll find him," Jodie said.

"I hope so," Dillon said. "He sure seems to be missing in action."

Jodie and I both froze in place before we shared a look.

"No, it couldn't be," I said.

"That would be a wild coincidence," she said.

"What?" Chester said.

I sent him a frown. I didn't want to say aloud in front of Dillon what Jodie and I were thinking but Chester would pick up on our thoughts in a second.

He did.

"Oooh," he said. "Well, that would be terrible."

"What's going on?" Dillon said.

"Come on, kid. Let's find a place for you and your truck to stay tonight," Jodie said. "Lock 'er up."

"Why? Why can't I just leave them and head back toward Evanston? I need to get home."

"We gotta find Lloyd before you can go. It's best that way," Jodie said.

Dillon scratched his head and shrugged because he was too young to know what else he could do. "Okay."

Chester and I took a moment to jump inside the back of the truck and take a closer look at the rare old machines. I was a little worried about their being left in the open police station parking lot.

"I can take them down to Salt Lake to a secure facility if you think I should," Jodie said.

"Tonight?" It was already after eight.

"I could if you think it's best."

"You have officers on duty at the station all night, right?" I said.

"Yes."

"Just have them check on the truck throughout the night. Unless we were being spied on, we're the only ones who know about them."

"Lloyd too," Jodie said.

"Let's hope so," I replied.

"I'll find him."

She and I got Dillon set up at the same hotel our visiting author was staying at. It was conveniently located near the police station. I didn't knock on Nathan's door as I walked out of the hotel with Jodie, but I angled toward it and heard what I thought was the *click-clack* of typewriter keys. He hadn't mentioned that he wrote on a typewriter, but I'd ask him about it.

Jodie dropped me off at my house, affectionately named Little Blue, and left me with thought-provoking parting words: "Hope Lloyd still has both feet."